Pra[illegible] TODAY
[illegible]ayne

"RaeAnn[illegible] my favorite authors.... [illegible]oing to be able to stop."

—*Fresh Fiction* on *Snow Angel Cove*

"A sometimes heartbreaking tale of love and relationships in a small Colorado town.... Poignant and sweet, this tale of second chances will appeal to fans of military-flavored sweet romance."

—*Publishers Weekly* on *Christmas in Snowflake Canyon*

"Once again, Thayne proves she has a knack for capturing those emotions that come from the heart.... Crisp storytelling and many amusing moments make for a delightful read."

—*RT Book Reviews* on *Willowleaf Lane*

"Thayne pens another winner by combining her huge, boisterous cast of familiar, lovable characters with a beautiful setting and a wonderful story. Her main characters are strong and three-dimensional, with enough heat between them to burn the pages."

—*RT Book Reviews* on *Currant Creek Valley*

"Hope's Crossing is a charming series that lives up to its name. Reading these stories of small-town life engage the reader's heart and emotions, inspiring hope and the belief miracles are possible."

—Debbie Macomber, #1 *New York Times* bestselling author, on *Sweet Laurel Falls*

"Thayne, once again, delivers a heartfelt story of a caring community and a caring romance between adults who have triumphed over tragedies."

—*Booklist* on *Woodrose Mountain*

"Thayne's series starter introduces the Colorado town of Hope's Crossing in what can be described as a cozy romance.... [A] gentle, easy read."

—*Publishers Weekly* on *Blackberry Summer*

Also available from RaeAnne Thayne and HQN Books

Snow Angel Cove
Wild Iris Ridge
Christmas in Snowflake Canyon
Willowleaf Lane
Currant Creek Valley
Sweet Laurel Falls
Woodrose Mountain
Blackberry Summer

Coming in October 2015

Evergreen Springs

RAEANNE THAYNE

REDEMPTION BAY

Recycling programs for this product may not exist in your area.

ISBN-13: 978-0-373-78506-3

Redemption Bay

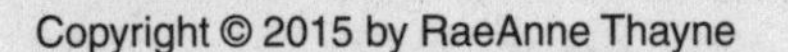

This edition published by arrangement with Harlequin Books S.A.

For questions and comments about the quality of this book, please contact us at CustomerService@Harlequin.com.

www.HQNBooks.com

Printed in U.S.A.

To the fantastic Jayme Maness for going above and beyond! I cannot thank you enough. Special thanks to Miranda Hutchins-Holman and Karen Whitmer Armes. Lindy-Grace and Hondo, thank you as well, for helping bring them to life. As always, I am eternally grateful for my amazing husband and children for putting up with my scattered deadline brain. Love you to the moon and back.

CHAPTER ONE

THIS WAS HER favorite kind of Haven Point evening.

McKenzie Shaw locked the front door of her shop, Point Made Flowers and Gifts. The day had been long and hectic, filled with customers and orders, which was wonderful, but also plenty of unavoidable mayoral business.

She was tired and wanted to stretch out on the terrace or her beloved swing, with her feet up and something cool at her elbow. The image beckoned but the sweetness of the view in front of her made her pause.

"Hold on," she said to Paprika, her cinnamon standard poodle. The dog gave her a long-suffering look but settled next to the bench in front of the store.

McKenzie sat and reached a hand down to pet Rika's curly hair. A few sailboats cut through the stunning blue waters of Lake Haven, silvery and bright in the fading light, with the rugged, snow-capped mountains as a backdrop.

She didn't stop nearly often enough to soak in the beautiful view or enjoy the June evening air, tart and clean from the mighty fir and pines growing in abundance around the lake.

A tourist couple walked past holding hands and

eating gelato cones from Carmela's, their hair backlit into golden halos by the setting sun. From a short distance away, she could hear children laughing and shrieking as they played on the beach at the city park and the alluring scent of grilling steak somewhere close by made her stomach grumble.

She loved every season here on the lake but the magnificent Haven Point summers were her favorite—especially lazy summer evenings filled with long shadows and spectacular sunsets.

Kayaking on the lake, watching children swim out to the floating docks, seeing old-timers in ancient boats casting gossamer lines out across the water. It was all part of the magic of Haven Point's short summer season.

The town heavily depended on the influx of tourists during the summer, though it didn't come close to the crowds enjoyed by the larger city to the north, Shelter Springs—especially since the Haven Point Inn burned down just before Christmas and had yet to be rebuilt.

Shelter Springs had more available lodging, more restaurants, more shopping—as well as more problems with parking, traffic congestion and crime, she reminded herself.

"Evening, Mayor," Mike Bailey called, waving as he rumbled past the store in the gorgeous old blue '57 Chevy pickup he'd restored.

She waved back, then nodded to Luis Robles, locking up his insurance agency across the street.

A soft, warm feeling of contentment seeped through

her. This was her town. These were her people. She was part of it, just like the Redemption Mountains across the lake. She had fought to earn that sense of belonging since the day she showed up, a lost, grieving, bewildered girl.

She had worked hard to earn the respect of her friends and neighbors. The chance to serve as the mayor had never been something she sought but she had accepted the challenge willingly. It wasn't about power or influence—not that one could find much of either in a small town like Haven Point. She simply wanted to do anything she could to make a difference in her community. She wanted to think she was serving with honor and dignity, but she was fully aware there were plenty in town who might disagree.

Her stomach growled, louder this time. That steak smelled as if it was charred to perfection. Too bad she didn't know who was grilling it or she might just stop by to say hello. McKenzie was briefly tempted to stop in at Serrano's or even grab a gelato of her own at Carmela's—stracciatella, her particular favorite—but she decided she would be better off taking Rika home.

"Come on, girl. Let's go."

The dog jumped to her feet, all eager, lanky grace, and McKenzie gripped the leash and headed off.

She lived not quite a mile from her shop downtown and she and Rika both looked forward all day to this evening walk along the trail that circled the lake.

As she walked, she waved at people walking, biking, driving, even boating past when the shoreline came into view. It was quite a workout for her arm but she didn't mind. Each wave was another reminder that this was her town and she loved it.

"Let's grill some chicken when we get home," she said aloud to Rika, whose tongue lolled out with appropriate enthusiasm.

Talking to her dog again. Not a good sign but she decided it was too beautiful an evening to worry about her decided lack of any social life to speak of. Town council meetings absolutely didn't count.

Her warm mood lasted until a few houses from her own, when an older gentleman out clipping the tall hedge in front of his trim brick home whirled to face her, almost as if he had been lying in wait for her—probably *exactly* what he had been doing.

"I need a word with you, missy."

Her stomach dropped. Darwin Twitchell—the bane of her existence and the three previous mayors before her.

"Mr. Twitchell. How are you this lovely evening?"

"Terrible," he growled. He wore a perpetual frown, much like his English bulldog, Petunia, who adored him. Of the two, Petunia clearly had the more appealing personality.

"I'm sorry to hear that," she answered, trying to be polite.

"Oh, I doubt that. I really do."

She tried so hard to be nice to Darwin. It was almost a point of honor with her, but he was one of those perpetually unhappy people who twisted everything around and made it so difficult to be kind.

As both a natural-born and determined optimist,

she struggled every time she had dealings with the man—which was at least two or three times a week when he came to her with some kind of beef about the city.

A Korean War combat vet, Darwin had recently become a widower. In the months since, he had become even more sour, if possible. Though arthritis gnarled his fingers and he relied on a cane for balance and support, he still somehow managed to keep his yard and house exquisite, without a stray leaf or overgrown branch.

She considered it one of life's great mysteries that a man who seemed to be a festering pile of frustration could expend so much effort and energy into making his property into a restful oasis of blooms and trailing vines and sturdy, beautifully placed trees.

A mystery she would try to puzzle out another day, she told herself. She had a chicken breast to grill—after she dealt with whatever stick he had up his hindquarters today. Dealing with irate citizens was part of her description as mayor, like it or not.

"How can I make things better for you this evening?" she asked politely.

"How long have you had your name on the door at the mayor's office in city hall?" he demanded.

"Six months, Mr. Twitchell." Six difficult, stress-filled months. Why, again, had she ever thought this whole mayoral gig was a good idea? Oh, yes. Because she loved this town. Perhaps not every single inhabitant, though.

"Six months." Darwin scowled. Or maybe he was

beaming with happiness and glee. It was hard to tell, since all his facial expressions looked the same. "And how long have I been warning you about that bridge over the Hell's Fury?"

The expression was a scowl, then. Not really a surprise.

She forced a smile. "Just about every week for the past six months, Mr. Twitchell."

"I don't know why I waste my breath. You obviously don't care, since you haven't done a damn thing about it since you've been in office."

She tried not to let that sting, especially considering all the things she *had* accomplished in six short months. He was a lifelong resident of this town, one of her constituents, and she owed it to him to try to address his concern. As much as she wanted to hug his adorably grumpy-faced dog and walk away.

"The public works director is aware of the problem. We've talked to the state about it. It's on the list. We're waiting on a couple of grants and appropriations to come through. When that happens, it will be at the top of our list, I promise you."

"When will that be?"

"I'm afraid I can't tell you exactly. As I'm sure you're aware, it costs a great deal of money for that kind of project. Right now the city cupboard is a little bare for a major infrastructure repair."

"If this were Shelter Springs, we would have had a dozen new bridges by now. My nephew, the mayor, would never let things go this long."

She had heard the same argument plenty of times

over the past six months. According to Darwin, Mayor Martin of Shelter Springs could walk the entire length of Lake Haven without getting the cuffs of his tailored slacks damp.

"Now, Mr. Twitchell, we have our challenges, yes. But the people of Shelter Springs have their own."

She would like at least one of their problems—more tax revenue than they knew what to do with.

Instead, her downtown was dead and most of the available property had been tied up for years by one man.

Ben Kilpatrick.

Just the thought of him made her grind her back teeth and grip Rika's leash a little more tightly.

"You'd better do something about that bridge or there's going to be trouble, mark my words," Darwin grunted.

"I appreciate the advice, Mr. Twitchell," she lied.

"And another thing. Garbage collection. That darn truck knocked over my can again for the third week in a row! Does that fool driver even know how to operate the thing?"

Apparently the mayor, by virtue of the office, was responsible for every single thing that went on within the city limits. Garbage collection was run by the county, as Mr. Twitchell fully knew.

"It might have something to do with the slope at the end of your driveway. It's a little tricky to set the can down just so."

"I don't know why we ever had to switch over to those stupid automated trucks. Who can even pull those big cans out to the street, unless they're a superhero or something? More trouble than it's worth, you ask me."

Who would ever be dim enough to ask Darwin Twitchell *anything*, unless he or she wanted to spend the rest of the day listening to his lengthy litany of complaints?

She drew in a deep breath, focusing on the scent of pine and lake instead of acrimony. Darwin was an object of pity. He had little to do but sit around and stew about everything wrong in his world, both globally and locally. The challenge of righting a tipped-over can probably represented all the things he could no longer do because of his age and physical limitations.

McKenzie forced a smile, trying her best to inject a little genuine compassion in it. "Next time the truck tips over your can when it's done taking your garbage, please leave it. I'll be happy to pick it up for you and roll it back to the house."

He harrumphed at that and she knew he would never consider leaving his can tipped over all day, waiting until she could get to it. He was so particular, he raked the gravel out on his parking strip if anybody so much as left a bike tire trail through it.

"Just find a damn garbage truck driver who knows what the Sam Hill he's doing. That's all I ask. Nobody cares anymore about doing a good job. They're all so busy on their computers, sending out nekked pictures of their whatsit."

She almost laughed aloud—why didn't anybody send *her* nekked pictures of their whatsit?—but she managed to contain it. "I'll talk to the county public works supervisor and ask him to remind the garbage collectors to be a little more careful."

"You do that. And take care of that bridge, too!"

He gripped his cane and made a sharp gesture to Petunia, who had the effrontery to be fraternizing with the enemy—or at least the enemy's cinnamon poodle—then shuffled back up his driveway with the dog trotting behind him.

She sighed and continued on her way. She wouldn't let one cranky old man ruin her enjoyment of this beautiful summer evening.

When she reached her lakeside house, however, she forgot all about Darwin and his perpetual complaints when she discovered a luxury SUV with California plates in the driveway of the house next to hers, with boat trailer and gleaming wooden boat attached.

Great.

Apparently someone had rented the Sloane house.

Normally she would be excited about new neighbors but in this case, she knew the tenants would only be temporary. Since moving to Shelter Springs, Carole Sloane-Hall had been renting out the house she received as a settlement in her divorce for a furnished vacation rental. Sometimes people stayed for a week or two, sometimes only a few days.

It was a lovely home, probably one of the most luxurious lakefront rentals within the city limits. Though not large, it had huge windows overlooking the lake, a wide flagstone terrace and a semiprivate boat dock—which, unfortunately, was shared between McKenzie's own property and Carole's rental house.

She wouldn't let it spoil her evening, she told herself. Usually the renters were very nice people, quiet and polite. She generally tried to act as friendly and welcoming as possible.

It wouldn't bother her at all except the two properties had virtually an open backyard because both needed access to the shared dock, with only some landscaping between the houses that ended several yards from the high water mark. Sometimes she found the lack of privacy a little disconcerting, with strangers temporarily living next door, but Carole assured her she planned to put the house on the market at the end of the summer. With everything else McKenzie had to worry about, she had relegated the vacation rental situation next door to a distant corner of her brain.

New neighbors or not, though, she still adored her own house. She had purchased it two years earlier and still felt a little rush of excitement when she unlocked the front door and walked over the threshold.

Over those two years, she had worked hard to make it her own, sprucing it up with new paint, taking down a few walls and adding one in a better spot. The biggest expense had been for the renovated master bath, which now contained a huge claw-foot tub, and the new kitchen with warm travertine countertops and the intricately tiled backsplash she had done herself.

This was hers and she loved every inch of it, almost more than she loved her little store downtown.

She walked through to the back door and let Rika off her leash. Though the yard was only fenced on one side, just as the Sloane house was fenced on the corresponding outer property edge, Rika was well trained and never left the yard.

Her cell phone rang as she was throwing together a quick lemon-tarragon marinade for the chicken.

Some days, she wanted to grab her kayak, paddle out to the middle of Lake Haven—where it was rumored to be so deep, the bottom had never been truly charted—and toss the stupid thing overboard.

This time when she saw the caller ID, she smiled, wiped her hands on a dish towel and quickly answered. “Hey, Devin.”

“Hey, sis. I can’t believe you’re holding out on me! Come on. Doesn’t your favorite sister get to be among the first to hear?”

She tucked the phone in her shoulder and returned to cutting the lemon for the marinade as she mentally reviewed her day for anything spill-worthy to her sister.

The store had been busy enough. She had busted the doddering and not-quite-right Mrs. Anglesey for trying to walk out of the store without paying for the pretty hand-beaded bracelet she tried on when she came into the store with her daughter.

But that sort of thing was a fairly regular occurrence whenever Beth and her mother came into the store and was handled easily enough, with flustered apologies from Beth and that baffled what-did-I-do-wrong? look from poor Mrs. Anglesey.

She didn't think Devin would be particularly interested in that or the great commission she earned by selling one of the beautiful carved horses an artist friend made in the wood shop behind his house to a tourist from Maine.

And then there was the pleasant encounter with Mr. Twitchell, but she doubted that was what her sister meant.

"Sorry. You lost me somewhere. I can't think of any news I have worth sharing."

"Seriously? You didn't think I would want to know that Ben Kilpatrick is back in town?"

The knife slipped from her hands and she narrowly avoided chopping the tip of her finger off. A greasy, angry ball formed in her stomach.

Ben Kilpatrick. The only person on earth she could honestly say she despised. She picked up the knife and stabbed it through the lemon, wishing it was his cold, black heart.

"You're joking," she said, though she couldn't imagine what her sister would find remotely funny about making up something so outlandish and horrible.

"True story," Devin assured her. "I heard it from Betty Orton while I was getting gas. Apparently he strolled into the grocery store a few hours ago, casual as a Sunday morning, and bought what looked to be at least a week's worth of groceries. She said he didn't look very happy to be back. He just frowned when she welcomed him back."

"It's a mistake. That's all. She mistook him for someone else."

"That's what I said, but Betty assured me she's known him all his life and taught him in Sunday school three years in a row and she's not likely to mistake him for someone else."

"I won't believe it until I see him," she said. "He hates Haven Point. That's fairly obvious, since he's done his best to drive our town into the ground."

"Not actively," Devin, who tended to see the good in just about everyone, was quick to point out.

"What's the difference? By completely ignoring the property he inherited after his father died, he accomplished the same thing as if he'd walked up and down Lake Street, setting a torch to the whole downtown."

She picked up the knife and started chopping the fresh tarragon with quick, angry movements. "You know how hard it's been the last five years since he inherited to keep tenants in the downtown businesses. Haven Point is dying because of one person. Ben Kilpatrick."

If she had only one goal for her next four years as mayor, she dreamed of revitalizing a town whose lifeblood was seeping away, business by business.

When she was a girl, downtown Haven Point had been bustling with activity, a magnet for everyone in town, with several gift and clothing boutiques for both men and women, restaurants and cafés, even a downtown movie theater.

She still ached when she thought of it, when she looked around at all the empty storefronts and the ramshackle buildings with peeling paint and broken shutters.

"It's his fault we've lost so many businesses and nothing has moved in to replace them. I mean, why go to all the trouble to open a business," she demanded, "if the landlord is going to be completely unresponsive and won't fix even the most basic problems?"

"You don't have to sell it to me, Kenz. I know. I went to your campaign rallies, remember?"

"Right. Sorry." It was definitely one of her hot buttons. She loved Haven Point and hated seeing its decline—much like old Mrs. Anglesey, who had once been an elegant, respected, contributing member of the community and now could barely get around even with her daughter's help and didn't remember whether she had paid for items in the store.

"It wasn't really his fault, anyway. He hired an incompetent crook of a property manager who was supposed to take care of things. It wasn't Ben's fault the man embezzled from him and didn't do the necessary upkeep to maintain the buildings."

"Oh, come on. Ben Kilpatrick is the chief operating officer for one of the most successful, fastest-growing companies in the world. You think he didn't know what was going on? If he had bothered to care, he would have paid more attention."

This was an argument she and Devin had had before. "At some point, you're going to have to let go," her sister said calmly. "Ben doesn't own any part of Haven Point now. He sold everything to Aidan Caine last year—which makes his presence in town even more puzzling. Why would he come back *now*, after all these years? It would seem to me, he has even *less* reason to show his face in town now."

McKenzie still wasn't buying the rumor that Ben had actually returned. He had been gone since he was seventeen years old. He didn't even come back for Joe Kilpatrick's funeral five years earlier—though she, for one, wasn't super surprised about that, since Joe had been a bastard to everyone in town and especially to his only surviving child.

"It doesn't make any sense. What possible reason would he have to come back now?"

"I don't know. Maybe he's here to make amends. Did you ever think of that?"

How could he ever make amends for what he had done to Haven Point—not to mention shattering all her girlish illusions?

Of course, she didn't mention that to Devin as she tossed the tarragon into the lemon juice while her sister continued speculating about Ben's motives for coming back to town.

Her sister probably had no idea about McKenzie's ridiculous crush on Ben, that when she was younger, she had foolishly considered him her ideal guy. Just thinking about it now made her cringe.

Yes, he had been gorgeous enough. Vivid blue eyes, long sooty eyelashes, the old clichéd chiseled jaw—not to mention that lock of sun-streaked brown hair that always seemed to be falling into his eyes, just begging for the right girl to push it back, as Belle did to the Prince after the Beast in her arms suddenly materialized into him.

Throw in that edge of pain she always sensed in him and his unending kindness and concern for his sickly younger sister and it was no wonder her thirteen-year-old self—best friends with that same sister—used to pine for him to notice her, despite the four-year difference in their ages.

It was so stupid, she didn't like admitting it, even to herself. All that had been an illusion, obviously. He might have been sweet and solicitous to Lily but that was his only redeeming quality. His actions these past five years had proved that, over and over.

Through the open kitchen window, she heard Rika start barking fiercely, probably at some poor hapless chipmunk or squirrel that dared venture into her territory.

"I'd better go," she said to Devin. "Rika's mad at something."

"Yeah, I've got to go, too. Looks like the Shelter Springs ambulance is on its way with a cardiac patient."

"Okay. Good luck. Go save a life."

Her sister was a dedicated, caring doctor at Lake Haven Hospital, as passionate about her patients as McKenzie was about their town.

"Let me know if you hear anything down at city hall about why Ben Kilpatrick has come back to our fair city after all these years."

"Sure. And then maybe you can tell me why you're so curious."

She could almost hear the shrug in Devin's voice. "Are you kidding me? It's not every day a gorgeous playboy billionaire comes to town."

And that was the crux of the matter. Somehow it seemed wholly unfair, a serious karmic calamity, that he had done so well for himself after he left town. If she had her way, he would be living in the proverbial van down by the river—or at least in one of his own dilapidated buildings.

Rika barked again and McKenzie hurried to the back door that led onto her terrace. She really hoped it wasn't a skunk. They weren't uncommon in the area, especially not this time of year. Her dog had encountered one the week before on their morning run on a favorite mountain trail and it had taken her three baths in the magic solution she found on the internet before she could allow Rika back into the house.

Her dog wasn't in the yard, she saw immediately. Now that she was outside, she realized the barking was more excited and playful than upset. All the more reason to hope she wasn't trying to make nice with some odoriferous little friend.

"Come," she called again. "Inside."

The dog bounded through a break in the bushes between the house next door, followed instantly by another dog—a beautiful German shepherd with classic markings.

She had been right. Rika *had* been making friends. She and the German shepherd looked tight as ticks, tails wagging as they raced exuberantly around the yard.

The dog must belong to the new renters of the

Sloane house. Carole would pitch a royal fit if she knew they had a dog over there. McKenzie knew it was strictly prohibited.

Now what was she supposed to do?

A man suddenly walked through the gap in landscaping. He had brown hair, but a sudden piercing ray of the setting sun obscured his features more than that.

She *really* didn't want a confrontation with the man, especially not on a Friday night when she had been so looking forward to a relaxing night at home. She supposed she could just call Carole or the property management company and let them deal with the situation.

That seemed a cop-out, since Carole had asked her to keep an eye on the place.

She forced a smile and approached the dog's owner. "Hi. Good evening. You must be renting the place from Carole. I'm McKenzie Shaw. I live next door. Rika, that dog you're playing catch with, is mine."

The man turned around and the pleasant evening around her seemed to go dark and still as she took in sun-streaked brown hair, steely blue eyes, chiseled jaw.

Her stomach dropped as if somebody had just picked her up and tossed her into the cold lake.

Ben Kilpatrick. Here. Staying in the house next door.

So much for her lovely evening at home.

CHAPTER TWO

For a moment, McKenzie could only stare at the man. It took her another minute before she could find her voice.

"This must be a record," she finally said. "The Haven Point rumor mill actually nailed it, for once. You *are* back."

Her sister was usually right but why did she have to be right about *this*, darn it?

Why was he here? She highly doubted he had come to make amends for all he had done. Judging by history, he was probably here to cause more trouble.

"Hello, McKenzie. Long time, and all that."

He gave her an almost-smile, though she didn't miss the rather bleak look in his blue eyes that made her suspect the rumor mill had something else right—Ben Kilpatrick wasn't any happier to find himself back in Haven Point than she was.

Even with the dark shadows in his gaze, he was far more gorgeous than he'd been when she was a girl. That chiseled jaw was more, well, chisel-y, his eyes seemed more intense, his features masculine and strong.

The last time she had seen Ben in person had been

at Lily's funeral. The sudden realization sent a wave of remembered grief washing over her for her friend and his sister, one of the most courageous people she had ever met. Lily had lost her battle against cystic fibrosis the year they both turned thirteen.

She pushed away the echoing sadness. Lily had been gone a long time. As much as she might despise Ben, McKenzie could never fault him for his care of his sister. In all the years she had been friends with Lily, she had never seen Ben be anything but loving and kind with her, patient under very difficult circumstances.

She had a long list of other sins she could lay at his feet, however, starting with the abrupt way he had left town right after the funeral and taken her idealism and trust with him.

"I'd like to say I'm happy to see you, but I've never been a very good liar."

"Oh, ouch."

His mouth quirked up in a smile and he appeared more amused than offended.

She had a hundred accusations she wanted to hurl at him, years of helpless frustration as she watched her town die inch by inch.

Instead, she focused on what was really the least important of them all.

"Is this your dog?" she demanded.

"No. Okay. Yes. Sort of. This is Hondo."

The dog's tongue lolled out and he appeared to beam broadly at his name.

"Like the John Wayne movie?"

"I suppose. I didn't name him."

The dog nosed her hand in a friendly way but McKenzie only frowned, refusing to be charmed by anything associated with Ben. Unlike Rika, she had a few standards. "Is he your dog or isn't he?"

"Technically, he's mine, I guess. Until a few weeks ago, he belonged to a good friend. He died unexpectedly but stipulated in his will that I take him. I'm not sure why. It's a temporary situation. Until I can find him a good home, I guess we're stuck with each other."

Naturally, he wouldn't want to take any unexpected responsibility that had been thrust on him. Why ruin a perfect track record? It was a wonder he bothered to feed and water the dog, if his treatment of the property he inherited in Haven Point was any indication.

"He's a beautiful dog. Unfortunately, the owner doesn't allow pets at the vacation rental. I'm sure the property management company informed you of that fact. As usual, you probably think the rules don't apply to you, right?"

His eyes widened a little at the direct frontal attack. Okay, she hadn't meant to add that last bit. She probably should have tried for politeness first but the hostility had sort of slipped out.

"Actually," he answered, a little stiffly, "when I was looking for a place to stay with Hondo while I'm in town, Carole was kind enough to make an exception to the no-pets rule."

McKenzie could just *bet* Carole would make an exception. She had always liked the other woman and considered them good friends for the short time Carole had been her next-door neighbor before the divorce, but she knew Carole was eager to add another husband to her collection—even one several years younger than she. A man with an amazingly attractive portfolio would only sweeten the deal.

Not to mention that sinful mouth and eyes the same deep blue as Lake Haven on a calm August morning.

She frowned. She didn't care about his sinful mouth, for heaven's sake.

"I've discovered in the few weeks since Hondo here came to live with me that he isn't crazy about hotels—and, quite frankly, vice versa. Since I'm not sure how long I'll be in town, a vacation rental seemed the most logical option. The dock was definitely a bonus."

"I saw the boat out front when I came home. It's a Killy, isn't it?"

His family's boatworks had been famous across the world for making beautiful wooden boats. Many older models were considered classics and were highly sought by collectors for their tight construction and classic lines. In only a few days, Haven Point would be hosting its annual wooden boat festival as part of Lake Haven Days, when collectors came from all over to share their love for the elegantly crafted boats.

"Yes. The Delphine, named for my grandmother."

The Delphine was one of the most expensive and hard-to-find of the older Killy models, she knew. While McKenzie wasn't exactly an expert on the boatworks and its history or products, she had chaired the

Lake Haven Days committee three years in a row at the request of the previous city administration and had come to know more than she ever expected about wooden boats and the passionate fans who adored them.

She never would have expected Ben to be the sentimental type, especially considering he was the one who made sure Kilpatrick Boatworks would never manufacture another Killy.

In one single afternoon five years earlier, he dealt a crippling blow to the town and his family's legacy when he closed the factory and put two hundred people out of work.

She curled her fingers into fists at the reminder. How dare he show up in the town he had irreparably damaged, towing behind him bold and painful evidence of all he had taken away? Was he *trying* to rub everybody's faces in it?

Grrr.

The words he had spoken suddenly penetrated the fog of anger around her.

I'm not sure how long I'll be in town.

Was he talking days, weeks, months? All of it spent *next door* to her?

How would she endure it, when some heretofore unknown violent part of her wished she could drag him behind his family's beautiful boat for two or three hours?

Having him next door was going to be torture. Her comfortable little house on the lake was her sanctuary. She desperately needed the calm oasis she found here on Redemption Bay, overlooking the raw, craggy mountains reflected in the vivid blue waters of the lake.

With him staying next door, she wouldn't be able to relax for an instant. She would always be aware he was there, just a few shrubs away.

She couldn't bear it.

Okay. Gloves officially coming off now. The idea that he had brought one of his family's boats back to town to float in Lake Haven in front of everyone like some kind of *taunt* was the last straw. Why bother being polite?

"I'll admit, I'm surprised to see you here. Last I heard, you despised Haven Point and never wanted to see the place again. You've certainly done your best to see us obliterated off the map."

He frowned. "I never despised Haven Point. That's a bit of an exaggeration, wouldn't you say?"

"What else would you call it? You deliberately let the downtown fall into ruins."

"I did?"

The jerk actually had the nerve to look surprised at the accusation.

"You must have driven through town on your way here. You had to have seen all the boarded-up buildings and vacant properties in *your* buildings."

"Not mine now," he pointed out. "Aidan Caine owns them."

"For five years they were yours!" she exclaimed. "And for five years you did absolutely *nothing* to take care of them except hire a completely incompetent property manager, who robbed you blind along with the tenants of your buildings."

He glowered at her, looking suddenly as dark and forbidding as thunderstorms over the Redemptions.

Rika whined a little and suddenly planted her haunches at McKenzie's feet. McKenzie highly doubted Ben would pose any sort of threat to her but she appreciated the moral support, anyway.

"I might have been less…attentive than I should have been," he said stiffly. "I've been a little busy the last few years. And, again, I haven't owned the property since I sold everything to Aidan."

"Regardless, the problem was created by *you*. Haven Point is practically a ghost town, with almost half of the businesses closing or relocating outside the city limits to Shelter Springs since Joe died. I'm the mayor of Haven Point. Did you know that?"

"I did not. Congratulations?"

"Condolences are more in order, thanks to you. It's a rough job, especially with our constantly plummeting tax revenue. It kills me to know we could have a thriving, active downtown filled with shops, restaurants, hotels, entertainment—if the man who owned most of the real estate in this town hadn't completely ignored his responsibilities for the last five years."

His jaw clenched for only a moment before his features smoothed out. "Wow. This is an interesting way to welcome someone to your town. Go directly on the attack."

She refused to feel guilty. He deserved every ounce

of her hostility and more. "I'm *very* welcoming to newcomers, in general."

"Just not to me."

Could he honestly blame her? He had created a huge mess and even with Aidan's cooperation now, she didn't know how to help her town find its way out.

"Let's be honest. You're not my favorite person right now."

"Message received, loud and clear, Mayor. I'll try to stay out of your way while I'm here. That might be a touch difficult, considering we're next-door neighbors and share a boat dock, but I'll do my best."

If it hadn't been such a long day—and if she weren't so darn *angry* at the man—she might have been able to muster a facsimile of politeness, but right now it didn't seem worth the effort. "How long are you staying?"

"I'm not sure," he hedged. "A week. Maybe two. Depends."

On what? His mood? The moon cycle? The futures market?

Why was he here?

He didn't seem inclined to be forthcoming about that particular question on his own and she couldn't figure out a way to ask, especially considering she had just unloaded years of frustration on him.

His reasons for being here were none of her business, really. He could travel anywhere he wanted. She was the mayor, not some petty megalomaniac who could demand to see his papers once he crossed over her town boundary.

McKenzie fought the urge to press a hand to her suddenly shaky insides. She had never been very good at confrontations and now that the heat of this one with Ben had passed, she felt a little quivery and unsettled. At the moment, she only wanted to go home, lock the door, run a hot bath and try to pretend the past fifteen minutes never happened.

She certainly wasn't going to bring her chicken breast out to the terrace to grill now. She would just have to sauté it or something, which wasn't nearly as good.

Darn the man for ruining what had promised to be such a beautiful evening.

"Good night, then. I'll do my best to keep Rika on my property."

"I don't mind her. I get the feeling the boundary between the houses has been fairly fluid. I see no reason to change that. She's welcome over there."

She nodded, but gripped her dog's collar tightly so her poodle wouldn't be tempted to go sniffing after Hondo again.

Cheap tart. Okay, so he was big and beautiful, with all those muscles. That didn't make him good for her.

The dogs, of course. She was talking about the dogs.

"Come, Rika."

After considerable effort, she managed to convince her dog to leave her new BFF and return to the house. The dog immediately plopped down onto her favorite spot on the rug in the sunroom.

Usually the room was McKenzie's favorite of the

house, too—but with those glass windows, she was entirely too aware of her new neighbor's presence next door. She closed all the blinds before she turned around and marched into the kitchen.

Her hands were shaking and her knees felt as weak as the first time she had gone backcountry skiing with her friend Paulo and they had nearly been caught in an avalanche when a cornice above them had broken free.

They had managed to ski out of the path just in time. Right now, she didn't feel as lucky as that day. She felt as if thousands of tons of snow and ice and rock had just tumbled over her head.

Ben Kilpatrick. Here, in Haven Point, after all these years, and tougher, harder, more sexy than ever.

Oh, she used to have such a *crush* on the man. It was humiliating, really, when she remembered how she had pined for him. He barely knew she was alive but she had watched him with almost stalker-like intensity. When she would visit Lily at Snow Angel Cove to bring her homework or hang out and talk about boys, McKenzie used to pray he would be there. She hoped every time that he would come into Lily's room—which had become basically a hospital room in later months as her condition regressed—to check on her at some point during the visit.

When he did stop by, he barely noticed McKenzie. She knew that. He plainly adored his ill younger sister and probably didn't know McKenzie existed.

He had been brooding and angry back then. Though she had never been quite sure why, she sensed the atmosphere at Snow Angel Cove hadn't been exactly nurturing and warm. She had always liked his mother, Lydia, but Joe was a serious A-hole most of the time, cold and cruel, especially to Ben.

Why was he here? And why now? It was the worst possible timing. She was heading into her busiest few weeks of the year. Lake Haven Days, the boat show, the Fourth of July town celebrations. She didn't expect to have five minutes to even breathe in the next week to ten days and now she had to worry about Ben Kilpatrick living next door.

It was enough to make a woman want to tear her hair out—or want to curl up in her bed under the blankets and pretend she didn't have a business *or* a town to run.

AFTER THEIR NEIGHBORS went inside their house, Ben led Hondo next door. The dog immediately found a stick under the big birch tree, carried it to the water's edge, then flopped down on his belly and started to chew it.

Ben watched him for a moment, then took a few more steps to a double swing overlooking the water just a few yards from the dock.

It was beautiful here. Wispy clouds encircled the tops of the Redemption Mountains and the setting sun painted them pink and coral and lavender, a scene perfectly reflected in the clear waters of the lake.

Because of the way the shoreline curved, he could see the lights of downtown begin to twinkle in the twilight and with a piercing cry, a red-tailed hawk suddenly soared from one of the tall pines that grew in such abundance around the lake, lending their crisp, tart scent to the scene.

Haven Point was an idyllic spot, really. How had he forgotten that over the years? Somehow he must have let the darkness and despair of his home life swallow the memory.

Yes, it was pretty. That didn't make him any happier at being forced to come back.

He could have said no.

He wasn't exactly an indentured servant. When Aidan asked him to take on this assignment after Marsh's sudden fatal heart attack, Ben could have told him to kiss off, to send someone else at Caine Tech.

Yes, they were facing a top-level decision but he could have picked two or three others on his team or Aidan's, people he trusted, who were likely to be more objective about Haven Point than he was.

It would have been the logical move—and Ben was nothing if not logical.

So why hadn't he? Why was he here on a beautiful late-June evening gazing out at a couple of colorful wood ducks swooping in to land on the water?

He didn't have a clear answer to that, even inside his own head. Something was tugging him back here and had been for some time. Closure, maybe? Some sense of unfinished business? He had left town so abruptly, the afternoon of Lily's funeral, and he hadn't been back since.

Whatever the reason drawing him to Haven Point, he was here now. Aidan had wanted him to take over for Marshall Phillips on this fact-finding assignment and Ben had agreed.

"I think it will be good for you to go back," Aidan said three days earlier when he came to Ben's house personally to ask him to come. "Take it from a man who survived a brain tumor. At some point in your life, before it's too late, you have to grab your ghosts by the throat and tell them to back the hell off. The only way to do that is to face them head-on."

He hadn't seen the point in arguing with Aidan that he didn't have ghosts, unless he were counting the painful memories of the younger sister he adored.

He didn't hate Haven Point. It was merely a small, beautifully situated town where he had once lived—one he had intended to spend the rest of his life without ever stepping foot in again.

"Besides," Aidan had continued with that logic that was always so damn hard for Ben to refute. "You were just saying how that Killy you've been working to renovate for the last year is done and ready for her maiden voyage. It seems fitting that you put her in the water for the first time at Lake Haven, where she came from."

Through the well-landscaped shrubs and trees, he caught sight of a figure moving past the window of the pretty little lake house next door.

He wasn't sure he would be able to tolerate living next door to Haven Point's vociferous mayor, even for a few days.

He remembered McKenzie. Those long-lashed dark eyes in her dusky skin, the inky hair, the dimples, which tended to flash equally, whether she was angry or happy.

How could he forget her, when she had been Lily's dearest and most loyal friend? While his sister's other friends seemed to have dropped off the edge of the earth after her condition deteriorated and she was forced to curtail most activity outside Snow Angel Cove, McKenzie had come faithfully at least two or three times a week, bringing homework and goodies and movies for the two of them to watch.

Yeah, he had been a self-absorbed, angry teenager, just trying to survive living in his father's house until he could graduate from high school and get the hell out. But even *he* had been able to see that McKenzie had made Lily's last year far more bearable—even *enjoyable*—than it would have been otherwise.

He would have liked to be able to thank her for that—but considering her animosity toward him, he wasn't sure she wanted to hear anything he had to say.

He inhaled deeply then let out a sigh. What had he expected? He had burned every bridge he'd ever crossed here and had walked away without looking back.

Now here he was again, fully aware that his history here with the people of this town—the difficult heritage he didn't like to remember—would make the job much harder than it would have been for Marshall.

CHAPTER THREE

AFTER A RESTLESS NIGHT filled with very strange dreams involving a certain sexy billionaire, McKenzie rose before sunrise and headed outside, leaving a disgruntled Rika behind. She grabbed her kayak and paddle from the shed next to the lake then launched it from the dock.

The rim of the sun started to appear above the high peaks of the Redemptions as she paddled south along the shoreline through clear, quiet water.

Only a few hardy anglers shared the water with her but they were way out in the deep water of the middle, probably going after the huge lake trout that could be found there. She hardly noticed them as she stroked through tendrils of mist that curled off the water on these mountain mornings.

A few loons flapped their feathers and moved away from her as she paddled in their direction. To her left, a fish jumped, going after all the little morning bugs that skimmed across the surface, and in the pine trees offshore on the other side, she heard an owl hoot as he returned to bed after a night prowling the forests. Sometimes it seemed like a dream that she really had a life here—a good one, too, filled with good friends, responsibilities she did her best to tackle, a thriving business she loved.

Things could have turned out very differently for her, the child of an overworked single mother who struggled every day to care for both of them.

When she considered what could have happened to her if she had ended up in foster care in California after her mother died, she had to cringe.

Okay. Things here hadn't exactly been perfect for her. She glanced at the shoreline, still in shadows as the sun continued its slow climb over the mountains. From here, she could see the house of her father and stepmother, where she had come to live when she was ten—a frightened, lost, grieving young girl.

Though nearly two decades had passed since the day Xochitl Vargas had arrived and been transformed slowly into McKenzie Shaw, she still felt the awkwardness of that first day when Richard had pulled into the driveway with her in the passenger seat of his BMW and her one suitcase of belongings in the trunk.

As uncomfortable as it had been for her, how much worse must it have been for her father, showing up in a small town like Haven Point with the half-Mexican love child he fathered with a paralegal during a business trip a decade earlier?

While it had taken her many years to come to this point, she had a more mature perspective now and could acknowledge the person who had been thrust in the *most* difficult situation—Adele, Devin's mother and Richard's wife.

She had opened her home and her family to the

by-product of a brief affair her husband had during a difficult time in their marriage. Maybe she hadn't been completely *enthusiastic* about the idea—or particularly warm and welcoming, for that matter, but she had done it.

McKenzie couldn't really say she blamed her. What woman would have been thrilled at being forced to face the evidence of her husband's infidelity every morning at the breakfast table?

Adele's coolness had been more than offset by Devin and Richard. Devin had been thrilled to have a new sister—even one just two years her junior—and Richard had gone out of his way to make up for the ten years he had never known she existed.

She felt a pang at the thought of her father, gone three years now. She missed him so much sometimes and would have dearly loved to ask his advice a hundred times a day.

Some distance past her childhood home—where Devin lived alone now since her mother had moved away after Richard's death—McKenzie pivoted the kayak around so she could paddle back home in time for work.

A few more boats had come out on the water by the time she made it back to Redemption Bay and reached the dock she shared temporarily with Ben. Even so, Lake Haven seemed quiet, serene.

Who could come here without feeling embraced by the beauty of the place?

Ben, probably. She frowned at the reminder as she hauled the kayak out of the water and carried it to the shed. He obviously hated it here—or why would he not have taken at least a passing interest in his holdings over the years?

As she headed out of the shed, she heard a low-throated bark and glanced over to the house next door just in time to see Ben and Hondo come out to the deck. The dog caught her attention first as he hurried down the deck steps to take care of what looked like urgent business. She smiled a little, then looked at Ben—and immediately wished she hadn't.

He wore only jeans and his hair was damp, as if he had just stepped out of the shower. He held a mug of something steamy and as she watched, he took a sip, then lowered the mug and appeared to be enjoying the sunrise bursting over the mountains.

She stood gawking like an idiot, unable to look away. Her insides felt shaky and hot and she remembered suddenly some of those weird dreams she'd had about him, filled with heat and steam and hunger.

He must have sensed her presence—or, who knows, maybe she whimpered or something. To her great dismay, he glanced in her direction and after an extremely awkward moment that seemed to stretch and tug between them like the taffy Carmela Rocca sold in her store, he lifted a hand in greeting.

With sudden chagrin, she remembered she was wearing a skintight wetsuit—the only way she had found to truly enjoy chilly morning paddles around the lake—and that from his vantage point, he had an entirely unobstructed view of her too-generous curves.

It couldn't be helped.

She nodded in response and then turned and walked with as much dignity as she could muster to her own house.

When she made it safely inside, she found Rika waiting by the door.

"Seriously?" she exclaimed to the dog. "You were out for fifteen minutes before I left. I can't believe you need to go again."

Her dog moved to the sunroom and whined, her attention solely focused on Ben's German shepherd. Apparently Rika was smitten.

"I'll let you out again in a minute—as soon as That Man lets his dog back in. You wouldn't want to fraternize with the enemy, would you?"

Rika looked mournful, obviously disagreeing, but she gave a resigned sigh and plopped onto the rug.

As she expected, Rika hadn't really needed to go out. When she saw the other dog was no longer in the yard, McKenzie opened the door but her dog only yawned and stretched out on the rug, just as if she hadn't been sleeping for most of the past ten hours.

McKenzie showered and dressed, then grabbed Rika's leash and the two of them took off into town.

By the time she reached downtown, she was brimming with energy from the walk and the early-morning paddle and hardly needed her usual coffee at Serrano's but she and Rika stopped, anyway.

The small columned city hall on Lake Street might be the political apex of Haven Point, with the old city library next door serving as the literary hub, but Serrano's, in its weathered redbrick building, was the social center of Haven Point.

The diner took up both stories of one of the downtown's oldest buildings and was founded by the current owner's great-grandparents, immigrants from Italy.

She tied Rika up in the small fenced grassy area Barbara Serrano and her husband had created just for visiting animals, then strolled through the glass door.

She loved walking inside the diner, that sense of slipping into an Old West time warp. From the mirrored wall behind the counter to the stamped-tin ceiling to the red leather chairs and old tables, Serrano's likely wasn't that different now than it had been a hundred years ago when it was founded. In the morning, the place smelled of pancakes, bacon and the best coffee in central Idaho.

Even more than the decor or the alluring scents, McKenzie loved the friendly welcome she always received when she walked inside.

A chorus of hellos rang out, almost as if people had spent hours practicing it together.

She waved to friends in general but made her way to the table of old-timers who had breakfast there each day, mostly to have somewhere to go and shoot the bull. She found them all completely adorable, BS and all, and always stopped to chat.

"Why, if it isn't the prettiest mayor west of the Mississippi."

"Morning, Ed." She smiled at Edwin Bybee. He was just about the happiest guy in town, with a kind word to everyone. It was remarkable to her, especially considering he was fighting stage-four liver cancer.

"How are you this morning?" she asked after kissing him on his wrinkled cheek.

"Oh, I can't complain. I'm still ticking, aren't I?"

"Was that you out on the lake this morning?" his constant companion, Archie Peralta, asked her.

He used to be the manager of the grocery store but retired when she was still in high school. She had worked for him in her first job as a bagger and cart retriever and had a deep fondness for him.

"It was indeed."

He gave a raspy laugh. "Thought so. That pink life jacket is a dead giveaway."

She grinned. "I hope I didn't scare the fish away."

"The cutthroat biting this morning?" asked Paul Weaver, whose family had a small dairy farm on the outskirts of town.

"You'll have to ask Archie here. He was the one with the line in the water that didn't seem to be moving much. I was only kayaking."

"Not this morning. They weren't going after the bait," Archie answered. "Don't know why anybody would bother going out on the water without a fishing rod."

"I'm only out there so I can watch you not catching anything," she retorted, which made the whole table bust up.

She spent a few more minutes talking to the group and was about to go order her coffee and head to the store when Barbara Serrano headed over with a go-cup for her all ready.

No wonder she loved the woman.

"Is it true?" Barbara asked, holding the coffee just out of McKenzie's reach as if they were playing a particularly cruel game of Monkey in the Middle.

"I don't know. I hope not," she answered automatically. "Is what true?"

"People have been talking all morning. Word is, Ben Kilpatrick is back in town."

Instantly, the diner seemed to go deathly silent, as if somebody had flipped a switch. The comfortable buzz of conversation, the occasional laughter, even the clatter of silverware seemed to shut down as everybody in the vicinity stopped as if Barbara had just doused them all with McKenzie's coffee.

"Kilpatrick. That son of a—" Ed bit off whatever harsh name he wanted to call Ben. His usually kindly, wrinkled face tightened into a scowl that shocked her, until she remembered that Ed as well as his only son had worked at the boatyard. After Kilpatrick's closed its doors five years ago, Ed's son and family had been forced to move away. She knew he lived in the Pacific Northwest along with Ed's only grandchildren.

Folks here took the closing of the boatworks hard, especially those who had worked there and been displaced in a single afternoon after Joe Kilpatrick's funeral.

"So is it true?" Barbara demanded. "Is he really back, after all this time?"

She sighed. "Yes. I can verify firsthand. Ben is in

town. He showed up last night, renting Carole's place next to mine."

Conversation immediately started up again, animated and annoyed.

"Why is he back? What kind of trouble is he planning to stir up now?" Archie asked.

"How much more damage can he do?" Ed glared at McKenzie as if all this was *her* fault. That was the problem with being the mayor, she was finding. Everybody expected her to solve their problems, from a neighbor who watered his garden all night to a streetlight that had gone out.

"I don't know why he's here," she confessed. "We only spoke for a moment last night. He did have an old Killy. Maybe he's here in advance of the boat festival."

It was a hollow explanation. She couldn't see Ben hauling a boat from California to the hometown he hated just to show off what even *she* could tell had been a very fine watercraft.

"What model?" Ed asked. For the moment, he seemed to forget his animosity toward Ben. The people who had worked at the boatworks took great pride in their product—probably why Killy boats were still so sought-after these days.

"He mentioned it was a Delphine."

"Oh, that is a fine boat," Archie said, almost reverently.

"One of our best," Ed agreed, in the same devout tones.

"I can't see that the kind of boat the man owns matters a good gosh darn," Barbara said. "I just want to know what he's doing *here* with it."

"I don't know," McKenzie admitted. "I can only promise you this. If he plans to cause more damage to this town than he already has, the jackass will have to get through me first."

"Is that right?"

An instant too late, she realized all conversation in their vicinity had ground to a halt again. She turned at the familiar low drawl and of course, there he was standing just a few feet away. He looked gorgeous, wearing those jeans—buttoned up now—and a tailored polo shirt and fancy high-tech watch that could probably cover her entire mortgage.

The air inside the diner seemed to suddenly plummet thirty degrees, as if a January cold front had just blown across the lake.

No one seemed to know what to say—which she found as shocking as Ben's presence here, since regulars usually had the opposite problem and never seemed to know when to shut up.

"Hello," Ben said.

She cleared her throat, grateful the dusky skin she inherited from her mother didn't show the heat she could feel soaking her cheeks. At least she hoped not.

"Um. Hi." He knew she didn't want him there, so she couldn't see the point in showing outright hostility to the man. Okay, any more than she already had. "Everyone. You remember Ben Kilpatrick, I'm sure."

Edwin opened his mouth to say something but Archie elbowed him in the ribs. While she would have liked to see them rip into Ben, this didn't seem the time or the place—and she had a feeling that as resentful as everyone in town might be toward him for his negligence, most people were too well-mannered to throw it in his lap the first time they met.

"Hear you've got yourself a Delphine," Archie said.

"I do. A 1965 model. She's a beauty."

"You restore her yourself?" Edwin asked.

"The easy parts. Mostly, I worked with a couple guys in the Bay area, who did the heavy lifting. I'm planning to put her in the water later today."

"You want to keep an eye out for crevice corrosion. As I recall, the Delphine was prone to that."

"I'll do that. Thanks."

"If you need a hand off-loading from your trailer, my grandson Jake works at the marina," Paul said. "Don't let the earring fool you. He'll treat your Delphine like a newborn babe."

Just once, she wished the residents of Haven Point weren't so darn nice. This man had single-handedly turned a thriving community into a shadow of itself—but here was Ed, who had been directly impacted by Ben's overnight decision to close the boatworks, giving him tips on the Delphine, for crying out loud, and Paul offering up his grandson's help.

Was she the only one willing to fight the good fight?

"As I recall," Ben said, "Serrano's was always the best place in town for breakfast. Is that still the case?"

"Sure enough," Archie answered.

"Try the Western omelet," Paul said. "You can't go wrong."

"I never met a Serrano's pancake I didn't like," Archie said.

Ben smiled. "Both sound good."

"Why don't you take a seat at the bar and you can see for yourself?" Barbara said.

"I prefer a table if you've got one free."

"Sure. I can swing that. Looks like a nice one just opened up by the front window. Just over there."

"I see it."

McKenzie glared at her friend. She would have thought Barbara, at least, would be on her side. Why give the man the best table in the house?

"Menus are at the table and I'll bring coffee in a minute."

"Thank you. Mayor Shaw. Can you join me for a moment? I need a quick word."

She could think of several words she would be happy to give him, free of charge, but she forced herself to remain calm.

Out the window, she could see Rika, who looked perfectly content, flopped onto her belly in a small patch of sunlight, watching the cars go past on Lake Street. "I'm in a rush, but I can spare a moment."

She followed him to the booth, trying not to notice the broad shoulders tapering down to a narrow waist. It seemed wrong, somehow. He was a tech geek businessman, right? He ought to be pale, hunched over and asthmatic, not brimming with tanned athletic grace.

An image popped into her mind of him that morning on his terrace wearing only those jeans, masculine and relaxed. She swallowed hard. She really needed to get out more. Her friends were always trying to set her up with a grandson here, a cousin there. Maybe she needed to stop fighting the would-be matchmakers and give in, once in a while.

She slid into the booth across from him, noting the lovely view of the lake and the mountains from here. She never got tired of looking at those calming blue waters.

"You're an early riser," he said.

She felt that heat rising on her features again and was grateful again he couldn't see her discomfort. "Wasting a beautiful June morning here is nothing short of criminal, as far as I'm concerned."

His mouth twitched a little. When he didn't quite make it into a full-fledged smile, she told herself the little clutch in her stomach couldn't possibly be disappointment. "Have you made a law against that, Mayor?"

"Not yet. I'll add it to the next town council agenda." She refused to be drawn to him. Everyone else might roll over like Rika for a good long belly scratch, but not her.

"I have to go open my store," she said shortly. "What did you want to talk to me about?"

"You want to know why I'm back in Haven Point. I thought about it overnight and decided it's only fair to tell you."

Ah. Finally. "I agree. We have the right to know, especially if you've come to town to figure out some other way to drive our economy into the ground."

He frowned. "I'm beginning to find that accusation and your hostile attitude more than a little tiresome."

"I'm so sorry," she said with a forced sweetness that made her teeth ache as if she'd just eaten an entire bag of that taffy she was thinking about earlier. "I guess something about you brings out the worst in me." *Could be the lasting damage you've done to my town, but that might be just a guess.* "Go on. Tell me why you're here."

He sighed. "I didn't expect to ever return but apparently I have a tough time saying no to some people."

"Aidan Caine."

He raised an eyebrow. "Did he contact you to let you know I was coming?"

"A lucky guess. You're the chief operations officer of Caine Tech and Aidan's right-hand man. Aidan just bought half the town. Aidan and his wife-to-be, Eliza, have wonderful taste and both love Haven Point—unlike some people I won't mention—and they've been working to revitalize it. Suddenly, you show up, obviously not happy about being here. I connected the dots. What did Aidan ask you to do?"

A muscle worked in his jaw. He glanced around Serrano's. If not for her own tension, she might have found it amusing how heads swiveled back to their meals as if everybody in the place wasn't watching him covertly—and some not even bothering with that.

He angled slightly toward the window, away from the other diners, and leaned forward, speaking in a low voice that forced her to incline forward as well, until their heads were just inches apart, far more intimate than she was completely comfortable with.

Up close, he smelled of toothpaste and some kind of expensive soap, woodsy and masculine and delicious.

Not that she noticed.

"This is a delicate situation and one that requires total discretion, as I'm sure you can understand. Unfounded rumors only stir the pot to overflowing and generally end up making a big mess."

"What sort of rumors should I have heard?"

"Nothing, I hope," he said. "I would like to keep it that way. Please don't share what I'm about to tell you with anyone. Not the town council, not your executive staff."

Which consisted of Anita Robles, her personal assistant at city hall and the real driving force behind the town. She supposed Dale Pierson, the public works director, might count as executive staff, but that was about it.

"Fine. I won't say anything," she said.

He studied her as if trying to gauge whether she meant it. Finally, he nodded. "The truth is, Caine Tech is expanding into a couple fresh areas and we have need of a new facility that would employ about three hundred people. Aidan is pushing to move those operations to Haven Point."

Her brain seemed to stall on "employ" and "three hundred people." Jobs. An economic base beyond tourism. That was *exactly* what Haven Point needed. It could mean new housing, stores, restaurants.

Bless Aidan and his sweet fiancée. If Eliza had

been there, McKenzie would have smooched her right on the lips.

As it was, she almost smooched Ben, since he was only a few inches away—until her brain kicked in again and she remembered exactly who sat across the table from her.

Her burgeoning excitement popped as if he had just blasted it with a shotgun. Very carefully, she eased away a little and entwined her fingers together in her lap. "Aidan asked you to come here," she said slowly. "In what capacity?"

He glanced out at the others in the restaurant then back at her. "Call it a fact-finding mission. In two weeks, I'm supposed to report to Aidan and the board of directors with a cost-benefit analysis of placing our new facility in Haven Point."

Just as she suspected. Her stomach dropped. So much for all those beautiful jobs and families and dreams of prosperity.

"Why would he send you? Aidan can't possibly think for a moment you're capable of offering an objective opinion," she hissed. "You hate it here with a passion."

"*Hate* is a strong word. I don't hate Haven Point. I'm indifferent. There's a big difference."

"Fine. You're *passionately indifferent*, though I don't know how it's possible not to love it here. Haven Point is a beautiful place filled with good, hardworking people who care about this town and about each other."

He leaned back in his seat. "That may be true but

I can't see that as a basis for investing millions in a new facility here. I'll be honest. I see real problems with Haven Point. For one thing, the distance to a major airport is a real concern. Boise is almost two hours away. It's fine for Aidan, who has his own private jet, but everybody else will have to travel here from Boise. Then you've got the matter of your inadequate infrastructure and few housing opportunities. All are negatives."

"Are there any positives?"

He remained stubbornly silent and she wanted to point out a hundred wonderful things about her town. Besides the kind neighbors and beautiful surroundings, she could have cited the relatively low cost of living, the well-educated population, the favorable tax conditions.

"I see," she said when his silence stretched out. "That's clear enough."

"It's a very pretty lake town, McKenzie, but when it comes to business decisions, that can't be enough. From my perspective, the negatives outweigh the positives. But I'm here and I'm keeping an open mind."

She doubted that was possible for him but she didn't see the point in arguing.

"Thank you for telling me."

"It seemed only fair. I should also let you know, part of my responsibility here is to study the possibility of placing the facility in Shelter Springs. It's larger, with better infrastructure and a bigger existing real estate market and commercial base. If we did that, Haven Point would probably see some trickle-down positive impact."

The waitress was heading in their direction and she used that as an excuse to jump from the booth. "I've got to go so I can open my store. Thank you for telling me why you're really here. I guess it's good to know what we're up against. You're going to change your mind. Mark my words. After you spend a week in Haven Point, you'll have no choice but to see we're the clear winner among all your contenders."

She had no idea how she was going to prove that to him, but she darn well intended to try.

CHAPTER FOUR

BEN WASN'T AT ALL SURE he liked that sudden militant gleam in the mayor's lovely dark gaze as she looked at him.

"I admire your confidence," he murmured. He considered it completely misguided and without merit, but he appreciated her determination and her loyalty.

"You'll see," she repeated, then grabbed her go-cup off the table and turned around and headed for the door.

He hated to disappoint her but he truly felt as if Haven Point was the weakest of the contenders. He intended to make a decision based on logic and reason. He was doing his best to keep an open mind but it wasn't easy.

He had offered up the town's greatest shortcomings, from his perspective. What he hadn't told her was that everywhere he looked in Haven Point, the past seemed to crowd him.

Being here again left him itchy, on edge. All the dark, ugly memories he thought he had firmly and succinctly dealt with long ago seemed to be creeping back to life, like skeletal, decomposing fingers suddenly poking over the side of an opened grave.

The waitress reached him finally. She poured coffee without asking and pulled out a notebook. "Have you decided yet?" she asked, her tone just shy of belligerent.

She looked familiar, a woman about his age and on the plump, comfortable side. Her name tag read Sharon and he suddenly placed her. Sharon Lowell. She had been in his grade and had dated one of his friends.

"Hi, Sharon. Good to see you again."

"Likewise." She offered a smile that didn't look close to genuine. It took him a moment to remember her brother and father had both worked at the boatworks.

McKenzie Shaw wasn't the only one in town who hated him. He wasn't used to that but he supposed he couldn't really blame them. Closing Kilpatrick Boatworks had been a necessary but difficult decision, when the business was steadily losing hundreds of thousands of dollars a year.

"Have you had time to look at the menu or do you need a few more minutes?"

"I'm ready. I believe I'll have a Greek omelet and a side of whole wheat toast."

"Right. You want hash browns or anything?"

"No. Just the eggs and toast."

"Got it." She nodded and walked away without even bothering to make the customary server small talk.

As soon as she left, he once more became conscious of all the gazes aimed in his direction, some simply curious, others openly hostile.

It was awkward all the way around. He and Aidan both should have expected this. He was apparently the least popular person in Haven Point.

At least in one respect, he was carrying on his father's legacy.

After looking out the window for a while at the desultory traffic passing by, he turned to the reliable diversion of his cell phone and started scrolling through and answering messages and emails.

After a few moments, a voice intruded into his digital distraction.

"Ben! I thought that was you."

He looked up and knew the man instantly, though he hadn't seen him in years. Probably not since Lily's funeral, when he had left Haven Point.

Dr. Russell Warrick, their family's longtime physician, was still handsome, though in his late fifties. He had brown hair threaded with gray, warm blue eyes and a trim, athletic build.

Lily had quite simply adored the man. As far as Ben's younger sister had been concerned, Dr. Warrick could do no wrong.

He had always been so calm and patient with her, Ben remembered, even in those difficult last days of hospice.

He stood up and held out his hand. "Dr. Warrick. Hello."

"Wow. It's great to see you, son! It's been far too long since you've been back this way."

He couldn't say he agreed but he smiled anyway, remembering a hundred different kindnesses over the years.

He gestured to the table across from him. "Join me, won't you?"

"I just finished but I'll sit for a moment to catch up. I'm due at the hospital for rounds but not for a while yet."

"How are you?" Ben asked when the physician sat down. "How's your family?"

Warrick had two sons, one a few years younger than Ben and another who had been around Lily and McKenzie's age.

"The boys are good. They both live in Boise and between the two have given me three beautiful grandchildren." He paused and sadness slanted across those blue eyes. "You may not have heard but I lost my wife a year ago."

He remembered the other woman as kind and matronly. "I'm very sorry for your loss."

"She was a good woman and I miss her every day, even a year later. I try to stay busy but, well, you know. I have cut back, though. I've taken on a go-getter young partner and she's doing most of the work these days. You may remember her from school, though I think she was a bit younger than you. Devin Shaw."

McKenzie's half sister, he recalled. He had never known her well but he remembered her as being scary-smart.

"So how long are you back in town?" Warrick asked him.

"I'm not sure," he hedged. "A week, maybe. Ten days."

"You're still working with Aidan at Caine Tech?"

"I am."

"He's a good man," Warrick said with a smile.

Ben still found it odd that his best friend had a life here that he loved. It was more than a little surreal that the world where he had lived his first seventeen years had merged with the world he had created since leaving—and he still felt more than a little guilty about selling Aidan his holdings here.

If he'd had any idea Aidan had a brain tumor when the other man offered an exorbitant amount for Snow Angel Cove and his commercial holdings in Haven Point, Ben never would have agreed to the deal. The whole situation still left a bad taste in his mouth, even though he had sold the property for far less than market value.

In the end, Aidan had come out ahead—as he usually did—but Ben knew the other man never would have even made an offer for property in this obscure corner of Idaho if the tendrils of a benign tumor hadn't been pressing on key decision-making areas of his brain at the time.

After Aidan's diagnosis, Ben had tried to back out of the deal and invalidate the sale but Aidan refused to let him. For reasons Ben still didn't understand, Aidan had fallen for this place and for Snow Angel Cove.

"You've done well for yourself with Caine, haven't you?" Warrick said.

"He's a good man," he answered.

From their first encounter when Caine Tech was just a start-up like thousands of others in Silicon Valley, they had clicked. They made a damn good team. Aidan was inarguably the tech wizard behind the success of the company but Ben liked to think he was the business genius.

"I could always tell you had big things ahead of you," Warrick said, with an odd note in his voice that almost sounded like pride.

Ben didn't know quite how to answer that so he remained silent.

"Your mother must be thrilled to have you back in town, even if it's only for a few weeks."

The band of tension around his shoulders seemed to ratchet a notch tighter. "I haven't had the chance to tell her," he said curtly. "I don't believe she's around, anyway. Last I heard she was going to Tuscany."

He should have called her, anyway. The moment he gave in and agreed to come to town on this assignment, he should have dropped her an email. Technically, Lydia lived in Shelter Springs—well, she had a condo there anyway, purchased after Big Joe died, but she lived there only in the summer months. Most of the time, she lived in the San Diego area, near one of her sisters, where she had moved after the divorce.

He wasn't estranged from his mother. They spoke on the phone or emailed weekly but theirs was a strained relationship.

Though he might tell himself he was over the past, he could never quite forgive his mother for the choices she made and he supposed that was the reason he preferred a casual, superficial relationship between them. Over the years, she had given up trying to forge a closer bond.

Dr. Warrick gave him a long, thoughtful look. “Shelter Springs is only a ten-minute drive, son. If she’s in town, I’m sure she would love to see you.”

He didn’t want to be rude to the man but he also didn’t particularly care to discuss with him the complicated relationship he and his mother shared. Especially not in a crowded diner.

“I’m sure you’re right,” he said in a noncommittal way.

The doctor seemed to sense he had overstepped. He gave a kindly smile and stood up.

“I should probably head to the hospital. Injured and sick people aren’t always the most patient people on earth. Pun intended.”

Ben forced a smile. “Good to see you,” he said. It was the truth. Russell Warrick was at least a friendly face in a town that didn’t seem very inclined to look favorably at his return.

Warrick studied him with that intense expression he sometimes wore when he looked at Ben. “I would love a chance to catch up more while you’re in town. Maybe we could arrange dinner sometime.”

“I would enjoy that,” Ben answered. “I’m staying in a rental on Redemption Bay. The old Sloane house.”

“I know it. Perfect. I’ll drop by one day soon so we can make arrangements.”

The doctor reached out a hand and shook Ben’s. “Good to see you, son. I mean it.”

With another of those kindly smiles, he walked out, leaving Ben alone with his memories and a restaurant full of people who didn't want him there.

RUSS WALKED OUT of the diner into the beautiful blue of an Idaho summer morning feeling shaky, off balance at the unexpected encounter. He walked a few dozen steps on autopilot, then turned into the small alley next to the restaurant used by delivery trucks. When he was sure no one could see him, he rubbed a hand over the ache in his chest.

Lydia's quiet, thoughtful boy had grown into a tall, handsome man. A man any parent would be proud of.

But, oh, the shadows in those blue eyes.

When he woke that morning and decided to grab a bite to eat at Serrano's before work, he never expected to find Ben drinking coffee and looking out at the lake.

How could he have? As far as he knew, Ben hadn't been back since the day of his sister's funeral.

He stood, lost in indecision, while the lake sparkled in the distance and the peaks of the Redemption Mountains gleamed white in the sunlight with snow that hadn't melted yet.

This had been easier when his wife was still alive. Joan had provided a necessary buffer, somehow, to keep him from doing something stupid.

She was gone now, bless her. After a year, he was finally learning to make his way without her, one baby step at a time.

Perhaps it was time he took a giant step into the

unknown and finally faced all the murky secrets of the past.

He picked up his cell phone. A quick web search revealed the number he had purposely avoided looking up for a year.

He was ridiculously aware that his palms were sweating as he selected "call" on the phone options.

It rang four times. Just before he was certain the call would go to voice mail, a slightly breathless voice answered. "Hello?"

He swallowed. "Lydia. Hello. It's Russ Warrick. Is this a bad time?"

After a long, awkward pause, she spoke again, clear surprise in her voice. "Russ. Hello. No. No. It's not a bad time. I was in the middle of yoga."

He tried not to picture her, limber and prettier at fifty-four than she had ever been.

"Sorry to interrupt. You can call me back when your class is over."

"No class. Just a video at home. I paused it. Really, this is fine. Is something wrong?"

"Why would you say that?"

"I haven't talked to you in forever," she said calmly. "You're not a man who calls out of the blue just to chat."

That was true enough. He had stayed away from her on purpose, hadn't called her once since Joanie died, even though he had been tempted a hundred times.

This was a stupid idea, he thought. Her relationship with Ben was none of his business. *She* was none of his business. But stupid or not, he had called her and couldn't just make an excuse now and hang up.

"Nothing's wrong, exactly. I had some information I thought might interest you."

"Oh?"

"I just bumped into Ben at Serrano's."

"Ben? *My* Ben?"

The singular pronoun sent pain clutching his heart. "Yes. Your Ben. I thought you might want to know."

Her tone shifted from shock to crisp disbelief. "That's impossible. I'm sure you've made a mistake. Ben will never come back to Haven Point. He's made that abundantly clear."

"No mistake. I spoke with him for a good ten minutes." A wonderful ten minutes. It had been so very long, he had absorbed every word, memorized each mannerism and vocal tone. "He's in town to help Aidan Caine with a project. Apparently he'll be here for a few weeks. I thought you might want to know."

"What makes you think I didn't already know?" she asked in a haughty tone. The essence of Lydia, bristly and distant on the outside but so very vulnerable beneath all the layers.

"Your reaction just now was a good giveaway." He fought hard to keep the dryness out of his tone. "He also seemed reluctant when I suggested he call you."

"So you thought you would step in to make things right between us by calling me, anyway. How very helpful of you."

Her hostility stung, though it wasn't unexpected. Lydia had erected a wall between them long ago, so high and so wide one would never guess they'd once been best friends…and much more.

"I'm sorry I bothered you," he said stiffly. "I know if *my* son were in town, I would want to know."

She didn't answer for a long moment, a silence thick and murky with secrets. Why wouldn't she tell him the truth, even after all these years?

"I'm sorry," she finally said, her voice subdued. "You're right. I'm a bear today. I think it's the low pressure system coming in. It's left me edgy. I was hoping the yoga would help center me. Perhaps I'd better get back to it. Thank you for telling me, Russell. You're right. I do want to know. I doubt Ben would have called to tell me himself, even though he knows I'm in the area for the summer. I appreciate that you stepped in."

"You're welcome."

He should say goodbye but he didn't want to hang up. Not yet. A cool and distant Lydia was better than nothing.

"How are you doing?" she asked after a moment. "I've been wondering."

She sounded genuinely interested, which was more than most people did when they asked that question. His standard response was to say he was fine then deflect the inquiries with a change in topic but that didn't seem right with Lydia.

Somehow there seemed more freedom here on the phone, when she wasn't standing in front of him with those deep green eyes.

He looked out at the lake, silvery in the sunlight.

"It's been a year and a few weeks now," he answered, his voice low. "I'm done with all the firsts now. First Christmas without her, first birthday, first wedding anniversary. There's an odd sort of relief in that, you know? In making it through. I believe I'm finally starting to get used to coming home to a quiet house."

"I'm so sorry, Russell," she said, her tone soft and rich with empathy.

"Thank you. You know a little about loss yourself."

"More than I'd care to. Yes. The first year was definitely the hardest after Lily died. I remember the first time I laughed again at a joke on a television show. I felt so terribly guilty afterward, I cried myself to sleep. But then I began to find more and more things to smile about and realized my life wasn't over, just different."

"Yes. That's it exactly. It's a perspective shift. I'm still finding my way but at least I don't feel like I'm floundering through quicksand anymore." He appreciated that she was willing to push beyond the usual platitudes and the superficial sympathy.

"I know I said it at the funeral but I truly am sorry for your loss. Joan was a wonderful woman."

"Thank you. She was." In light of the direction the conversation had taken, he thought perhaps he should just say goodbye and hang up, but it felt so very good to talk to her. He didn't want it to end.

"The hardest thing for me is eating alone. Would you…go to dinner with me sometime?"

Silence met his question and his palms seemed

suddenly sweaty. Lord. Why was this so much harder at fifty-seven than it had been at seventeen?

"Yes," she finally said. "Yes, I think I would like that very much."

The sun suddenly seemed blinding off the water. "Great. Perfect. What about Sunday? There's a concert at the park afterward, if you'd like to go. Bluegrass, apparently." He wouldn't have known that except he was staring right at the poster on the wall outside the diner.

"Why don't we start with dinner, then we can go from there." She sounded overwhelmed suddenly, as if she regretted agreeing to go. He wondered if this was as awkward for her as for him.

"Dinner is a good start. A very good start. I'll see you then."

And with luck, he would find a way to see Ben before then, too, one more time—and maybe finally, after all these years, together they could pull back the lid containing all the secrets between them.

CHAPTER FIVE

McKenzie gazed around her workroom at the women gathered there.

Her troops.

Her sister, Devin, sat next to Megan Hamilton, who owned the inn that had burned down last year, and across from Lindy-Grace Keegan, McKenzie's right hand at the store. All around the battered table in the workroom of Point Made Flowers and Gifts sat her dearest friends, the other members of the Haven Point Helping Hands.

Her heart swelled as she gazed at their beautiful faces. One urgent phone call, that's all it had taken, and she had fifteen women willing to drop everything on a busy Saturday morning to see what they could do to help.

Hazel Selby Brewer and her sister Eppie had obviously been playing tennis, at least judging by their matching white skirts and short-sleeved sweaters that showed off their knobby knees, varicose veins and age spots. Though a year apart—Irish twins, they always informed people proudly—they dressed almost identically. The two were inseparable and had even married twin brothers—though since Hazel's husband, Donald, died two years earlier, Eppie's husband, Ronald, had taken over escorting both women around town.

Hazel and Eppie wore their wrinkles well. They were the oldest of the Helping Hands at eighty-three and eighty-two. The youngest, Samantha Fremont and her best friend, Katrina Bailey, were in their early twenties. They dressed in short shorts and tight T-shirts and both looked a bit hungover, as if they'd partied a little too late on Friday night at the Mad Dog, which had featured a live band the night before.

In between the two ends of the spectrum were housewives, a real estate agent, a couple of teachers. They weren't particular about who could come to the Helping Hands meetings.

She loved every single one of them.

McKenzie drew in a deep breath that smelled of flowers and raffia and sage. "Thank you all for coming to meet with us. I know everybody is crazy busy right now, especially on a summer Saturday with Lake Haven Days in less than a week. I hardly have time to take a shower most days, and I imagine it's the same for all of you. I can't tell you how much I appreciate each one of you for dropping everything and coming for this impromptu meeting."

"What's going on?" Linda Fremont demanded. "Marie wouldn't tell me anything."

"Because I don't *know* anything," Marie Caldwell said in a testy tone. "All I heard from Hazel was that Kenzie had called an emergency meeting and it was all hands on deck. That's the message I got and the message I passed along."

"It had better be important," Linda Fremont said, her features as sour as ever. "I need to be at the store. This is one of our busiest days of the summer."

McKenzie gave a patient smile. Linda didn't need to be there, since her daughter Samantha had come as well and could have passed along any message—but then Linda would have had to miss something, which she would have found intolerable.

"This won't take long, I promise." She tried her best to be sweet to Linda, even when the woman was at her most annoying. Which was quite often, unfortunately.

"I think I can guess what this is about," Barbara Serrano said. "Does it have anything to do with our unexpected visitor and your companion at the diner this morning?"

Only a few people looked confused—but that was still a few more than McKenzie had expected. She had anticipated the news of Ben's return would have already spread through Haven Point like a late-October frost, touching everything in its path.

"Who was it?" Sam Fremont asked, blue eyes widening with interest. "Are you dating somebody, Kenz?"

"No! Absolutely not! Anyway, why would I call an emergency meeting to tell you all about my date?"

"Breaking news?" Devin asked.

She glared at her sister. "It wasn't a date. I can't believe you all haven't heard this already, but, okay. Here it is. Ben Kilpatrick is back in town."

This caused a minor stir. Sam and Kat gaped at

each other, probably trying to figure out how they had missed the news that a gorgeous billionaire bachelor was suddenly in their humble midst. Hazel and Eppie also looked shocked. Other than that, most of the women wore expressions ranging from curiosity to disgruntlement to outright anger.

"Betty Orton came into the store this morning and told me but I didn't believe it."

"Why didn't you say anything, Mom?" Sam demanded.

"I just said, I didn't believe it. What's the point of passing along gossip without a shred of proof?" she said. McKenzie almost rolled her eyes. Linda delighted in sharing any tidbit she heard and rarely bothered to authenticate any of it.

"It seemed impossible to me and that's what I told Betty. How can he dare show his face here after what he's done to this town?" Linda glowered.

"I'll admit I was pretty surprised, too, when he sauntered into the diner this morning like the cock of the walk."

"Oh, he was always such a polite boy," Hazel exclaimed. "And so handsome. Remember how handsome he was, Eppie?"

Eppie beamed. "Oh, yes. I remember, with those brooding blue eyes. Like a young Paul Newman in *From the Terrace*."

"Oooh, I loved that movie," her sister exclaimed.

"Is he still as handsome, Mayor?" Eppie asked.

"Well, yes, Eppie dear. But that's not the point."

"What does he want?" Linda Fremont demanded.

"Let me guess. He and Aidan are going to raze the whole downtown and build a golf course."

"What?" Hazel exclaimed. "That's not right! We don't need a golf course! Shelter Springs already has one. That would be just plain crazy!"

"We could take up golf next, Hazel," Eppie protested. "I think it would be fun."

Okay, she dearly loved all these women and they had been amazingly sweet to her over the years but sometimes during these meetings, McKenzie felt as if she was trying to grab hold of a whole herd of greased piglets.

Did piglets run in herds?

She pushed away the stupid random thought. "Nobody is building a golf course, I promise. Look, our time is limited here. Lindy-Grace and I have a busy Saturday ahead of us and I know the rest of you do, too. Let's try to stay focused so we can all get back to it. The truth is, as much as I would like to, I can't tell you exactly what Ben is doing here—I don't know specifics anyway and he's asked me to keep what little I *do* know to myself."

"Then what's the point of calling a meeting if you're going to be Miss Locked Lips?" Marie demanded.

"The truth is, I need your help. I know you all love Haven Point as much as I do. None of us is happy about what's happened here the last five years. This has been a dark time for us."

Because of what she intended to ask, she was careful not to remind them the town had suffered mostly because Ben had ignored his responsibilities and let the downtown fall into disrepair.

"This is our chance to turn things around," she went on. "Aidan and Ben are considering something that might improve things around here. That's all I can say about it right now. Trust me, this would be very good for us."

"What do you need us to do?" Ever wise, her friend Julia Winston, one of the librarians at the Haven Point library, struck to the heart of the matter.

She sighed, looking around the assembly of her dearest friends. "This is difficult for me to ask. I know how you all feel about Ben. I share your feelings, believe me."

"You mean, you think he's hotter than a billy goat with a blowtorch?" Hazel asked.

Eppie laughed and so did just about everybody else in the room, even Devin. McKenzie felt her face heat, finding it extremely difficult to be appropriately mayoral and dignified around this crowd.

"Okay, first of all, how hot can a billy goat with a blowtorch really get? And why does he have a blowtorch in the first place? But that's not the point, is it? No. The point is, it's extremely important that while Ben is here, we work very hard to show Haven Point in the best possible light."

"How do you propose we do that?" Devin asked.

"That's where I need your help. I need some ideas about how we can prove to him that this town is warm and neighborly, that he won't find a better place anywhere in the mountain west."

"I think we need to kill the man with kindness, even when we want to strangle him," Lindy-Grace suggested.

"Excellent. Excellent. If you see him on the street, stop and say hello. Show him genuine interest. Be neighborly and welcoming."

"That would have been easier if he hadn't made such a mess of things," Marie protested.

"If it were easy, I wouldn't have to call an emergency meeting and beg you all to help me," McKenzie said.

"You don't have to beg," Eppie said. "Hazel and I will be nice to him—so nice, he'll think he's died and gone to heaven and has two wrinkly old angels at his beck and call."

Oh, gosh. That was an image she didn't need. "Don't overdo, ladies. Just be kind. That's all I ask."

"You want us to suck up to Ben Kilpatrick, after everything he's done?" Linda Fremont demanded.

"Not suck up to him, exactly. Just put aside your anger for now in the interest of helping the town. An investment, if you will, in something that could pay off for all of us. And please ask your brothers and husbands and fathers to do the same."

She wasn't sure it would work—or if it was even right. He shouldn't get a pass for all the things he had done to harm this town, simply because he was here on behalf of Aidan.

"He did come at a great time for seeing Haven Point at its best," Julia said.

"Right. One of the busiest but most fun weeks of

the year, with Lake Days next week along with our July Fourth celebrations *and* all the events surrounding the wooden boat show."

"Don't forget the service auction just a few days after that," Lindy-Grace said.

She nodded, heartened by the response. At least they weren't throwing tomatoes at her just yet. "Exactly. The timing couldn't be more perfect, really, unless Ben were to show up during the Lights on the Lake Festival. Since he's not here at Christmastime, we'll have to take what we can get. This is a perfect chance to showcase the best Haven Point has to offer. I will make sure he is invited to everything, from the mayor's kickoff luncheon this week to the barbecue at the beach park to the fireworks."

Linda sniffed. "I don't think we should have to kiss that man's ass, no matter how hot Eppie and Hazel might think it is."

It was indeed a fine backside, but McKenzie wasn't about to admit that.

"I completely understand your feelings, Linda, and I'm not saying they're off base. You have to do what you think is right. I will add that, like it or not, Ben could hold the future of our little town in his hands. I just want him to see that any decision he makes will have real impact on a town and a group of people who have already been through a great deal."

Most of the women in the group seemed to be on her side, though she sensed a few siding with Linda Fremont.

"Be nice to him. That's possibly a tall order, but manageable by most," Devin said. "What else?"

"That's where I need your input. A good old-fashioned Helping Hands brainstorming session. Go."

AS SHE HOPED, she was able to keep the meeting to less than an hour, and most of that was spent keeping the Brewer sisters from drooling over a picture of Ben with Aidan Caine that Kat Bailey had found on Google on her smartphone.

Finally, game plan in hand, everybody went their separate ways except Lindy-Grace and Devin, who stayed to help pick up paper plates and cups from the few snacks McKenzie had been able to score at the last minute.

"That went pretty well, don't you think?" McKenzie asked both of them, her two closest confidantes.

"I don't know." Devin shook her head. "Linda is a pretty tough sell, as always."

"I know. She can give stubborn lessons to a three-year-old. I just hope she doesn't sabotage anything. Slash his tires or key his car or something."

"Sam will keep her in check. Don't worry."

McKenzie sometimes thought she did nothing *but* worry. With her luck, she had probably picked up an ulcer in the few hours since Ben had told her the reason behind his return.

Whatever Aidan and Ben might eventually decide about the new facility was completely beyond her control but that didn't stop her from fretting about all the possible ways she could help sway him toward Haven Point.

"I know. She's not vicious anyway, just sometimes a little...opinionated," she answered, which was a little like saying the surrounding mountains received a little snow during their legendary winters.

"She might be angry at Ben but she's not stupid," Devin said with that calm rationale McKenzie envied so much. "She won't do anything to screw up this chance if it means a single dollar more profit for the boutique she loves."

"I suppose you're right."

"She's definitely right," LG chimed in. "Anyway, enough boring talk about the fate of Haven Point. Let's talk about me."

"A far more interesting topic," McKenzie agreed.

Lindy-Grace grinned. "I know. You're still taking my kids Sunday night, right? I know it's a huge favor and terrible timing, right after Lake Haven Days, but I can't tell you how desperately Mac and I need some alone time, if you know what I mean."

"No. I have no idea what you mean," she said with studied innocence.

Her sister snorted. "That's because you need to get out more. When was the last time you went to dinner with anybody besides the city council?"

"You're one to talk. Have you even had a date since medical school?"

"Yes. I'll have you know, just last week Archie and Ed bought me breakfast at Serrano's. Apparently they like the way I fill out a lab coat."

"Who doesn't? You've always been a big hit with the over-seventy crowd."

"A girl's got to take what she can get sometimes. So. Operation Charm Ben's Socks Off. What do you need me to do?"

For some weird reason, the idea of Devin charming socks—or anything else—off Ben bothered her far more than it should, but she told herself she was being ridiculous.

"If I end up siccing my vicious dog on him because he's driving me crazy next door, you can stitch him up for me," she suggested.

Devin laughed and ruffled Rika's curly head. "Sounds like a plan." She glanced at her watch. "If you need me to do anything else, you know where to find me. I'd better run. I've got a hundred errands to run on my first day off in weeks."

"Okay. See you. Thanks for making time today for the emergency summit."

"No problem." Devin hugged her and McKenzie wrapped her arms around her sister, deeply grateful for the bond between them. When McKenzie showed up out of the blue all those years ago, Devin could have been cold and distant, resentful and embarrassed about having an illegitimate half sister thrust into her world.

Instead, Devin had literally and physically embraced her from the very beginning and had never been anything but kind and loving.

"So you didn't answer me about next weekend," LG pushed after Devin left.

"Yes. I am planning on your two wild children staying at my place. I can't wait." LG's boys were completely adorable, even though McKenzie was exhausted just thinking about entertaining them for thirty-six hours. "We're going to have a fabulous time. I'm stocking up on all the sugary sweets I can find and fully intend to send them back to you with an epic sugar high bordering on illegal."

Lindy-Grace laughed, though it didn't mask the worry in her eyes. McKenzie suspected by a few things her friend let slip that her marriage wasn't completely rosy. Mac Keegan could be a jerk sometimes, loud and annoying with a tendency to drink a little too much on the weekends and ignore his hardworking wife and cute kids.

If dinner and a night away at the small romantic boutique inn where Eliza Hayward used to work would help reignite their burners, McKenzie was more than willing to help out.

Now, if only she could help her town as easily.

HE SERIOUSLY WANTED to deck Aidan Caine.

The man might be a genius and Ben's closest friend, but right now, if the other man happened to walk through the doors of the small Haven Point city offices, Ben would be tempted to take him out with one punch.

He wasn't much happier right now with McKenzie Shaw, the little trickster.

When the mayor called him that morning and asked him to meet her here, he expected they would have a quiet, closed-door meeting at city hall, a chance for her to give her spiel extolling the magnificent virtues of her town.

He had every intention of nodding politely while he tuned her out and went to some distant happy place in his brain—somewhere with palm trees rustling in the trade winds, for instance, or an alpine meadow somewhere with granite boulders surrounding a glacial-fed lake.

Instead of a personal, private discussion with McKenzie, he had showed up to what appeared to be a full-fledged breakfast banquet, apparently attended by every business owner and dignitary in town.

McKenzie bustled through the middle of everything looking like an exotic butterfly in a field of gorse. Her features were animated and bright, her hands constantly in motion as she floated from group to group like a good hostess, making everyone feel comfortable.

This was definitely her party. A sign over the head table read Haven Point Mayor's Advisory Council. If he had known she planned to embroil him in a small-town political meeting, he *definitely* would have come up with some excuse. An emergency appendectomy, maybe.

Everyone seemed to be staring at him out of their peripheral vision. It was almost amusing to watch people whip their heads away and try to pretend they weren't watching whenever he would happen to catch their gaze. The noise volume in the room seemed unnaturally loud—a little too much conversation and convivial laughter to be real.

So much for his plans to come into town under the radar, carry out Aidan's wishes about the feasibility study, then sneak out again without anyone making a fuss. He supposed he'd deep-sixed that idea the moment he decided to go to Serrano's for breakfast a few days earlier.

If everyone in town didn't know by now exactly why Ben was here, they likely suspected it had something to do with Caine Tech.

He had been shortsighted not to realize that his return after all these years would stir up the town's curiosity like poking a hornets' nest with a stick. He had too much baggage here, too many connections to everyone.

"How are you enjoying the Sloane house?"

He glanced at Roxy Nash, the real estate agent who had worked with Ben's assistant to arrange the rental property on Redemption Bay. She had the long, lean build of a marathon runner and a hungry look in her eyes that he suspected had nothing to do with food.

"Good. It's a beautiful spot overlooking the mountains."

"Have you had a chance to take that boat out yet?"

"A few times."

"And how's it running, after all these years?"

He shrugged. "It's a Kilpatrick. Still as tight as ever."

"Your family made good boats, from what I hear, though that was before my time in town."

"Yes."

The little twinge of guilt took him by surprise. Closing the boatworks had been the right decision at the time—the only choice, really. The company had been losing money steadily for years because of market factors and Joe's general mismanagement.

"I've always loved Redemption Bay," Roxy went on. "It's a great location, within the city limits but far enough on the outskirts that you sort of feel like you're out there on your own and the walking path from downtown to the bay around the lake is a huge bonus."

"It's been nice so far," he answered.

She looked around—surprising a few people who quickly turned away from them—then pitched her voice low. "You know, if you're interested in purchasing a place of your own in town now that you've sold Snow Angel Cove to Aidan, I might have a few possibilities. The property three houses over from where you're staying now, just on the edge of the bay, is about to go on the market. I'm not supposed to say anything yet but I think you can get it for a steal."

Yeah, that wasn't happening. He forced a smile. "Thanks. I appreciate that."

"Are you thinking about moving back?" When Ben wasn't looking, Russ Warrick had approached them and now he faced Ben with an arrested expression.

"No," he was quick to answer. He didn't need *that* rumor going the rounds in Haven Point now. "Aidan keeps me plenty busy in San Jose, believe me. I'm not coming back."

He would have liked to leave the matter there but Dr. Warrick wouldn't let him.

"You should seriously think about it, son. I know you've sold your holdings to Aidan but your roots in Haven Point go as deep as an oak."

"I've been gone a long time, Doc. I've got a pretty good life in California. Some trees are able to throw down roots just fine in a new place."

"Maybe. It's worth considering, though."

The doctor wanted something from him and Ben didn't have the first idea what that might be. He was actually grateful when McKenzie went to the front of the room and asked everyone to take a seat so the breakfast could begin.

Before he could figure out a way to sneak out, McKenzie pointed at him and then at an empty seat near her, clearly ordering him to sit. Bossy thing, wasn't she? At least she wasn't making him sit at the head table or something.

Not sure why he wasn't obeying his instincts to leave, he slipped into the seat as McKenzie went to the microphone. He was struck by how lovely she was, with that dusky skin and dark hair and the high cheekbones that made her look like some sort of Aztec princess.

"Thank you all for coming to the annual mayor's Lake Haven Days Luncheon, which as you know kicks off four days of crazy fun here in Haven Point. I've been to several of these but this is my first one in the hot seat. I've got to say, I much prefer sitting where you are, eating lousy pastries and exchanging gossip with my neighbors, than having to stand here at the microphone and say something pithy."

"Then maybe you shouldn't have thrown your hat into the ring for mayor," a burly man with a big dark beard said from the audience.

When the general laughter subsided, McKenzie made a face. "As you will recall, Larry, I didn't precisely throw any hats here. I was nominated at an election meeting I was unable to attend because I had the flu. But that's beside the point."

So that explained how she had become mayor of Haven Point. She hadn't seemed avidly political to him. It made sense that she had stepped up out of a sense of civic duty.

"The point is, Lake Haven Days provides a priceless opportunity for those of us lucky enough to call this place our home to pause and reflect about all the things we find meaningful about living here. The lake is a big part of it and that's what we celebrate with the wooden boat festival, but there's more. It's about the neighbors who show up at 6:00 a.m. with their tractors to plow your driveway after a big storm. About the basketful of tomatoes another neighbor might drop off on your doorstep or the dinner in your refrigerator when you've got the flu.

"We all have the chance to give back next week with our annual community service auction. As members of the mayor's advisory council, I expect every one of you to participate. You can donate something from your business to be auctioned off or if you have a particular skill or talent, you can donate that instead.

Larry, I know you make a mean Dutch-oven chicken dinner, since I've been lucky enough to be invited over for it, and I'm sure someone in town would be thrilled to bid on that. Karen, with your graphic arts skills, I'm sure someone in this room would love to bid for an hour of your time to help them redesign a logo or a website banner. I expect everyone to help."

Ben heard a little good-natured grumbling but people mostly seemed receptive to her order. In his role as the public face at Caine Tech, he had become very good at assessing the mood of a crowd and right now he could see that McKenzie seemed very well-liked among her constituents. She came across as energetic, enthusiastic and warm.

"Will you still be in town for the service auction?" Doc Warrick asked him after McKenzie ended her welcoming speech and sat down.

"I don't know yet, to tell you the truth. I haven't figured out how long I'm staying."

"It's only another week and some change. If you are still here, the service auction is an event you should not miss. If you want to know this town's heart, you should see us in action."

He wasn't really interested in seeing the town's heart. He had seen enough when he lived here, watching them all kiss up to Joe, even though his father had been an ass and a bully.

"I'll keep that in mind," he said with a polite smile.

Yeah, he was going to wring McKenzie's lovely little neck. She should have told him what he was getting into when she invited him here to meet her.

Breakfast was served buffet style. While everyone left their chairs to queue up at the platters filled with pastries, fruit and bagels, Ben opted to remain in his seat to enjoy a surprisingly good coffee.

A moment later, he was joined by a vaguely familiar older man with a shock of white hair and sun-wrinkled features.

He set his plate down and eased into the chair with stiff, jerky movements. "Young Kilpatrick, isn't it? Ben."

He nodded.

"Thought so. You've changed a bit from the days when you were a punk driving too fast up and down the street but I could recognize your mother's eyes. Lovely woman, your mother. How is she these days?"

"Good. Thank you." He assumed as much, anyway. With a niggle of guilt, he remembered Doc Warrick's conviction that he should tell his mother he was back. He hadn't called Lydia yet. Maybe after breakfast.

"Do you remember me? Mick Sargent."

Right. He had worked at the boatworks as long as Ben could remember. The man had always been kind to him.

"Was that you I saw the other day out on the water in an original Delphine?"

"Yes."

"Named for your grandmother," Mick said with a solemn nod. "From where I sat on shore, she looked sleek and feisty—much like the original Delphine, as I recall."

He smiled at this, wishing he remembered the woman.

Those who had known her, universally spoke of her with admiration and respect.

"Did you restore her yourself?"

He shook his head. "When I found her, she was in terrible shape, rotting out. I sent her to someone I know in the Bay Area and he managed to find mostly original parts to bring her back to her glory."

"She is looking fine, at least the quick glimpse I got on the water. It's only right you should bring her back here. Good decision, son."

"Thank you."

"I've got a Verlaine myself. She's not quite as smooth as the Delphine but she's solid and dependable."

"Good."

"I don't think I'm alone in hoping the reason you're back in town might have something to do with new plans to open the boatworks again. Fine-crafted wooden boats have made a big comeback in recent years. Look at you, pouring all kinds of money and time into restoring a Delphine. You're not the only one who sees the beauty there."

He hoped he wasn't going to have to defend his decision to close the factory all morning long. "I'm not in the boat-building business anymore," he said quietly, hoping this would be the end of it. "My job at Caine Tech takes all my time and energy."

"That's fine for you," Mick said in a low, even tone that matched his own. "What about for the people of this town? You've got obligations here, like it or not."

He wasn't responsible for these people. He barely knew them! Simply because his father had once owned the company that had once been the town's largest employer did not make Ben some sort of feudal lord, for heaven's sake.

He was saved from having to answer when another guy of about the same age as Mick sat down on his other side and asked Sargent a question about irrigation water shares.

Ben used their conversation as an excuse to get up. He started to head for the exit, hoping McKenzie wouldn't notice. Unfortunately, at the same moment she began to walk toward him. She wore a tailored white shirt and a chunky blue-and-green necklace that reminded him of sunlight shifting across the lake. All that lovely dark hair was tangled up in some kind of a twist behind her head. She probably thought it made her look crisp and businesslike but he only wanted to pull a few pins out and trail his fingers through the soft strands.

The impulse came out of the blue, shocking him to the core, and he curled his fingers into his palm to keep from acting on it.

"Hi, Ben. I hope you're enjoying breakfast. I wasn't sure you would come."

"I get the impression people don't say no very often to the Haven Point mayor."

Her mouth twisted into a wry expression. "You'd be surprised. Most people have absolutely no problem saying no to me."

"That's fairly shocking. I can't believe I'm the only one in town who considers you a force of nature."

She laughed a little but it still relaxed the tension

in her features. "Not a force of nature. Mostly a pain in the butt. I have a…bad habit of putting high expectations on people. Some have even called them unrealistic."

Who? Her family? He had been a teenager when McKenzie came to town and could clearly remember hearing gossip around town about the big-eyed, exotic-looking daughter who had suddenly shown up and moved in with the local attorney and his family.

It had set tongues wagging all around town. McKenzie had obviously been the product of an affair, as she was a few years younger than the Shaws' only other living child, Devin.

What had life been like for her in that household? Adele Shaw had always struck him as a nice woman but she wasn't a saint, by any stretch of the imagination. It couldn't have been easy for her to have her husband's love child suddenly thrust upon her.

He didn't have the local monopoly on shitty childhoods, he suddenly realized.

"When you have unrealistic expectations of people, you're setting yourself up for a firestorm of disappointment," he said. "That's a tough way to go through life."

She shrugged. "I may be naive, but I like to put my faith in people, even if it's overly optimistic. In my experience, if you demand much of people, they usually want to rise to meet those expectations."

Or they fight back and do their damnedest to shatter them, he thought, but didn't say.

"I overheard you talking boats with Mick Sargent."

"*He* was talking about boats. I was mostly listening."

Her smile was like the sun sliding over the peaks of the Redemptions after a miserable night. "That's usually all you can do once Mick settles in for a chat. He's a character. Eighty-three years old and still going strong."

"He seemed old when I was a kid. I remember seeing him work a sander and wondering if he was going to keel over any minute."

"Isn't perspective a funny thing? When I was a girl, thirty seemed absolutely ancient. Now that I'm staring it right in the face, I feel like I'm still a baby."

"You *are* still a baby. You're probably the youngest mayor in the history of Haven Point, aren't you? Though apparently not by choice."

"Not really. I never sought this position and didn't want it."

"Why did you accept the nomination? Nobody can force you to run for office in this country, unless there's some bizarre Haven Point compulsory service bylaw I don't know about."

She sighed. "You're absolutely right. I could have said no."

"But you didn't."

She gave a shrug that seemed both eloquent and simple. "This is my town and I love it here. People here embraced me when I was a strange kid who showed up out of nowhere. They have supported my business and opened their hearts to me in friendship. Haven Point isn't perfect. We have our problems, like any other town—the economy being at the top of the list—but in general, this is a warm, caring place."

She looked around the room. "I love this community—and if I can make it a better place to live for my neighbors and friends, I have an obligation to step up and do my part."

He studied her, wondering if her earnestness could possibly be genuine. Yeah, he might be a cynic, but it seemed a little too good to be true. No one could possibly have this rosy a view of her hometown.

"And how's that working out for you so far?"

He regretted the caustic words immediately, especially when her lovely dark eyes clouded and her mouth tightened.

"Great. And as a delightful perk of my job, I get to entertain all the visiting ass—" She caught herself at the last second before she could complete that particular sentiment and quickly amended the thought. "Er, *awesome* dignitaries."

He deserved the original pejorative, he acknowledged. Finding himself the center of attention left him feeling awkward and uncomfortable and he was taking his unease out on McKenzie. Though she had misled him about the meeting, he still didn't have the right to be a jerk to her.

"A difficult task, no doubt."

"Sometimes. Last month, we had a delegation from the state clean water board. I got to enjoy four hours of stories about inorganics and metals, nitrates and nitrites. I now know more about water treatment procedures than I ever dreamed."

She held up a finger suddenly. "That reminds me. I meant to mention to you that's another big plus about Haven Point, by the way. We have a very plentiful supply of exceptionally clean drinking water. In fact, I've got an extra copy of their report that might be useful to you and Aidan. Follow me and you can take it with you."

Without waiting for an answer, she turned around and headed down the hallway. Since he didn't seem to have too many options unless he wanted to stand here by himself and deal with more of those sidelong glances, he followed her.

CHAPTER SIX

YES, THAT'S RIGHT, PEOPLE. Your stately, dignified mayor of Haven Point had almost called Ben Kilpatrick an A-hole.

On the way to her office, McKenzie wanted to stop in the hallway and bang her head against the wall a few dozen times but she forced herself to keep walking.

The man brought out the absolute worst in her. Okay, he had been a jerk but she was supposed to at least *try* to be nice to him. She was trying to convince the man to bring a major tech facility to her community that would be a total game changer and yet she couldn't refrain from calling him names, deserved or not.

For heaven's sake, what *was* it about him that brought out the worst in her and turned her into a second-grader in pigtails, sticking her tongue out at the cutest boy in school?

Forty-eight hours earlier, she had lectured all her friends to do whatever was necessary to be nice to the man during the short time he would be in town. Why couldn't she take a little of her own advice?

She unlocked her office and led the way inside.

It wasn't the most extravagant office in the world—on the small side, utilitarian, with a basic oak desk and matching credenza and a couple of visitor chairs that had probably been ugly and uncomfortable even back in the eighties, when they had obviously been purchased.

If she had to guess, she would imagine about ten of her offices would probably fit into his private office space at Caine Tech, but she still experienced a burst of pride when she saw her nameplate on the desk.

She might not have ever aspired to the job but she could still appreciate that Mayor McKenzie Shaw had a lovely ring to it.

"You're welcome to sit down." She gestured to the uncomfortable guest chairs while she headed behind her desk. Somehow she wasn't surprised when he remained standing.

She began to sift through the papers stacked neatly on the desk. "Where is it? Let me see. I know it's here somewhere. Sorry things are a little disorganized, with the festival this week and all."

She moved aside a report from the police chief asking for an increase in his budget and another from the public works director informing her the sewer line on a third of the city streets needed to be replaced, then she finally found what she was seeking at the bottom of the pile.

"Here you go. The latest from the state water agency. This is an extra copy. You can take this one or I can also shoot you a digital version if you'd rather have that. It clearly states that Haven Point has a plentiful supply of remarkably clean water."

"Thanks."

He took the report but her insides sank when he barely looked at it.

Haven Point was fighting a losing battle. He had told her that. She was suddenly convinced it would take nothing short of a miracle to convince Ben Kilpatrick that the hometown he had walked away from without a second glance was worthy of another chance.

So what? McKenzie was a big believer in miracles. Her sister was proof that they really could happen. When she was only a teenager, Devin had defied doctors who had offered the family little but pessimism about her survival chances after her cancer diagnosis—and now her sister was a physician herself and had been cancer free for more than a decade.

In her experience, most miracles came to people who worked hard to make them happen. Why not in this situation? Once Ben spent a little more time in Haven Point and came to know the people who lived here, surely he would be able to embrace the possibilities.

She drew in a breath and waded into the fray. "You must be aware this is a really big week for us around here."

"Lake Haven Days. That's got to be a big tourist draw."

"Yes. In the last few years, Shelter Springs has tried to copy it by coming up with their own Lake Festival, but the original Lake Haven Days is still a much bigger draw."

"Naturally."

She shrugged. "We have history and tradition, not to mention the wooden boat festival and an amazing parade. This year, it so happens that Lake Haven Days coincides with the July Fourth weekend so we've also got the fireworks on Saturday night to cap off everything. It's going to be a great week."

"Busy for you, I'm sure."

"Yes. And one of my responsibilities as mayor is to escort visiting dignitaries."

"Or assholes. Depending on circumstances."

Once more, she had to be grateful she didn't blush. "Often, they're both. But that's not the point."

He watched with an expectant look and she was suddenly aware butterflies danced through her insides, as if she were asking him on a date or something. Stupid. She most definitely was not.

"We've got several exciting events planned, as you can imagine."

"A full day, I'm sure."

"Yes. And I have been asked to escort you as one of our guests of honor to some of the main Lake Haven Days events, particularly the parade, the barbecue and the fireworks on Saturday."

He lifted an eyebrow. "Asked by whom?"

"You name it. The town council. My friends. The Chamber of Commerce. I believe a few strangers on the street might have mentioned it."

It was only a slight exaggeration. Three people had

suggested it to her when she went shopping for milk the evening before. "Apparently no one wants you to miss Lake Days and all the fun associated with it."

"Why does anybody care what I do while I'm in town? I'm just a random tourist, as far as most people are concerned. Isn't that right, Mayor?"

She bristled at any implication that she had been indiscreet.

"I haven't given anyone specifics about Caine Tech and the new facility, I swear, not even my town council. But, Ben, come on. Be realistic. When you show up out of the blue after all these years—when you didn't even bother to come back for your father's funeral—you have to expect that people are going to be a little suspicious. The moment you drove over the city line, rumors started flying like baseballs in April. I've heard the most outlandish things—apparently you and Aidan are planning everything from a huge new ski resort to an amusement park to a nudist colony up at Snow Angel Cove."

"I'm 99.9 percent sure the nudist colony is a big no."

"So there's still a chance?"

He gave an unexpected laugh, low and throaty, that slid down her spine like a caress.

"Not in this lifetime, anyway. From what I've heard, Eliza is too busy transforming Snow Angel Cove into a home for Aidan and Maddie."

"She's done a beautiful job. You've been up there, haven't you, to see what she and Aidan have done to the place?"

His smile slipped away and shadows returned to the depths of his Paul Newman blue eyes. “No reason to.”

She bristled. “Tell me you can’t possibly have something against Eliza or Maddie. If you do, I might start to think you really are, erm, a dignitary.”

His mouth quirked but the shadows remained in his eyes. “I am many things—an, erm, dignitary among them, at times—but not in this particular case. I love Eliza and Maddie both. They’ve been wonderful for Aidan. Together, they’ve helped him slow down a little and enjoy his life more.”

“Good. I’m glad you agree—otherwise I might have to hurt you.”

She simply adored the lovely and sweet Eliza Hayward, who would be marrying Aidan in a quiet ceremony at the end of the summer, and Eliza’s adorable but fragile little girl, Madelyn, had stolen hearts all over town the moment they both came to Haven Point.

“So why haven’t you been to visit them up at the house since you came back to town? It seems like it would be the polite thing to do, since you and Aidan are BFFs and Eliza is the woman he’s going to marry. I hope it’s not something ridiculous about not wanting to see anybody else live in your childhood home—because that would just be wrong and I would have to tell you to get over yourself already.”

She heard the echo of her words but couldn’t believe they were coming out of her mouth. Nice. She was supposed to be nice. For crying out loud. Couldn’t she manage that for ten little minutes?

Fortunately, Aidan seemed more amused than offended. His mouth twisted a little into an almost-smile.

"You can be sure I would have been up to visit them within the first few days, except they're not home right now. They've been spending a few weeks at Aidan's place on the coast. Last I heard, Maddie couldn't wait to ride horses on the beach."

"She does like horses."

It was an understatement. Eliza's daughter was notoriously horse-mad. A month ago, McKenzie had gone riding with them at the ranch and Maddie had been over the moon the whole time to ride her favorite horse, Cinnamon.

"I had an email from Aidan last night that said they're going to try to make it back to town for Lake Haven Days this weekend. He's not sure they'll be able to."

"Oh, I hope so. If they do, they'll have a wonderful time. So will you."

"Will I?"

She tried not to squirm under that intense gaze. "Yes. Consider this your official invitation to be one of the mayoral guests of honor for the parade, the boat festival and the barbecue. It's a great chance to mingle with the people of Haven Point. How else can you make a truly informed decision about the new Caine Tech facility?"

"How else, indeed?" he murmured in a voice as dry as the dust on the fake plants above her credenza.

She was certain he would shut her down immediately but after a long, considering moment, he nodded.

"Sure. Since my trip here coincides with Lake Haven Days, I suppose I should make a point not to miss all the fun."

Shock tied her tongue for several seconds but she finally managed to pull herself together. "Great. That's great. Most of the fun is Saturday. The parade, the boat races and so forth. I'll make sure you have a seat in the VIP section on Main and Lake Streets and we can go from there."

"Okay. I'll be there."

She told herself the little burst of anticipation was only because she would have that many more chances to convince him Haven Point and Caine Tech were a perfect match.

Somehow she didn't quite believe it.

BEN HAD EXPECTED to feel many emotions upon his return to Haven Point. This unaccustomed feeling of contentment would never have been among them.

He stood on the back lawn of the vacation rental watching a trio of Canada geese, wings outstretched, come in for a landing on water that glowed orange and red in reflection of the dying sun.

Sunsets and sunrises on Lake Haven were nothing less than glorious. Each morning as the sun peeked above the Redemptions, the day seemed like a gift and each night the dazzling sunset was like a benediction.

He had seen more beautiful sunsets, certainly. In Bali a few months ago, he had had an almost spiritual experience watching the sun sink behind the Tanah Lot temple with the ocean as a stunning backdrop. A year ago, he had been in Venice, watching light and color dance across the unearthly beauty of the canals.

But something about this moment—the panting, adoring dog beside him, the quiet lap of the water against the shore, the mountain breeze that played soft, low music on the dragonfly wind chimes hanging off the edge of the house—struck him as close to perfect.

He drew in a breath crisply scented with pine and sage—a scent that resonated deeply, striking old memory chords inside him.

His father. The rocky beach at Snow Angel Cove. A fishing rod and a can full of worms and a pure, perfect summer evening like this one.

He pushed away the memory, relegating it to the jumbled corner of his mind with all the other debris he preferred not to examine too closely.

Hondo planted his haunches in the dirt and gave what sounded like a canine sigh, as if to say *Get on with it, already.*

"Sorry." Ben picked up the tennis ball the dog had dropped at his feet a few minutes earlier. "I'm still with you. Let's do this."

He tossed the ball, which went a little farther than he intended, through the shrubs toward McKenzie's house.

Undeterred by silly things like boundaries, Hondo went after it. He was probably hoping to find his friend, the pretty cinnamon standard poodle, but she was inside and had been there since McKenzie left with her kayak an hour earlier.

Not that Ben was a crazy stalker or anything, but he happened to be in the kitchen at the window when he saw her return with the dog earlier and then head down to the little shed near the water to pull out her kayak. When they lived thirty feet apart, it was a little hard to miss her comings and goings.

Hondo brought the ball back and Ben made a point of throwing it for a while in the opposite direction from McKenzie's house.

He had to stop thinking about her. All day long, he hadn't been able to get her out of his head. This sudden attraction seemed to have blossomed out of nowhere and he wasn't sure what to do about it.

What was it about her that fascinated him? She was lovely, certainly, all big dark eyes and long eyelashes and high cheekbones. He had seen plenty of beautiful women, just as he had seen other beautiful sunsets, but something about McKenzie tugged and pulled at him.

It was only this place that had him behaving in ways that were completely untypical, like aching for a soft, small-town mayor who expected things from him he could never deliver.

If he were smart, he would go inside and spend the rest of the evening with paperwork. Something kept him out here, waiting for her.

The lake was filled with recreational watercraft of all descriptions, from pontoon boats to Jet Skis to old fishing boats. That didn't stop him, several moments later, from picking out a single kayak as it moved swiftly toward his Delphine.

She reached the shore and climbed out, then started to pull the kayak the last few feet to dry land. She wore a pair of cargo shorts over a bright red one-piece swimsuit and an unfastened life jacket, which exposed plenty of luscious skin.

A wise man who found himself fighting an attraction he knew would end badly should probably wave politely and head inside his house.

While Ben usually prided himself on his logic and common sense when it came to women—and everything else—he was halfway across the lawn without even thinking about the wisdom of spending more time with her. He couldn't seem to help himself.

"Evening."

She glanced up and he saw surprise and disquiet in her expression before she nodded politely.

"Hi."

"Need a hand?"

Her eyes seemed to sparkle in the fading rays of the sun as she looked first at him, then down at the kayak. "This thing weighs all of thirty pounds. I think I can handle it."

"So can I. You stow it in the shed, right?"

Without waiting for an answer, he picked it up and carried it toward the small red structure. He didn't miss the little frustrated huff she gave at his high-handedness but she didn't argue, only picked up the double-bladed paddle and followed him, shrugging out of her life jacket on the way.

"Just there is fine, next to the lawn mower. Right. That works."

He set it down and she hung the life jacket and paddle next to the door.

"Thanks for your help," she said as she led the way back out of the small structure.

"You're welcome." It was a little hard to reconcile this fresh-faced, vibrant woman with the flyaway braid and the bright eyes to the buttoned-down, self-contained mayor who had hosted breakfast that morning in a tailored skirt and high heels.

He wasn't sure which one attracted him more.

"Lovely evening, isn't it?" he said, to distract himself from the sudden impulse to reach forward and push a stray tendril of hair behind her ear.

"The best." She smiled. "July is one of my favorite months on Lake Haven. At least in the top twelve."

He smiled and suddenly realized that was one of the things he found most attractive about McKenzie. He smiled more often around her than he remembered doing in a long time.

He had spent far too much time being serious since he had left Haven Point. First, he had thrown himself into his studies and after meeting Aidan and teaming up with him to build Caine Tech into the powerhouse it was today, he had dedicated every spare moment to the company.

His social life usually consisted of entertaining vendors and clients, traveling to trade shows, attending charity benefits.

For so long, he had been fiercely driven to push out

the harsh voice in his head telling him he was lazy and stupid and worthless.

At some point along his journey—perhaps after his father died—that voice had stopped mattering to him, but those workaholic habits still consumed him.

Watching the changes that had come over Aidan these past few months since he and Eliza connected had been both illuminating and disconcerting. Aidan had learned to relax, to slow down a little and savor the life he was building with Eliza and Maddie.

Ben knew that was one of the reasons his friend had encouraged him to take this assignment to spend a few quiet weeks in Haven Point after Marsh Phillips's unexpected death.

It was working, at least when it came to McKenzie. Right now, he wasn't thinking about Caine Tech. Instead, he had a sudden fierce urge to be out on the water with her, kayaking through golden-hued ripples and sending those Canada geese into flight.

"Have you had dinner?" he asked on impulse. "I was about to throw a steak on the grill. It would be no trouble to toss on another one."

She blinked at him in the fading sun, obviously caught off guard by the invitation.

Another thing he enjoyed about McKenzie—she wasn't very good at shielding her emotions. In her eyes, he saw surprise and confusion and, if he wasn't mistaken, an unwilling but unmistakable attraction.

So she felt this little sizzle between them, too. The realization heightened his own awareness of her.

"I haven't had dinner," she admitted. "A steak

sounds delicious. Maybe I can whip up a salad and cut up some vegetables."

Just as she finished the sentence, Hondo suddenly gave his deep-throated stranger-danger bark and planted his paws in a protective stance in front of both of them.

"Hello? Is anyone there?" a familiar woman's voice called.

Tension suddenly gripped his shoulders, strengthened a moment later when his mother walked around the side of the house.

She looked lovely and feminine, as always, well-dressed in a sundress and scarf with strappy sandals and big Jackie O sunglasses. She always looked to him at least a decade younger than her true age, with only a few laugh lines at the corners of the blue eyes he had inherited.

She must have gained those after she divorced his father and walked away, because he didn't remember her laughing much during his childhood.

As always when faced with his mother, he was filled with that conflicting jumble of emotions—resentment and love and frustration, all wrapped into one big, delightful ball of angst he hated.

Lydia's face brightened when she spotted him standing with McKenzie. "Here you are. I rang the doorbell but you didn't answer. I thought you weren't here, even though that must be your vehicle in the driveway, and then I thought I heard voices back here and a dog. I'm so glad I caught you."

Lydia approached them, smiling brightly. He tried to hide his discomfort as he dutifully kissed her cheek.

"Mom. Hi."

"Hello, my dear. Why didn't you tell me you were coming to town? Imagine my surprise when Russ called me a few days ago and told me he bumped into you at Serrano's. I waited for you to call. When you didn't, I decided to take matters into my own hands, since I'm meeting someone in town for dinner."

He had no reason to feel guilty. He had seen his mother just a few months earlier when he flew down to San Diego for her birthday. "I wasn't sure you would be here," he answered. "Didn't you tell me you were heading to Tuscany over the summer? Some kind of extended art history class, wasn't it?"

She made a face. "It sounded like fun but it didn't quite happen the way I planned. My friend Cynthia backed out at the last minute after she was lucky enough to be blessed with new twin granddaughters. They're absolutely darling, by the way. Not that I'm hinting or anything."

Right. She had hinted plenty that she thought it was past time he started looking for something a little more stable than his steady string of short-lived relationships.

"Anyway, I didn't want to go to Italy by myself—what's the fun in that?—so I decided to spend July here at the condo, where I could see my sisters."

He did not understand at all how his mother could feel such a connection to this place. Yes, she had grown up in Haven Point and several of her multitude of siblings had chosen to settle in the area. Maybe that connection to her younger life compensated somehow for the memories she must have of her unhappy marriage.

"I stopped by yesterday but you weren't here. We must have missed each other."

Yet another layer of tension and guilt knotted the muscles in his shoulders. He loved his mother and would love the kind of relationship Aidan Caine had with his father, Dermot, but every time he was with her, he couldn't seem to shake all those difficult memories of the times she stood by and didn't protect him.

He suddenly remembered his manners. "Mom, you remember McKenzie Shaw, I'm sure. She used to come around the house sometimes to hang out with Lily."

His sister's name seemed to shiver between the three of them, as heavy and dangerous as a claymore. McKenzie drew in a quick breath and Lydia's mouth tightened for a moment before she straightened it out into a warm smile she aimed in McKenzie's direction.

"Of course!" she exclaimed. "I should have recognized you instantly. It's been years, but I still remember those beautiful dark eyes and long eyelashes of yours. You were such a good friend to Lily."

McKenzie smiled, though it looked a little sad around the edges.

"Lovely to see you again, Mrs. Kilpatrick. I would hug you but I just came off the kayak and I'm drenched."

"Please. Call me Lydia. And I certainly don't care about a little damp."

Before McKenzie could back away, his mother stepped forward and embraced her. McKenzie looked startled at first and then touched as she hugged Lydia back.

His mother often had that effect on people. Most saw her as a calm, lovely person who drew people to her.

He did his best to see her through that prism but it was sometimes difficult when the view was obstructed by murky pain and disappointment.

"How are you?" Lydia asked, folding her fingers around McKenzie's. "I understand you're the one who bought that charming floral and gift shop in town. My sister Janet was telling me the other day she can't walk out without spending a fortune."

"Just what I like to hear. You'll have to stop in while you're in the area."

"I'll definitely do that. Is this handsome fellow yours?" She scratched Hondo's chin and the dog immediately became enamored of her, too.

McKenzie shook her head, looking a little surprised. "Actually, he's your son's."

His mother's jaw dropped and she stared at him in disbelief. "You got a dog, after all these years? This is huge! Why didn't you tell me?"

"He's not mine," Ben said stiffly. "A friend passed away a few weeks ago and I temporarily ended up with Hondo. I'm looking for a good home for him before I head back to California. You're not looking for a German shepherd, are you?"

"No, though I would love a handsome boy like this. Yes, I would. I would. I'll ask around."

"Thanks," he answered stiffly.

Most of the time, Ben felt as if he handled his life pretty well, other than the tendency to work too much.

He had friends, a good life in California, an amazingly successful career.

So why did he have so much trouble forging a healthy adult relationship with his mother? He always felt suffocated by her expectations and choked by her disappointment when he was unable to meet them.

Sometimes he worried that something fundamental had been crushed out of him after his father stopped loving him, as if some healthy emotional development had been stunted along the way.

"Was there some reason you stopped by?" he asked.

Only when McKenzie frowned at him did he realize how cold, almost hostile, his words and tone sounded. For an instant, he felt uncomfortably like his father, wielding words like a samurai sword to jab and wound, always aiming for the weakest spot.

Lydia only smiled, though some of the delight in her eyes seemed to have seeped away. "When my only son shows up in the same zip code, of course I'm going to stop by to say hello. Your aunt Janet and I were hoping you could come for dinner with us while you're here."

He didn't answer for a moment—too *long* a moment. The hesitation was obvious to all three of them.

"I don't know," he finally said. "I'm here on business and my schedule is quite packed while I'm here. Mayor Shaw and I were just working out the details of all my obligations. I don't know when I'll have a moment to spare. I'm going to have to check my calendar but I'll see what I can do."

"I see. Of course. I know you're a busy man." She

wore that same calm smile he hated, the one that reminded him painfully of the polite facade she used to exhibit to the world during his childhood, even during the worst times with Lily. That smile was carefully crafted to give no evidence that behind it their life was quietly falling apart.

"Do let me know. Your aunt would love to see you while you're here."

"I'll do that."

"Good. I'll be in touch, then. I should run. I have a… date, if you can believe that."

He wasn't sure how he was supposed to respond to that.

"Not a date, I suppose. Just an outing with an old friend. Russell Warrick. We're meeting for dinner."

"Have fun, then."

She gave a short laugh. "I'll try."

After an awkward moment, she reached out and hugged him and he was instantly awash in her familiar apple-scented shampoo and the perfume she still used, after all these years.

"Goodbye, son," she murmured "It really is wonderful to see you. Please call."

"I'll walk you to your car."

"No need. I can find my way. I'll call you."

She hurried away as if she were escaping rising floodwaters, leaving behind a thick silence.

"You lied to your mother," McKenzie finally said.

He made a face, though he felt ridiculously guilty about it. "I've heard people do, on occasion."

"You didn't have to drag me into it. I only asked

you to attend the Lake Haven Days celebrations on Saturday. You could have spent any one of the other evenings you're in town having dinner with your mother and aunt Janet."

"And I probably will."

He would call her in the morning and set up something else, he told himself. Even if it was an evening filled with awkwardness and the resurrection of memories he preferred to stuff down most of the time.

"Are we still on to grill tonight?" he said, trying to change the subject. "I'm starving."

She looked as if she wanted to say more about his mother, but to his relief, she only smiled. "Sure. Let me go change into dry clothes."

"Great. I'll grab the steaks and meet you here in a few moments," he said, grateful he had acted on the impulse and asked her to share a meal with him.

An evening with McKenzie Shaw was guaranteed to keep him from thinking about his mother and the ball of emotion that wouldn't stay submerged, no matter how hard he tried.

CHAPTER SEVEN

SHE COULD HANDLE THIS.

She was a strong, competent, professional woman, chief executive for a town of four thousand people and owner of her own successful business.

A simple meal on a lovely summer evening posed no challenge, as long as she focused on her goal—to convince Ben Kilpatrick he was completely wrong about Haven Point, that the aging infrastructure could be quickly and easily updated and that this would be the absolutely perfect location for Caine Tech's new facility.

All while ignoring the unwanted attraction that simmered just under her skin and made stringing two thoughts together at a time a daunting endeavor.

What did a woman wear when she was taking on an impossible task?

McKenzie sighed as she slipped out of her board shorts and her swimming suit. Board shorts. Good grief. And not even cute ones. These were a raggedy pair she had bought off the closeout rack of a big-box store in Boise last fall. The evening had seemed too warm for the wetsuit and this had been the next best thing—but had she really just talked to the elegantly put-together Lydia Kilpatrick dressed like a surfer chick?

She fought down embarrassment as she jumped in the shower fast and hurriedly changed, opting for a favorite pair of capris and a red cotton knit shirt, simple but flattering. As she dressed, her mind continued to stray toward Ben and his mother.

What was the reason for the tension percolating between them? It had been impossible to miss, from the sudden tightness in Ben's posture to that yearning she had glimpsed in his mother's eyes when she looked at her son.

Add in the fact that he hadn't bothered to let his mother know he was in town and it was obvious the two of them had issues. Did the chasm have anything to do with the divorce of Lydia and Big Joe? Or maybe it was related to the reasons Ben clearly didn't like Haven Point and hadn't been back since Lily's funeral.

Not that it was any of her business, McKenzie reminded herself as she yanked a brush through her hair and quickly twisted it into a casual updo.

She had a tendency to try to repair other people's relationships. Some people played tennis or liked to knit. She liked to fix people and mend fences.

All her girlfriends came to her for relationship advice—and she had been the one to suggest to Lindy-Grace that a night away might be the ticket to reigniting the spark she and Mac seemed to have extinguished along the way.

She didn't have to dig very deeply to understand why she liked to fix things. She had grown up in such chaos, first with a struggling single mother, then being thrust into the life of a father who hadn't known she existed for the first decade of her life.

Standing by so helplessly and watching her mother slip away, day by day, and then moving here with the Shaws and struggling to find acceptance in their home had created a deep urge in her to help people heal their relationships while they could.

Ben didn't need or want her interference, she reminded herself as she carefully touched up her makeup. She heard a sound and looked down to find Rika in the hallway outside the bathroom, gazing through the doorway at her with a quizzical sort of look.

"What? You've never seen me put on mascara before?"

Her poodle seemed to shrug, settling down on her front paws to watch the interesting proceedings.

Okay, maybe it had been a while since she took such care with her appearance. In her position as mayor, she actually tried to go easy on the girlie stuff. It was hard enough as a reasonably attractive young woman—emphasis on young—to prove her competency when it came to city business.

She generally went out of her way to look professional, not soft and pretty.

She gazed at her reflection in the mirror, tempted for a moment to break out the eye makeup remover, scrub her face clean for the night and forget the whole thing.

This wasn't a date and she needed to remember that.

Of course, it had been so long since she'd been on an actual date, no wonder Rika looked confused.

One of the downsides of living in a small town—the dating pool of available men was a little on the shallow side. The pool of *attractive* available men in the area was more like a puddle.

It was a little depressing to realize her last serious relationship had ended three years earlier, when she left Chicago to come home and they had both decided they didn't care enough to cope with the headaches of a long-distance thing.

These days, most of her interactions with members of the opposite sex involved taking complaints from citizens like Darwin Twitchell, arm-wrestling the four Good Old Boys on the city council—the GOBs, as she thought of them in her head—or consulting with the fire and police chiefs.

While both men definitely had a yum factor, the fire chief happened to be married to one of her close friends and she had dated the police chief in high school, before they both decided they made better friends than anything else.

She could handle a simple dinner with Ben Kilpatrick. She might be attracted to the man on a purely physical level but she still hadn't forgiven him for all those years when he had neglected her town.

She could still be polite, she told herself as she quickly threw together a salad, then let Rika out the back door and followed her.

The evening air was sweet and lovely. She heard

the soft slap of waves against the dock and the peeps and coos of night creatures on the lake.

He had switched on all the exterior lights to his house against the gathering darkness and also had turned on the gas fire pit on the patio. It sent flickering light and shadows across the trees and bushes around the yard.

Ben stood at the gas grill, illuminated clearly by one of the lights on the house. He looked dark and gorgeous. When he caught sight of her, he smiled and a host of butterflies suddenly started flapping wildly inside her.

Okay, this was ridiculous. She could be professional, mayoral, polite. She had left her giddy teenage years behind her a long time ago.

Rika bounded ahead of her to brush noses with Hondo—the little traitor. The two of them romped and danced around as if they hadn't seen each other in weeks. It would have been adorable if she wasn't suddenly nervous.

Get a grip. It's only dinner. McKenzie drew in a calming breath and walked the rest of the way across the lawn, wielding the salad bowl and the other small bag she carried like a shield.

She told herself she was completely misreading the flash of appreciation in his eyes. It was a trick of the low light conditions. Even if it was truly there and not just a figment of her overactive imagination, she couldn't afford to pay attention to it.

"I was afraid you might have changed your mind and decided you weren't in the mood for steak."

She *should* have changed her mind. It would have been the wiser choice, to make some excuse and heat up a frozen dinner, her usual culinary option.

Try as she might, she had a feeling she was going to have a very tough time remaining professional around him.

"It just took me a minute to throw together a salad," she answered, deciding not to mention the lipstick and the extra layer of mascara, for obvious reasons.

"Looks great."

He was talking about the salad. That's all.

She held up the small bag. "When I came home from work, I picked some early green beans from the garden. You can sauté them on the grill or I can borrow your stove and cook them inside."

He smiled. "Yum. Haricot verts."

"Right. Well, here in Idaho we call them plain old green beans, not some fancy French term."

"I had some delicious plain old green beans in Paris last month when I was there visiting the Caine Tech office in Europe but I'm sure they still won't compare to fresh-picked from a high mountain garden."

He lived a fast-paced life she couldn't even imagine. "When you were a kid living here on the lake, did you ever guess that one day you would be traveling the world, moving and shaking for Caine Tech?"

"Not for an instant. Of course, when I lived here, Caine Tech didn't exist—except in Aidan's imagination, maybe."

"You know what I mean. Some people have their lives planned out, minute by minute. I just wondered if this was your master plan from the beginning, to end up where you are now."

"I didn't have a master plan. I just wanted to get through high school so I could get out of that house and this town."

The bitterness in his voice took her by surprise—both that he felt so strongly about leaving Haven Point and that he would confide in her about it.

It made her wonder all over again about his childhood. She had always sensed the house wasn't a joyful place. Sadness seemed to seep through the chinking between the log walls. She had always assumed it was because Lily's terminal cystic fibrosis and her valiant efforts to stay alive had become the focus of the family. Now she wondered if the reason was something deeper, something that had to do with the coolness between Ben and his mother.

She sensed somehow that Joe Kilpatrick was the key to all of it.

Few people in town had liked Joe. He had been a difficult man, a bully and a petty tyrant who demanded special treatment from everyone because Kilpatrick Boatworks was the largest employer in town.

McKenzie's interactions with him had been minimal, just a few encounters when he had come into Lily's room to check on her, but he had always seemed solicitous.

She had seen him yell at Ben once, she suddenly remembered. She had been helping Lily with her schoolwork one evening and had gone downstairs to find a glass of water for her. Ben had been sitting at the kitchen table, white-faced, while Joe called him some particularly nasty names. She didn't remember details, only how embarrassed she had been and how she had crept back to Lily's room without the glass of water.

"Was it so very terrible, growing up at Snow Angel Cove?" she asked quietly.

He gazed at her for a long moment, a muscle flexing in his jaw. Finally, he shrugged. "Who doesn't come from a little dysfunction?"

She certainly could agree with that, especially given her own situation.

"These steaks are almost done," he said, giving her the distinct impression he was trying to avoid the topic. "I think we can sauté your beans out here on the side burner of the grill. I just need to grab a pan."

He headed into the house and she took a seat at the cast-iron table on the patio, watching the last rays of the sun gleaming on the water.

Hondo and Rika sprawled out side by side on the flagstone terrace, the best of friends despite their short acquaintance.

She envied dogs for that. They didn't need to know someone's life history or probe into all their dark corners. They gave their affection with uncomplicated abandon.

He returned a moment later with an olive-oil spritzer and a frying pan, along with a couple of plates.

She was suddenly struck by the surreal moment. Ben Kilpatrick—tech billionaire, hometown boy, the man whose name she had cursed for years—was fixing her dinner. It didn't seem quite real that she was here with him. They had even shared a bit of civil conversation while the night settled in around them and their dogs dozed together.

"If you'd like, I can take care of the haricot verts," she said, with the clear accent she had attained in three years of high school French.

"Great, since I have no idea what I'm doing with anything but steak." That devastating smile flashed and her resident butterflies responded accordingly.

She ignored them and headed for the grill. From the larger bag of beans, she pulled the small zipper bag containing the unsalted butter, minced garlic and shallots she used in her recipe. A few moments, a shake of the pan, and she was basically done.

He plated the steaks and handed them to her to add the beans, then Ben carried them to the table, where he had already set out a couple of glasses and a bottle of wine.

"This all looks perfect. When I offered to grill a steak for you, I had no idea I was setting myself up for a gourmet meal."

"Hardly that. I am competent in the kitchen but that's as far as it goes."

For all her nerves, it turned into one of the most lovely meals she had enjoyed in a long time. Once she convinced herself to call a truce for the evening, she discovered Ben was filled with wry observations and wide-ranging interests that made for fascinating conversation.

He told her more about his recent visit to Paris and

the unforgettable trip he took down the Amazon River on a fishing boat the previous summer. She found herself fascinated by his travels, and by the man himself.

"So what about you?" he asked, when the conversation dragged a little. "I think I've talked about myself more tonight than I have in longer than I can remember. You told me you became mayor by default. What about the rest of it? Your business. This house. Why stay in Haven Point? Didn't you ever want to see what might be out there in the big, wide world?"

She sipped at her wine. "I've seen the big, wide world and I like my small one much better, thanks very much."

"Have you?"

"For your information, Mr. Skeptic, I have an MBA from Northwestern and after graduation, I worked for two years in middle management of a major bank in Chicago."

"Really?"

She had shocked him. He gaped at her as if she had suddenly jumped up and started badonka donking on the table.

"I know this will come as a surprise to you, but I'm not a complete hayseed."

"I never said you were any sort of hayseed," he protested.

"Admit it. You were thinking it."

"Not a hayseed. I would never go that far. Okay, maybe I thought your focus was a little…narrow."

"My focus is just right. I've lived in a big city, with all the excitement and restaurants and nightlife. I loved it while I was there but only after I came home to Haven Point did I realize I was always playing a role there. It wasn't me."

"Why did you come back?"

She played with the stem of her wineglass. "My father had a massive heart attack three years ago. From his hospital bed, he begged me to come back and run his business holdings here. He was an attorney but he had also branched off in later years and had taken on various business endeavors over the years—a couple of condo developments in Shelter Springs, a sporting goods store in town, a few fast-food outlets. He was doing too much, which probably contributed to his heart attack."

"He asked you to give up your life and your job in Chicago to come back here and, just like that, you did it?"

"Of course." She was a little surprised he even made it sound like a question. "He needed help. What else could I do?"

"I don't know. He could have sold his holdings or taken on someone local to manage them for him."

"Great advice. I have two words for you. Fletcher Barnes."

He winced at the reminder of the property manager he had hired, who had caused such trouble here while Ben wasn't paying attention. "Point taken."

"Here's the thing. I had a great job in Chicago and they were very good to me there. I had friends and an active social life, but it only took me a few weeks back home to realize I was much happier here."

"Do you still manage your father's business interests?"

She shook her head. "He died of another heart attack about six months after I came back. I consider those six months a gift. He and I spent a great deal of time together—out on the water, hiking in the mountains, watching old movies together."

Rika made a little snuffly noise in her sleep and McKenzie smiled over at her dog and at a sudden tender memory. "He even gave me Rika for my birthday, a few months after I came back. Adele would never let Devin or me have pets. She thought they were too much trouble and didn't like the mess, but since I had moved into a little rental of my own up near the Hell's Fury, Dad thought I needed a fierce guard dog to keep me company. You can see how well that turned out. She's great company and I truly adore her but she's not so great in the fierce-guard-dog arena."

"We all have our strengths."

She laughed. "Yes. Rika's strength is that she loves everyone. She's a great salesperson in the store, though somebody could probably rob me blind and she would just lick them to death."

"I'm learning Hondo is quite social for a German shepherd, but he's protective enough to get the job done."

"Have you decided what you're going to do with him?"

He gazed at the two dogs. "No," he answered. "I'm looking around for a good home. Are you sure Rika doesn't want some company? Between the two of them, they would scare away even the hardiest of intruders for you."

She smiled, entirely too drawn to him here in the moonlight. "Tempting. But no. One dog is more than enough for me to handle."

"I'll figure something out. Maybe Aidan will take him here at Snow Angel Cove. He's already got a couple of dogs. He probably won't notice one more."

"Or you could keep him, as your friend intended."

He made a face. "That's probably not going to happen. But anyway, back to you. You ran your father's holdings here. Then what? How did you move from Point A to Point Made Flowers and Gifts?"

He was very quick to change the subject when it touched on uncomfortable topics he didn't want to discuss. She thought about pressing him, then decided this was another area that wasn't her business.

"After my father died, Devin and Adele and I decided to sell everything. I used my share of the inheritance to buy my store—which is everything I could have dreamed and more."

"Sounds like you've figured things out."

She frowned as he poked a spot she never realized was tender. "For me, yes. I'm no COO of a Fortune 500 company. I run a small floral and gift shop in a tiny struggling town in Idaho. It might not be much, but I've worked hard to make it a success and I couldn't be happier."

She regretted her testy tone as soon as she heard it out loud.

"I have nothing but admiration for anyone who finds something she truly loves."

"I suppose I can be a little touchy. Sometimes I wonder if I should be doing more with my MBA, but I truly do love living here. When I try to imagine myself doing something else, leaving Haven Point, the picture just won't jell, you know?"

"I get it," he answered.

He sounded sincere and genuinely interested in the choices she had made that led her here.

It made it difficult to blow on the embers of her anger at him. She was finding it increasingly tough to remember her objective when the two of them were alone on a lovely summer evening with flames dancing in the gas fire pit and stars spreading out above them in a bright spangle.

She was supposed to be convincing him of the wisdom of moving the new Caine Tech facility to Haven Point. This would probably be a good place for her to talk about how great the town was—about the decent, hardworking people who lived here, who only wanted opportunities to keep their children from moving away.

No. She wouldn't push the matter tonight. No sense belaboring the point and stirring up possible conflict between them.

The impulsive decision had nothing to do with those butterflies or the warm light in his eyes or the lovely evening with its sweetly scented breeze.

That's what she told herself, anyway.

Though she was tempted to sit out here with him

in this quiet peace for two or three more hours, she didn't think that would be very wise, either.

"I should probably go. I've got an early-morning meeting with the police chief."

She was flattered to see what looked like disappointment flash in his gaze—though, again, that might have been the result of an extremely overactive imagination.

"Of course."

She stood up and started to clear away dishes but Ben held out a hand.

"Don't worry about things here. I can take care of the cleanup."

"And I can help," she said in a matter-of-fact tone that discouraged arguments.

She picked up as many dishes as she could carry and headed into the house. The kitchen was small but modern, with gleaming granite countertops and stainless appliances—much nicer than her own.

She rinsed her plate. "Clean or dirty?" she asked, gesturing to the dishwasher.

"Dirty. But, again, I can load them. You're a guest."

She simply smiled and set them in along with a few other plates and a couple of cereal bowls. "I don't mind helping," she answered.

"I get the feeling you're someone who likes to be in charge."

"Sometimes," she admitted.

Okay, most of the time. She had become used to taking care of herself from an early age. Her mother had been sick for two years before she died, so McKenzie had been forced to step up.

After she came here, her father had done his best to reinforce that she didn't need to work for her room and board. Despite his best efforts, McKenzie had always felt the need to please both him and Adele and was always taking on tasks without being asked.

"Is that a problem for you?" she asked Ben now. "Most men are a little threatened by a strong woman."

"Only weak men are threatened by strong women. Lucky for me, I'm not a weak man."

He was standing very close, she suddenly realized, so close, she could smell that delicious soap again, the clean, masculine scent of him. Something flared in his gaze, something that left her suddenly breathless, dizzy.

She opened her mouth to draw a breath and saw his gaze land there, almost as if he wanted to kiss her.

He didn't edge forward but she sensed his muscles gathering to do it. Before he could pass that point of no return, she edged away, toward the door.

So much for all her talk about being a strong woman. If she were truly as strong and sure of herself as she liked to think, she would be making out with Ben Kilpatrick right now.

She was fiercely attracted to him and was beginning to think—amazing as it seemed—that he just might be feeling the same. She wouldn't do anything about it, however. The situation between them was complicated enough without throwing that into the mix.

She swallowed hard and forced a casual smile that

made her feel as if her face was going to crack into fake little pieces. "Thanks for dinner. Next time, my treat."

He watched her, his eyes unreadable. "I'll look forward to it," he murmured.

The butterflies inside her seemed to go into hyperdrive. "I'll see you later, then. Good night."

She gave him another of those quick, fake smiles and hurried outside.

"Come on, Rika. Time to go home."

The dog whined a little but in the end, she brushed noses with Hondo, lumbered to her feet and followed McKenzie as she hurried across the lawn to the safe solitude of her house.

WHAT JUST HAPPENED HERE?

Had he really come a heartbeat away from almost kissing the stubborn, frustrating, beautiful mayor of Haven Point?

Ben stood in the kitchen of the rental house, trying to figure out if he was more astonished at himself for nearly kissing her or more disappointed that she had pulled away before he could follow through.

McKenzie Shaw was a lovely woman. She was also completely unavailable to him—*so* unavailable, in fact, that he couldn't believe he had entertained the impulse to kiss her for even an instant, no matter how softly romantic the evening had been.

He had a feeling McKenzie was the sort of woman who wouldn't be happy with a quick affair, no matter what sort of currents zipped between them, and that's all he wanted.

He enjoyed short-term, casual relationships with women who expected very little from him. He had always told himself he wasn't interested in anything more—especially not terrifying words like *marriage* and *family.*

His home life as a kid had been an exercise in misery—dysfunctional didn't begin to cover it—and his job had always been where he felt confident, comfortable. Safe.

Even as he thought it, his mind traveled toward Aidan and Eliza, seeing the two of them draw closer together these past several months.

Lately, he found himself watching his best friend with the woman he had fallen for and her little girl. Aidan had become a different person, more relaxed, more lighthearted.

They were like two lost, wandering souls who had finally found their way to each other.

While he might envy Aidan a little for the peace he had found with Eliza, Ben had no intention of following the path the two of them had laid out.

He was perfectly happy with his life the way things were.

Materially, he had everything he could possibly want. A beautiful house in the hills outside San Jose and another one on Big Sur. A private jet at his disposal. A career he loved.

Because of him, his mother had enough money for beautiful houses in Tuscany *and* Paris if she wanted.

He was fiercely proud of all he had achieved, despite his father's harsh voice in his head, telling him he would never amount to anything.

Hondo scratched on the door to come back in. The dog greeted him with that same constant, dopey affection. He scratched at the sweet spot between his ears.

Okay, maybe lately Ben had sensed an emptiness to his life, a certain sort of *void* he wasn't sure how to fill. He certainly didn't need to start by jumping into something with a woman as completely inappropriate as McKenzie Shaw.

She was the last person who should interest him, whether he was looking for a quick fling or something longer term. She was inexorably linked to this town, like the crystal-blue waters of Lake Haven and the steep, craggy peaks of the Redemption Mountains.

He would just have to be careful to keep things between them on a purely professional basis. As they had enjoyed a lovely evening together, he could only hope maybe she wouldn't give him the skunk eye every time she saw him.

He decided to consider that progress.

CHAPTER EIGHT

HER FIRST OFFICIAL Lake Haven Days as mayor was turning out to be an unqualified success.

McKenzie couldn't help the burst of pride as she walked back up Lake Street after climbing out of Carl Christopher's beautifully restored 1959 Thunderbird at the end of the parade route.

She had been half dreading the parade since her election in November. A whole hour of being the center of attention, of having to wave her little heart out and be "on" for all that time seemed exhausting and, quite honestly, more than a bit mortifying.

In reality, riding with the city council near the beginning of the parade in Carl's beautiful red convertible—behind the grand marshal—had actually been tons of fun.

It provided an entirely new perspective, the chance to see everybody along the parade route—small children waving little flags in honor of Independence Day, teenagers trying to look too cool to catch the taffy and bubble gum tossed their way, the older people on their lawn chairs clustered in groups who waved back with enthusiasm and vigor and clapped along with the military marching band coming up behind the convertible.

A dozen times during the parade, she had been aware of a goofy, warm burst of pride as she smiled at neighbors and friends on the perfect July morning, with the beautiful lake and mountains as a backdrop. Her town. How grateful she was to be part of it.

As she had been riding at the beginning of the parade, she decided to walk back to the grandstand at the intersection of Lake Street and Main to catch the last half. Though she had quite a walk, she didn't mind. It gave her a chance to wave again and even stop to visit with a few people along the way.

She paused on her way to watch the high school band go past and couldn't help thinking how much they had improved since the year before, thanks in large part to the infusion of a musical family with two sets of twins at the high school.

"Great parade, Mayor," a woman's voice called out.

She glanced over and found Eppie and Hazel, along with Eppie's husband, Ronald, the surviving husband who squired around both sisters.

"Thank you, my dear," she answered Eppie. She headed toward them and leaned down to kiss both their wrinkled cheeks along with Ronald's. He smiled at her but said nothing—which wasn't unusual for him.

"Why, in all our years here, I think this is one of the very finest Lake Haven Days parades we've ever seen," Hazel said. "And it's so wonderful that it's on July Fourth this year."

Eppie's blue eyes twinkled at her sister. "You just like all those hunky firefighters who came through first."

Hazel cooled herself vigorously with a red, white and blue fan. "Not true," she protested in indignation, then gave an impish grin. "It was all those soldiers who came through before the firefighters. You know I do love a man in uniform."

They both gave earthy laughs that made McKenzie shake her head. "Ronald, make these women behave themselves."

He gave her a long-suffering look, the darling. "Believe me, I wish I could."

She laughed and kissed his cheek again, hugged both women and continued on her way.

After several more stops to chat, she made it to the courthouse, where special guests had positions of honor on risers brought over from the baseball field at the high school.

This is where the city council members' families sat to wait for them as well as members of the Lake Haven Days organizing committee, the grand marshal's family and other town dignitaries.

Much to her surprise, Ben was sitting on the third row back wearing a baseball cap and sandwiched between Carmela Rocca and Roxy Nash, who looked as if they were talking over each other a mile a minute.

He spotted her and sent her a helpless *save me* sort of look, which she ignored. Instead, she gave him a smile and wave and headed over to sit by Edwin and Archie.

As it turned out, she had been so busy visiting on her way back to the grandstand that she caught only about five minutes of actual parade. She was able to see the search-and-rescue mounted posse riding past in formation, followed by a couple of young teens on an all-terrain vehicle and wagon on horse manure cleanup duty. After that came a flatbed trailer hauling one of the junior dance troupes, then Mike Bailey's classic blue pickup bearing poster-board signs promoting his friend Luis Robles's insurance company, and then finally one more patrol car to signal the parade was over.

Everybody clapped and stood up as it went past and the Lake Haven Parade became just another memory.

"Great parade, Mayor," Edwin said with his customary smile.

"Thanks, but I didn't have much to do with it. Marie and her committee did a great job," she said, smiling at Marie, who had somewhat reluctantly agreed to organize the event this year.

Ben looked as if he was trying to head in her direction but he kept getting waylaid by people trying to talk to him.

She was struck again by the memory of that moment in his kitchen when he had almost kissed her. In the five days since, she had relived that moment a hundred times—the pulse of blood in her ears, the catch in her breathing, the thick anticipation curling through her.

And then the raw disappointment and regret when she had walked away.

She hadn't seen him since, other than occasional glimpses in the evenings as he threw a ball for Hondo in the yard and once when she watched the two of them take off for a sunset cruise in his Killy.

How much longer would it take for him to realize he loved that dog and wouldn't be able to find him a new home?

"Nice parade, Mayor."

She turned at the welcome distraction from her thoughts to find one of her least favorite people in town, Gil Franklin.

"Thanks, Gil."

The man considered himself her biggest rival. She mostly considered him a pain in the butt. He had served as mayor three consecutive terms until health reasons forced him to step down.

She hadn't been completely truthful when she told Ben no one else had wanted the job. Gil would have liked to keep the job as mayor until his deathbed but his wife decided twelve years was long enough.

He made no secret that he thought she was far too young and inexperienced to do a good job as city administrator and was continually offering her what he probably thought was kindly advice but which she took as anything but kind.

"Personally, I wouldn't have permitted those belly dancers, but I guess some people must not share my delicate sensibilities."

"Apparently not."

Ordinarily, she would have laughed at this overt criticism but this was the same kind of caustic nonsense he always tried to pull and she was growing a little tired of it.

"It was nice to see old Coach Radford as the grand marshal. Good man. Good man."

"He is, indeed."

"He led the Haven Point Eagles to an undefeated season and state championship back when my oldest was on the football team."

"Yes. I know. That's one of several reasons he was selected. That and his many years of service on the library board of directors."

"He's a great coach—but I do have to say, I find him a bit of an interesting choice this year, don't you think?"

Not at all. She had even been the one to suggest Coach Radford's name to the Lake Haven Days committee.

"I'm not sure what you mean."

Gil shrugged and his mustache quivered. "It's just that I would have thought Aidan Caine the logical choice, considering how we all hope he has big plans to revitalize this town. Never hurts to send a few perks the man's way. You can't go wrong with a genuine gesture of goodwill."

If they had selected Aidan, Gil would have found some reason to complain with the choice. She made herself smile politely.

"Good advice, as always. Thanks, Gil. We'll definitely take that into consideration for next year."

He gave a careful look around to see who might be standing near them before he turned back to her and spoke in a low voice.

"Speaking of Caine, what's the story with Ben Kilpatrick coming back to town after all these years? Are he and Aidan up to something together?"

She wouldn't tell him, even if she could, which made her feel about eight years old. "That's something you're going to have to take up with Ben, Gil."

"I just might do that," he said pompously. "We have the right to know what they're planning for our town. The town hall meeting Aidan had with everyone after the holidays was well and good, where he talked about how he wants to revitalize the downtown area and some of his plans for new businesses, but I, for one, would like to see a few more specifics before we roll over and let the likes of Ben Kilpatrick walk all over us."

"Nobody is letting anyone walk anywhere."

"Ben Kilpatrick. Well, personally I think he's got serious balls to show up after all he's done to destroy this town. He ought to be tarred and feathered and run out of town on a rail. Instead, everybody's sucking up to him like he's some kind of hero. When I think of all the times I tried to get him to do something with the property he owned here during my time as mayor, I get mad enough to chew nails."

As annoyed as she could get with Gil, the reminder felt as if he had poked her under the ribs with one of those figurative nails he wanted to chew.

She looked around the downtown area at all the shuttered buildings, the peeling paint. Aidan was working on revitalizing the buildings but it was a slow process, one property at a time.

If only Caine Tech would move the facility here,

perhaps her town could begin to heal again. How could she convince Ben?

"He's here now," she said to Gil. "There's a chance we can all work together to turn things around in Haven Point, but not if we let anger and resentment for the mistakes of the past stand in the way of progress. He trusted the wrong people and they took advantage of him and of this town and he didn't care enough to check on them. Great harm was done here. We all know that, but at some point, we have to let that anger go and move on, for the good of Haven Point."

Gil suddenly looked over her shoulder with a pained sort of look and she knew before she even heard his voice that when she turned, she would find Ben standing there.

"Nice speech, Mayor."

How much had he heard? Most of it, probably. She could feel her face heat to be caught talking about him—but she hadn't said anything to Gil that she hadn't already said to Ben.

"I'm glad you think so," she answered. "I'm working on letting go of my anger. Can you say the same?"

He gazed down at her out of those blue eyes the same color as the lake. For one arrested moment, she felt as if the rest of the crowd had just slipped away. The noise and laughter, the traffic that had resumed after the parade—all of it seemed to fade away, leaving only the two of them standing with a sweet summer breeze blowing off the lake.

With perfect, almost painful, clarity, she remembered that moment in his kitchen—the house settling around them, the tingling in her stomach, the soft hoot of an owl outside.

Oh, for crying out loud. She needed to shove that memory away once and for all. He hadn't kissed her, thank heavens. She could still hold on to a *little* bit of sanity.

She drew in a sharp breath and jerked her gaze away. "Ben. You remember Gil Franklin. He was the previous mayor."

Ben nodded to the older man. "Hello. Good to see you again. I went to school with your son, Scott, right?"

"Right. My oldest. The two of you played ball together."

"I remember. He was a great shortstop with a hot bat. How is he?"

"Good. Good. He still plays in a couple of rec leagues and still has a hot bat. He's an electrician in Boise. You would not *believe* the work coming his way. He could work round the clock if he wanted. He and his wife built a house last year that has to be five thousand square feet, at least, with six bedrooms and a four-car garage, including a guest suite that's like a four-star hotel. The wife and I go stay with them whenever we can and it's like having our own little condominium in the city."

"That's great. Good for Scott."

Ben sounded genuinely happy for the other man, something she found a little endearing. Compared to his own success as the chief operating officer at Caine Tech, a five-thousand-square-foot house, even with a four-star guest suite, was probably nothing.

Gil went on to talk about his two other children, girls much younger than Ben that he probably had never even met, but Ben still made polite conversation with the man and seemed genuinely interested.

It offered fresh perspective on the man she wasn't completely comfortable about, that he could share small talk and set others at ease. She didn't know how long Gil would have kept up the mostly one-sided conversation if his wife, Nancy, hadn't stepped up with an impatient look.

"Gil, we'd better go. Aren't you supposed to be selling brooms and raffle tickets for the Lions Club over at the fair? Hi, McKenzie."

She smiled at Mrs. Franklin, who volunteered at the library several days a week. "Hello. Good to see you."

"If I didn't have my wife to keep me on schedule, I wouldn't remember to breathe in the morning—at least according to her." Gil shook his balding head. "But she's right, I do have to run. Good to talk to you, Kilpatrick."

How had Gil so easily shifted from being antagonistic and angry toward Ben to just about eating out of his hand? Ben had a way of making people think he was genuinely interested in them. Was it an act or sincere? And had she been stupid enough to fall for the same thing?

After Gil and Nancy took off for the fair, she and Ben were alone—except for the dozens of other people still hanging out at the grandstand, anyway.

"So," she began. "You haven't been to a Lake Haven Days in years."

"Looks like a few more people come out than I remember."

"It's become a big summer event in the region. People come from miles around to enjoy the lake and our quaint small-town celebration. There are a dozen activities going on around town. A quilt show, an antiques sale, a craft fair over at Lake Park. There's a baseball tournament over at the sports complex all day long and a tractor pull over at the fairgrounds. Oh, and don't forget the wooden boat festival. There's a regatta down at the marina and a boat show. People come from hundreds of miles away to show off their boats. You'll see plenty of Kilpatricks."

"That sounds good. I think I'll wander over to the regatta." He looked down at her. "You don't have to entertain me all day, you know. I can probably find my way there on my own."

He was giving her an excellent out so she didn't have to spend the day trying to resist temptation. She had a dozen things to do as part of her mayoral responsibilities. No matter the activity, from the Dutch-oven cook-off to the horseshoe tournament, people expected the mayor to show up.

It was also going to be a crazy-busy day at the store, with all the increased downtown traffic, but Lindy-Grace had assured her she could handle things.

No other demands were urgent. She mentally scanned the day's schedule and decided she could adjust things and spend an hour or so with Ben at the boat show.

None of the other activities were nearly as appealing, which ought to set off alarm bells in her head.

She rationalized that an important part of her responsibilities as mayor was to promote Haven Point, to convince Ben that Caine Tech could come up with no better community for the company's new facility.

How could she possibly accomplish her goal if she went out of her way to avoid the man?

She could manage to handle this inconvenient attraction for an hour or so. It was the least she could do for the town and the people she loved.

"Great. Let's head for the marina, then."

DESPITE THE CLOUDS of earlier in the morning that had clung to the mountain peaks in fragile wisps, the day had turned out to be a beautiful one.

The breeze off the lake was sweet and the perfect temperature for a late morning in July, pleasant and mild.

Ben walked beside McKenzie, struggling to accept the rather unnerving realization that for this exact moment in time, he couldn't imagine anywhere else he would rather be.

He frowned, gazing out at the lake. Something must be wrong with him—either that, or the pleasure of McKenzie's company was crowding out all common sense.

The Haven Point mayor was a woman of many facets—the crisply efficient businesswoman, the enthusiastic cheerleader for her town, the devoted sister. He was very much enjoying the process of discovering all these mysterious nooks and crannies of her.

He certainly found her attractive. Something about those big eyes and her high cheekbones—not to mention the way she became so adorably flustered every time he touched her—slid around and through him like that warm summer breeze.

She felt it, too. He could see it in the way she avoided his gaze and the way her fingers trembled just a little. That was possibly the most enticing thing about the whole situation. She wanted him and she didn't *want* to want him.

He sighed, losing a little of his enjoyment of the moment. He couldn't—and, more important, *wouldn't*—do anything to pursue it. She might be fighting an unwilling attraction to him right now, but that wouldn't last five seconds after he told her he had absolutely no intention of ever letting Aidan put a Caine Tech facility here.

He decided not to worry about that. Wasn't Aidan always pushing him to live in the moment? Right now he had no desire to waste a perfectly gorgeous summer afternoon beside a mountain lake by letting tomorrow's worry ruin things for him.

"The boat show portion of Lake Haven Days looks like it's grown a bit more than I would have expected," he said as they approached the marina.

"Kind of surprising, I know. You would think the wooden boat festival might have died off after you closed Kilpatrick Boatworks, but if anything it's grown exponentially in the last five years as your family's boats and other companies' wooden crafts have grown in popularity."

He refused to let her make him feel guilty about what had come down to a business decision.

"They're actually collector's items these days," she went on. "But then, I guess you know that. You've got a Killy yourself."

"Yes. It wasn't easy to find, either."

"The people of Haven Point made good boats," she said simply. "People who worked at the boatworks took pride in their craft."

He took pride in it, too, the legacy from his grandfather and his great-grandfather. Taking his Delphine out on the water gave him a thrill every single time.

"With the new popularity, have you thought about reopening the boatworks on a limited basis? Maybe reduce the number of boats you produced, in order to maintain that exclusivity. You've still got a building over on the south end of the lake."

"I don't own the building anymore," he reminded her gently. "Aidan does. You would have to ask him."

She made an impatient gesture. "You're the Kilpatrick. You must still own the rights to the company."

He did. He still owned whatever was left of Kilpatrick Boatworks and if he were so inclined, he could probably lease the building from Aidan for a nominal fee.

The idea was ridiculous, though. He was the chief operating officer at Caine Tech, one of the largest tech companies in the world. He didn't have time to be playing around with an obsolete boatworks in a tiny town he didn't even like to visit anymore.

As they neared the marina and the viewing area—more bleachers, probably borrowed from the high school—he pushed the idea completely out of his head as completely unreasonable.

Again, McKenzie seemed to know everyone in town. She stopped at least a half-dozen times to chat, always with that bright, sunny smile that drew people to her like iron shavings to a magnet.

They were making their way slowly to the bleachers when McKenzie suddenly pointed. "Look! Isn't that your mother?"

He glanced over and discovered Lydia standing with a group of people—Doc Warrick, Ben's aunt Janet and her husband, his uncle Boyd.

An outlandish hat with a broad white brim decorated with purple and yellow hats perched atop Lydia's perfect hair, making her look as if she were on her way to the Kentucky Derby, not the Lake Haven Wooden Boat Festival.

As usual, she looked young and pretty, far too young to have a thirty-four-year-old son.

"That's my mom," he answered, filled with the usual chaotic mix of resentment, love and sadness.

"I have to find out where she got that fabulous hat," McKenzie declared.

Before he could suggest otherwise, she took off toward the group. He figured he could either stand here like an idiot or head in that direction after her.

He didn't really have much choice, did he? It was

probably too late for him to take off for his rental house, grab the keys to his own Killy and take off with Hondo for an afternoon lake cruise.

With a sigh, he followed McKenzie toward his mother.

He knew the moment Lydia spotted him. Her eyes widened for an instant then softened with a deep emotion that left him feeling restless.

He also knew the instant she realized he and McKenzie had come together. The soft yearning in her eyes switched to something curious and speculative. Yeah, he wasn't crazy about seeing that, either.

"Darling! And Mayor Shaw. Hello!"

He dutifully leaned in and kissed her cheek and was immediately enveloped with the familiar scent of her.

When he drew away, he kissed his aunt's cheek and hugged his uncle, earning a lecture from the former about how disappointed she was that he hadn't come to visit while he was in town. He managed to deflect it, then turned to shake hands with Dr. Warrick, who looked at him with that same unnerving intensity as always.

What *was* it with the man?

"Wonderful parade this morning," Dr. Warrick said to McKenzie with a smile. "Every year I think it can't get any better and every year I'm proved wrong."

"No pressure for next year, right?" She smiled warmly at the doctor. They were obviously fond of each other, which he somehow didn't find surprising.

They shared a few common traits, Ben suddenly

realized. Doc Warrick had the same warm, approachable mien that made people want to spill out all their troubles. In McKenzie's case, he had the impression from the short time he spent in her company that people not only wanted to spill their troubles to her but to also hand them over for her to handle.

"I sure wish Shelter Springs had something like Lake Haven Days," his aunt said. "Our festival is ridiculous compared to this. Lake Days. We barely even have a parade."

"You're always welcome at the Haven Point celebration," McKenzie said.

A starter pistol suddenly went off with a sharp report and they all looked out to the lake.

"Oh, it looks like the regatta is starting," his mother said, stating the obvious. "We were about to find seats. We would love you both to join us!"

He wanted to say no but he didn't know how when everyone looked so eager.

To his great surprise, McKenzie came to his rescue. Apparently she saw him as just one more person who needed her help.

"We can stay for a few moments, but I'm afraid we both have other obligations. Today is a pretty busy day for me, as I'm sure you can imagine."

"McKenzie is the mayor of Haven Point," Doc Warrick explained to Ben's aunt and uncle, who were looking a little confused.

"You must have so many responsibilities during Lake Haven Days," Lydia said with a sympathetic smile.

Before Lily got so sick, his mother had been one of the social leaders of the town, he suddenly remembered. As the wife of the town's largest employer, she had served on dozens of committees. Garden clubs, charity events, golf fund-raisers.

After Lily's diagnosis, his mother had walked away from everything to take care of his sister. Driving her to appointments in Boise, doing breathing treatments with her, staying overnight in her room whenever she was in the hospital. He loved and admired his mother for that—something he had never once told her, he realized, feeling suddenly small and selfish.

"Yes. Everybody seems to want the mayor to show up to this event or that. I promised Coach Jones and the kids I would show up at their soccer tournament and then, of course, I have obligations at the barbecue and Dutch-oven dinner in town."

"Nice of you to help the mayor carry out her duties, son," Doc Warrick said with an approving smile.

"Yes. So nice," Lydia echoed.

He really didn't like that speculative gleam in his mother's eyes. He didn't want anyone—especially not Lydia—thinking there was something brewing between him and McKenzie.

Okay, there *might* be, but he didn't want his mother thinking about it.

To his relief, the boat races quickly captured everyone's attention. He shifted to a more comfortable spot on the bleachers—if that was possible—and enjoyed the sunlight gleaming off polished wooden hulls and the water rippling away in their wake.

After several moments of being engrossed by the action he became distracted by his mother's conversation with McKenzie.

"I've been thinking a great deal about you since I saw you the other day," said his mother.

"Oh?"

Lydia captured the mayor's slim but capable hand. "You were such a good friend to our Lily. I've never forgotten it, in all these years. She didn't have all that many, you know. It was hard for some of the girls, especially in later years when it became more difficult for Lily to hike and ride bikes and swim in the lake and all the other things young people like to do."

McKenzie gave a strained smile, looking uncomfortable. His mother apparently didn't notice.

"I cannot tell you how much it meant to me when you would come to Snow Angel Cove so often, just to sit and talk to her, especially near the end when she was so ill."

"I cared a great deal about Lily," McKenzie murmured. "It wasn't a one-sided friendship, believe me. She was very wise and helped me through some pretty hard times. She always had such a wonderful attitude and I learned so very much from watching the grace and strength she showed in dealing with the difficult hand she had been dealt. I became a much better person because of her. I want you to know, I still miss her and think of her often."

"Oh, my dear. Thank you for saying that." His mother's eyes dampened and to his embarrassment,

Ben's felt that way, too, before he firmed his jaw and willed away the emotion.

He had adored his younger sister. She had been sweet and funny, smart and compassionate. He often thought how very unfair it was that such a wonderful soul had been afflicted with a deadly disease.

The reality of her cystic fibrosis and the particularly deadly version of her particular variation of it had been like another member of their family, inescapable and always present.

By the time she died, his family had been held together by that reality and nothing else. He had left Haven Point right after the funeral, graduating from high school a month early and taking off to California, where he already had a scholarship at Cal Poly.

His mother had filed for divorce weeks later and moved out, leaving Joe alone at Snow Angel Cove with all the ghosts.

He pushed away the memories, yet another thing he didn't want to deal with today.

He preferred to think of his sister as she had been before those last terrible years of the illness, teasing and kind, always quick to comfort him after Joe would go on the attack.

A cell phone suddenly rang out. McKenzie's, he realized, when she pulled it out of her pocket.

"Hi, Anita," she said. Her assistant at city hall, he remembered from the breakfast earlier in the week, a battle-ax with salt-and-pepper hair and a stare that could likely bend metal.

"Yes," McKenzie said. "The check is all written out. It's in my desk drawer. I assumed we could mail it next week."

She listened. "Really? They're being that way about it after we've used them for our fireworks for fifteen years? No, it's not your fault, Anita, although this is exactly why I wanted you to have the key to my desk. Yes. I can be there in ten minutes. I'm just at the marina. Tell them to relax."

She listened to the conversation for a moment more. Apparently Anita wanted to give her an earful.

"It's fine, I promise," McKenzie finally said. "Thanks. Sorry you had to deal with it. You're a rock star, my friend. See you in a few."

She was a good leader, he thought. Calm in a crisis, supportive and encouraging. He wouldn't mind having her on his team at Caine Tech—if not for this inconvenient heat that sizzled under his skin when she was near.

"I've got to run," she said after she hung up. "I'm really sorry."

He rose from the bleachers and reached a hand to help her up. "No problem. I'll walk you back to the city offices."

"That's really not necessary if you want to stay here and watch the races a little longer. We can meet up for the barbecue later."

"I'll walk you back," he said firmly. He *also* was used to being in charge, which made him wonder what the two of them would be like in the bedroom—not exactly the appropriate image when his mother was sitting a few feet away.

"I'm sorry you have to go," Lydia said, with a disappointed look.

"It can't be helped," Ben said. "Goodbye. It was good to see you."

It wasn't a lie, he was a little surprised to realize. She looked fresh and lovely in the afternoon sun, so confident and happy that he still had a hard time reconciling her to the woman who had been beaten to dust—emotionally, not physically—by his bastard of a father.

He leaned in and kissed his mother's cheek, then his aunt's, and finally shook hands with his uncle and Russ Warrick.

"Lovely to see you, my dear." Lydia smiled at McKenzie and clasped one of her hands in both of her own. "We must go to lunch before I go back to San Diego next month."

"Yes. I would enjoy that."

"And you." She gave him a steady look. "You still haven't told me when we can get together for dinner before you leave."

He couldn't avoid it, he knew, so he might as well quit trying. Maybe it wouldn't be as awkward and uncomfortable as he feared—at least if he could figure out a way to drag McKenzie along. Somehow she made everything seem more palatable.

"What about next Friday night? I'm supposed to be leaving the day after that."

"Perfect. It's a date."

She looked painfully happy at the prospect and he tried not to let that fill him with guilt as he and McKenzie headed off on the trail around the lake that led them back downtown.

CHAPTER NINE

LYDIA WATCHED HER SON walk away, so tall and handsome, along with that sweet McKenzie Shaw. They were talking as they walked, Ben's head down to hear what McKenzie was saying. Though she couldn't see his face, she sensed he was smiling, something he did far too seldom.

She didn't think she was imagining the little hint of sizzle between them, like a pot of water just beginning a low boil.

How long had *that* been going on? She had no idea. She and her son lived completely different lives, bifurcated by history and pain and all the mistakes she had made. He answered her calls and her emails but was always careful to keep a safe, protective distance between them.

She sighed as the color and beauty of the day seemed to leach away a little, like sheets left too long to flap under the sun. She had been so looking forward to this day, ever since Russ asked her to spend it with him. She had dressed and put on her makeup and fixed her hair, as giddy as she had been at seventeen whenever he would come home from college to take her out.

This had seemed the chance for a new start between them. He had mourned his dear wife for a year and she had been alone for so very long.

He had even kissed her cheek when he picked her up, a casual, friendly sort of gesture that had still made her shiver.

For the first time in forever, she had started to let herself dream again, to imagine having someone in her life. Not just anyone, but Russ. The man she had loved since she was a young, silly girl, enamored of an older college boy.

Now, seeing Ben, she was reminded again of all the secrets and lies between them.

Her breathing suddenly felt ragged and tight and emotions crowded her throat.

She and Russ could never be together. She had ruined any chance of that by the foolish choices she had made so long ago.

She wrapped her arms around herself, chilled suddenly, though the July sun was warm on her shoulders.

"Are you all right?"

He was so concerned, so solicitous, and she felt tiny and worthless in contrast.

"Do you mind taking me home? I'm sorry. I suddenly have a terrible headache. I'm not sure if it's the sun or the excitement or perhaps the noise, but my head is killing me."

Disappointment flickered in his eyes but he hid it quickly. He had become very good at hiding his emotions from her over the years. Had he just become better at it or was she merely worse at reading him?

"I don't mind at all. Are you all right to walk to the car or would you like me to go get it and pick you up here?"

"I can walk. Thank you."

"A little movement might help you feel better."

He rose and helped her up from the uncomfortable metal bleachers, then tucked her arm in the crook of his elbow and strolled toward his luxury SUV, parked a block away.

Feeling perfectly wretched, she said little as they walked along the busy sidewalk. He seemed lost in thought as well, his mouth tight. He was probably regretting ever asking her out. A fine date she made, turning into a mess after only a few hours.

He settled her into the passenger seat, then drove back through the Lake Haven Days crowds, along the lake toward Shelter Springs and her condo.

"Ben looks good, doesn't he?" Russ said.

She didn't like talking about her son with him, for a hundred different reasons. "Yes. He has grown into a fine man," she answered, her voice rather more short than she intended.

He *was* a fine man, not because of anything his mother had done. She hadn't protected him when she should have. She hadn't given him the safe, warm childhood every boy deserved. Instead, she had put him in a terrible situation, one filled with uncertainty and pain.

Russ was quiet for a long moment, then he gave a heavy sigh, a sound so full of sorrow that she looked away from the road and her own grim thoughts.

"You're never going to tell me the truth, are you?"

Her heart began to pound as she took in the suddenly harsh lines of his face. No. He couldn't...

"I...don't know what you mean," she began.

"Lydia. For the love of God. Enough."

Though his voice was low, it vibrated with emotion, a fierce, barely controlled anger she had never heard before.

No, she had heard it, she suddenly realized. It had been there for a long time, simmering just below the surface like the churning, superheated waters of a dormant geyser, waiting to burst free.

An instant later, Russ turned into a small empty scenic pullout on the road, with a few picnic tables and a trash can. Across the lake, the Redemption Mountains rose in all their amazing beauty, jagged and raw—exactly like her nerves.

No. Not now. Were they really going to have this conversation now? She couldn't do it, not after all the years of lies and secrets.

He put the Range Rover in Park but didn't turn off the engine. The air-conditioning blew on her and she was suddenly so very cold, she was afraid she would turn to pure ice.

"For more than twenty years, I've been trying to convince myself you would tell me eventually."

"T-twenty years?" Dear God. Had he known that whole time?

"I was certain you would tell me, when you thought the time was right. I knew you had your reasons for keeping the secret and I had to respect your wishes.

Maybe it was better not to have it out in the open between them. I thought for sure you would tell me after Lily died, then again after your divorce. Then Joe died and I thought, *surely she'll tell me now.* Even last year when you came to Joanie's funeral, I was certain at last you would tell me. Today, just now, I've finally faced the truth that you never planned to tell me anything. If you had your way, you would go to your grave with this always between us."

The headache she had been halfway pretending earlier growled to life in actuality, pulsing through the veins of her temples as if it had a life and a heartbeat of its own.

How had she made such a huge mess of her life and that of others? So many lives had been damaged, some irreparably, because she had once been so very weak and afraid.

She tried one more time, clinging to the pretense that had sustained her all this time.

"I…don't know what you're—"

"Shut up. Just shut up. No more!"

The geyser burst through the thin surface, hot and bubbly, terrifying and beautiful at the same time.

She had a flashback to the last half of her marriage, to all those times she had cowered like the weak, pitiful creature she had been as Joe spewed venom and anger and filth at her.

Whore. Bitch. Slut.

She wrapped her arms tightly around herself. Though she wanted to shrink back against the seat, to become small and invisible and meaningless, she had come too far to sink into old habits. She forced herself to straighten her spine and face him head-on.

"Please don't speak to me like that," she said.

To his very great credit, he looked sick, his skin suddenly pasty and his eyes haunted.

"I'm sorry. You're… I shouldn't have… I'm sorry. I'm just… I'm so tired of the lies, Lydia. Please. For once, in thirty-five years, don't you think I deserve the truth?"

He was still handsome. Noble, even, though that seemed a ridiculous word to use for a man in the twenty-first century. Age had been extraordinarily kind to him. He hadn't gained a paunch, his bearing was still tall and straight, his features even stronger than they had been when he was a young man.

She had loved him for so very long but she had never been worthy of him. She had let fear make every decision for her and now he would hate her, as she deserved.

She had a sudden flashback to another summer afternoon, the two of them hiking up into the Redemptions with a couple of blankets in a bedroll, a canteen and the eager thrill of anticipation shivering through their veins. All they wanted was a place to be alone together and they had found it in a beautiful secluded clearing. She had loved him more than she ever believed possible and with every ounce of her heart, she had given herself to him in those beautiful fumbling moments before he left.

Now she drew in a shaky breath and wiped away a tear she hadn't even realized had escaped.

"How long have you known?" she asked quietly.

"Oh, no. I'm not going to let you talk around the subject. Say it, Lydia. For once, just say it. I deserve to hear you tell me the truth in your own words, after all these years."

"Fine. I'll tell you. Ben is yours." The words seemed strange, rusty after all these years of being buried so deeply inside. "I was pregnant when you left that last time. I was pregnant two months later when I married Joe. But you knew that already, didn't you?"

As she had feared, throwing the words into the open between them gave them power and weight, made them more real and terrifying.

"How?" he demanded. "We were only together a handful of times and we were...careful."

"Not careful enough, apparently. And you're the physician. You know it only takes once."

She had always thought it must have happened that last magical night before he left, when her heart had been aching. She had wanted their relationship to go on forever but even then she had known it must end. He was obligated to the army, for medical school first and then his obligatory service with them.

She couldn't follow him, as much as they both had wanted that. How could she? Her mother had just died a few months earlier and her father was struggling so much with her six younger siblings. Daddy not only needed her income as a secretary at the boatworks but he also needed her help in the evenings with the others while he worked the night shift and took care of the small needy flock of his Baptist congregation.

"When did you figure it out?" she asked.

"Lily," he answered.

The single word clarified everything. When Lily was first diagnosed with cystic fibrosis around age six, they had pursued genetic testing. As part of that, Ben's blood was tested as well to see if he was a carrier of the condition.

Everything had changed. That was when Joe had found out Ben wasn't his, too, when their semblance of a happy home had disintegrated into accusations and bitter betrayal.

She should have realized Russ would know. Though he hadn't performed the genetic testing—that had been done at the children's hospital in Boise—as Lily's primary care physician, he would have had access to all her records.

"All these years," she whispered. "More than two decades."

"Forever," he answered and she had to close her eyes at the pain in his voice.

"Why didn't you tell me, Lyddie?"

"I didn't know myself until I was more than a month along. That was a few weeks after the letter from you, if you'll recall, telling me in no uncertain terms to date someone else and move on with my life."

"I remember."

"I didn't want to date anyone else. I only wanted you. But when Joe started asking me out—the son of my boss—I didn't know how to tell him no. We had only gone out a few times when he...told me he was falling in love with me. I wanted to break things off.

It was too fast, too soon, and I wasn't ready. My heart was still yours. Then I found out I was pregnant."

Her heart pulsed with remembered terror. "You have to realize the position I was in. The daughter of a Baptist minister, alone and frightened."

"Lyddie."

"I didn't know what to do. I couldn't kill our baby, even though that would have been the…logical choice. I thought about running away, going somewhere far away where no one knew me and giving up the child for adoption, but I didn't know if I could do that to my daddy, who was still grieving and lost, struggling with all those kids."

She gazed out the window at the mountains and the lake, this place she loved. She couldn't look at Russ while she told him the next part. "Around that time, Joe started begging me to marry him. His father was pressuring him to settle down because of his health issues, so that Joe could take over at Kilpatrick's. It seemed the perfect solution. I finally agreed and he was…so happy. I just felt sick at what I had done—lies upon lies upon lies—but by that time, I didn't know how to get out of it."

She twisted her hands together in her lap. "We had Ben seven and a half months after we were married. He was small for his age, I guess, though you'd never know now by looking at him, and Joe never realized he was full term. As I held my baby and saw how proud and pleased Joe was, I resolved I would be a good wife, to make up for my terrible deception. I was. I promise. Though some part of my heart always belonged to you, I tried to love my husband and make Snow Angel Cove a home for us."

"And then Lily was diagnosed with cystic fibrosis."

"Yes." She sighed. "Everything changed the year she turned six, when we received the diagnosis. Ben was ten. By then, you had returned to town and opened your practice. It was so hard not to tell you. I wanted to, a hundred times, but you had married Joan and the two of you were obviously happy. She was pregnant with your second child and I couldn't see ruining more lives."

"And your marriage to Joe? How was it?"

It was a question she didn't want to answer. By necessity, she had become an intensely private person and didn't even like looking at these facets of her life *herself*, let alone sharing them with him.

Though she had tried to love her husband, she had never quite been able to pull it off. She had pretended as best she could but when one person loved the other more, things never turned out well. Joe must have sensed the truth. Eventually he started pulling away, finding passion with other women, which made her even less able to care for him.

"We were falling apart, even before Lily's diagnosis," she admitted quietly. "And then...well, things went sharply downhill."

She drew in a breath, fighting down emotions that clawed at her chest to be free.

"The worst was Ben. He and Joe had always had a...great relationship. Joe would take him fishing, they would go out on the boats, they would go on camping trips. Joe took such pride that Ben was a natural athlete, good at baseball and basketball and soccer. And he was so very smart, always with his nose in a book. When he found out after Lily's diagnosis that Ben couldn't possibly be his, it was like Joe turned off every positive emotion he had ever felt toward him. He became cold and harsh, yelling at him over the smallest infraction. I know it was… bewildering and hurtful for Ben, to go from having a father's love to losing it overnight. He had to stand by and watch Joe give all that love and care to Lily and absolutely none to him."

She was weeping now, her nose dripping, her eyes streaming. She didn't care. She deserved every splotch, every tear. "I should have left, packed up both children and gone somewhere. I saw what it was doing to Ben, how something good and bright inside my wonderful, kind son was shriveling more every day. Instead, again I did nothing. I never protected him. I kept him in that house and let Joe emotionally batter my baby, day after day."

She shuddered out a sob and then another.

"You were in a difficult position." Russell reached for her hand and folded it in his much larger, warmer one.

She didn't want his kindness, his understanding. She didn't deserve even a portion of it.

"That's what I told myself. I had a hundred excuses for staying there. Joe never touched Ben with his fists, so it wasn't really that bad, right? Besides that, Lily adored her father and he was a different man with her. How could I choose between my children, to protect one at great cost to the other? Anyway, where could I have taken them, me with no education and no resources, and still be able to provide the medical care she needed?"

"So you stayed."

"I stayed. I tried to shower Ben with the love his father withheld with such cruelty but…it was never enough. Somehow, despite me, despite Joe, despite all my terrible choices, Ben has grown into a good man. A man anyone should be proud to have as his son."

"I am," Russ said quietly. "I have always been proud of him."

She looked back now and saw a hundred kindnesses over the years that she had somehow overlooked. Russ going to Ben's ball games, sitting by himself in the bleachers. Russ showing interest in his activities and interests, always taking a moment to stop and visit with Ben when he would come to the house to check on Lily.

She was overwhelmed, suddenly, when she realized how much love and concern he had showered on the son he had secretly known was his.

As he handed her a tissue from a box in the car's inside door panel, she wiped at her streaming eyes, seeing everything through a new perspective.

He had known, all this time, and hadn't said a word.

"Of course he would be a good man," she whispered. "How could he be anything else? He's the son of the best person I have ever known."

"Lyddie."

He was crying, too, she suddenly realized. His eyes

were red and swollen and his fingers clenched hers tightly.

They sat for a long moment, fingers entwined together as they used to do during movies and plays and hamburgers at Serrano's, back when they were young and innocent and deeply in love.

"I am so sorry, Russell. Sorry I didn't tell you all those years ago, sorry I didn't tell you when you came back to Haven Point, sorry I didn't tell you a thousand times over." She drew in a shaky breath and faced him with all the love she had never lost for him in her expression. "But I will never, for one moment, be sorry I had the incredible chance to be your son's mother."

He gazed at her, eyes brimming, then he reached for her. As she slid into his arms, they cried together for all those years, for the pain of the past and for mistakes and missed chances while the July breeze murmured in the pines and rippled the healing waters of Lake Haven.

CHAPTER TEN

AS MCKENZIE AND BEN left the marina, the adorable old-timers from Serrano's were heading in. She stopped to talk to them for a moment, kissed their cheeks, then hurried on her way to city hall. She didn't miss the way Edwin gave a semi-friendly nod to Ben as they left.

"You know, you really didn't have to leave," she said after a few moments. "You seemed to be enjoying the boat races. You should stay."

"Do they still do the toy sailboat race?"

"Yes, over at the pond by Hell's Fury Park."

"That used to be my favorite. I'd completely forgotten it. It was the highlight of my year. I would start planning next year's boat the day after Lake Haven Days ended and I worked hard on it all year."

"Did your dad help you?"

It was obviously the wrong thing to say. His mouth tightened and he looked over the water. "No," he said shortly. They lapsed into silence and she winced at her own stupidity.

Of course his father hadn't helped. Why would she ask such a question, other than that her own father had helped both her and Devin make sailboats each year for the toy boat races? Joe hadn't been that sort of father.

His father had been a jerk, but his mother was a sweet, kind woman. Why the distance between them?

"Can I ask you an extremely personal question that is absolutely none of my business?" she asked as they walked.

He gave a rough-sounding laugh. "In my experience, when somebody starts a train of conversation with a leading question like that one, it's very hard to pull the brakes and shove them off."

She smiled, mostly out of relief that he seemed more amused than offended. She was already being nosy. She might as well go all the way. Blame it on that really annoying habit she had of trying to fix things.

"Your mom. She's terrific. Lydia was always so nice to me when I was a kid and everybody in town admires her. You, on the other hand, act like you can't stand being in the same time zone with her. What gives?"

She held her breath as a wealth of emotions crossed his features like egrets skimming the surface of the lake. He was so very good at containing them that she only caught a glimpse before his features turned stony again.

"You're right. That is an extremely personal question. And you're also right, it's absolutely none of your business."

"I told you. What's the answer?"

Again, he gave that rough laugh that made all her

nerve endings flutter. That laugh seemed to shiver between them, forming a tensile, strong connection.

She didn't want to be connected to Ben Kilpatrick. McKenzie frowned at herself. If she were wise, she would be doing everything she could to protect herself, not finding more things to tug her toward him.

"This isn't a conversation I can have with you while we're walking down Lake Street with half the town listening in."

He hadn't completely ruled out that he would tell her, she realized.

"Fine," she answered. "You can tell me later. Maybe at the fireworks. And don't think I'll forget, either. When I want to know something, Dev says I'm like a pit bull with lockjaw. But cuter."

He smiled. "I would have to agree."

He reached out to grab her elbow and it took her a second to realize he was only keeping her from stumbling off a curb she hadn't been paying attention to.

His hand was warm on her bare skin, though, and sent little tingly currents up to her shoulder and down again to her fingertips.

He didn't move his hand, even after all danger of her stumbling like an idiot was past, and they walked that way together the rest of the way to the redbrick two-story city hall, with its wide front steps and traditional white cupola on top.

She didn't want to stop walking, even though she knew she had responsibilities here. Couldn't they keep going? It had been a long time since she had walked beside a fascinating man whose touch made her feel so…warm.

But no. She had things to do here and couldn't just throw all sense of caution into the lake.

"Thanks for walking me back."

"No problem."

"Are you heading back to your mom and the boat races?"

He shook his head. "I should go check on Hondo. He's been inside for several hours and is probably ready to run a bit. Want me to let Rika out for a while?"

"That would be terrific. Thank you! My schedule is so packed today I'm not sure when I'll have time to get her. I was just about to text the girl who helps me out with Rika to go home and let her out, but I'm not sure if I can reach her."

"I can handle it. I'm going back and it's just a matter of walking next door."

"If you're sure, I would appreciate it. There's a spare key under the red flowerpot on the front porch."

"Red flowerpot. Got it."

"Thanks. I owe you. Seriously."

He gave her a long, slow smile. "I'm sure I can come up with some way for you to repay me."

Her insides shivered again, her mind on that moment in his kitchen when he had nearly kissed her. Her imagination orbited in a hundred different directions until he brought her firmly back to earth.

"We can start with you backing off the nosy questions about my relationship with my mother."

"You wish," she muttered.

"Or you could take a break for five minutes from being Haven Point's number one cheerleader."

"That could be a tough one, too," she admitted. "Speaking of which, you're coming to the barbecue and Dutch-oven dinner in a few hours, right? You have to come. Fabulous food, good people and a killer view you won't find anywhere else but right here in Haven Point."

He snorted. "Rah rah. You only need some pom-poms."

"Well? Will you be there?" she pressed.

"If I make it, I'll find you."

"Great. I'll see you then. Thanks. Red flowerpot."

"I know."

He started to walk away. Then, as an afterthought, he came back and brushed her cheek with his mouth—after which he stepped away with a baffled sort of look, as if he didn't quite understand himself.

"I'll see you," he said, then walked quickly away, leaving her stunned and breathless and aching for something more.

As she expected, she was crazy busy the rest of the day, bouncing between baseball games, horseshoe tournaments, public appearances and assorted crises in need of management. She was so busy, she didn't have time to think about Ben more than, oh, three or four dozen times.

By evening, she kept looking for him to show up

at the town barbecue and Dutch-oven dinner but he was nowhere in evidence.

Dratted man.

She did her best not to look for him obsessively. Instead, she was busy talking to residents of her town. She was making her way through, shaking hands and chatting, when she spotted Devin and their friend Wynona Bailey, who was on the Haven Point police department.

After disengaging from a dry conversation with a couple retired bankers who always wanted to talk to her about her time in Chicago, she made her way to her friends.

"Hey there." Wynona grinned, looking far too petite, blonde, young and feminine to be a tough police officer—though that was probably sexist and ageist of her, McKenzie acknowledged.

Devin looked around. "Where's your gorgeous gazillionaire? I thought you were trying to take him around to all the Lake Haven Days events so you could introduce him to more of the delights of our fair town."

She thought so, too. It would have been a good plan, if the man hadn't run off that afternoon and made himself scarce the rest of the day.

"Okay, let's be clear. I don't *have* a gorgeous gazillionaire. If I did, do you honestly think I'd be hanging around here with you two instead of spending the summer in my villa on the Côte d'Azur?"

Devin and Wyn laughed.

"Seriously. Where's Ben?" her sister pressed. "I

saw you with him this morning. Where did you lose him?"

"Oh, *that* gorgeous gazillionaire." She shrugged. "Don't know. He headed back to his place earlier in the day to take care of his dog and let Rika out for me. Apparently he was sidetracked there. I'm still hoping he makes it."

"He'll be missing some great food if he doesn't show," Wyn said.

"You're not on duty?" she asked. "I would have thought Lake Haven Days called for all hands on deck."

"I'm on call." Wyn pointed to her radio. "And I have to go on in an hour. I figured I needed sustenance before my shift and there's nothing better than Dutch-oven potatoes."

She pointed to the plate of cheesy, oniony, bacony potatoes that did emit a mouthwatering aroma.

"Your arteries may disagree," Devin said mildly. "And you can trust me on that. I'm a doctor."

"Did they teach you how to be a buzzkill in that fancy medical school?" Wyn retorted, taking another forkful of her potatoes with obvious enjoyment.

"Yes. We had a whole class in our third year. How to ruin every future social occasion with dire health warnings."

"And of course, you aced it, like always," McKenzie teased.

"Naturally." Devin grinned.

McKenzie stayed to chat with her sister and Wynona for a few more moments before she was drawn away by someone else who wanted to talk to her about a problem with water levels on the Hell's Fury River.

After breaking away, she headed over and grabbed a plate of food for herself—and couldn't resist including a small portion of the cheesy potatoes. She had to hope Devin didn't catch her at it.

She took a seat at the table and listened to the laughter, the live music, the conversation of her community.

"You have room for one more?"

She glanced up and saw Ben had made it at last. She smiled broadly, telling herself the little pulse of excitement in her chest was only because now he would have the chance to experience one of her favorite sides of this town.

"Of course. But you don't have any food."

"I actually grabbed a sandwich before I came over."

"Why would you possibly want to miss out on this?" She pointed at her plate, brimming with delicious items.

"I know. I must be crazy. I *have* heard I must try the Dutch-oven cherry cobbler and homemade ice cream."

Her mouth watered. "Yes. Definitely."

"Can I get you some?"

"That would be terrific. Thanks."

He headed away and she was busy telling her nerves to settle down when she suddenly heard a commotion near the table where the volunteer fire department was serving up the desserts.

"You're a son of a bitch like your old man and you always have been."

No alcohol was served at the community barbecue but judging by the belligerent tone and slurred words, somebody had brought his own to the party.

She knew that voice, McKenzie realized as dread soaked through her.

Jim Welch—big, tough, bellicose all the time. A terrible combination.

She cringed. Of all the people for Ben to bump into tonight. Hoping to deflect what had the potential to be an ugly scene, she slid away from the table and hurried over to the two men.

"My dad had forty years with Kilpatrick Boatworks," Welch snarled. "He gave his whole life to that company, his blood and his sweat. Then he and everybody else in this town lost their jobs in a single afternoon."

"It wasn't a single afternoon," Ben corrected firmly, looking not at all intimidated by an angry man, five inches taller and who outweighed him by at least a hundred pounds.

"We gave very generous severance packages to every employee," he went on. "We provided early retirement with fully vested pension benefits to anyone within seven years of retirement age and also provided full-tuition vocational training waivers for up to five years after the factory closed. Every effort was made to make sure no one was left out in the cold."

McKenzie blinked, momentarily distracted. This was the first she had heard about it. The way some people talked, one day the factory was open, the next everyone was out of a job. Maybe that would teach her not to listen to some people until she had the full story.

"That's a dirty lie. *Some* people were left out in the cold. My old man was one of them. He was too old to learn how to do something else! Boatbuilding was all he ever knew."

Jimmy all but chest-bumped Ben, who didn't give an inch. McKenzie clenched her fists, ready to step in. Jimmy had a reputation for starting bar fights down at the Mad Dog Brewery. Last Christmas at the Lights on the Lake Festival, he had actually gone after Aidan Caine.

She didn't know how she could possibly stop a mad bull on a rampage—though she was wearing red—but she wasn't about to let a bully like Jimmy ruin all the progress she wanted to think she had made convincing Ben this was a good place for Caine Tech to expand.

Ben seemed to be handling the situation without her. "I didn't want to close the factory," he said with firm control, "but it had been losing money steadily for a decade. Since I had no interest or aptitude to run it, I made an offer to the employees to buy me out. They weren't interested, either—and couldn't have found financing anyway, given the company's extensive losses. Like it or not, closing the plant was an inevitability. It should have been done years earlier."

That seemed to piss off Jimmy even more. His face turned mottled and red. He looked around the crowd that had gathered, a crowd whose mood McKenzie couldn't quite sense.

"Screw inevi—" The word was apparently too much for Jimmy's alcohol-impaired brain to work around. "Whatever. Screw that, you smug bastard."

Before McKenzie could move or think, he threw a hard punch. Ben clearly had the advantage, not being similarly impaired. He easily sidestepped the right hook. Carried by his own momentum, Jimmy stumbled into a table. It took him a moment to clamber to his feet again. He would have gone for Ben again, but McKenzie had finally engaged her own brain enough to move between the two men.

She wasn't thinking about any risk to life and limb, too focused on worrying. This was a disaster. How would Ben ever see what a nice community Haven Point was if he was attacked at the town barbecue?

"That's enough, Jimmy."

He turned red-rimmed eyes to her. "You stay out of this, Shaw. Mind your own business."

She had a sudden flashback of being ten years old, new in town, being bullied on the school bus every day by Jimmy and a couple of his friends. She made an easy target—new to town, half-Hispanic, illegitimate, virtually dumped on a family that didn't know what to do with her.

She hadn't learned to stand up for herself for a year or two. Once she learned to fight back—and fight back dirty, if she had to—Jimmy had left her alone.

This was the same principle. Stand up to the bullies and they inevitably backed down.

"This *is* my business," she snapped. "I am the mayor of Haven Point and Ben is here as my guest. I don't like to see my guests mistreated."

Unfortunately, she had forgotten that a drunk bully didn't have the usual common sense. Jimmy turned his belligerence on her, his huge fists clenched. "You want to pucker up because he works for Aidan Caine now and is swimming in green, go ahead. I don't give a shit about all that. To me, he's still the asshole who ruined this town when he closed the boatworks. Why should he be welcome anywhere in Haven Point? Who's with me?"

McKenzie was upset to see a few heads nodding but the majority of people in the vicinity frowned.

"Settle down, Welch," somebody said. "This isn't the time or place. There are kids here."

"He's my guest," McKenzie repeated fiercely, "and as such, I expect him to be treated with courtesy and respect."

"Just because you're screwing him doesn't mean the rest of us have to bend over, too."

McKenzie wanted to roll her eyes. Jimmy was *such* an idiot.

Ben apparently didn't find that as amusing as she did. He took a step forward, suddenly looking hard and dangerous and not at all the sort of man anyone with an ounce of sense would want to mess with.

"That's enough," he growled. "You're going to want to shut up now."

"Says who?"

"Says me," McKenzie snapped, even though some

part of her wanted to turn into a soft, gooey mess. She couldn't remember the last time anyone besides Devin had stood up for her. How was she possibly supposed to resist Ben's chivalry—misguided though it was?

"Go home, Jimmy, and sober up," she said firmly. "You're not welcome here."

"I pay my taxes! I can be here if I want."

"Not if I say you can't. Don't make me call Chief Emmett."

"Let me get this straight. You're kicking me out, yet you let this son of a bitch stay and eat the food my taxes pay for, after what he's done to this town?"

"That's about the size of it. Yeah."

He glared. "Screw this. And screw you, too."

She should have been braced for it but he shoved past her—and shoved *her* on the way. Caught off guard, she stumbled and fell, her head hitting the edge of a table as she went down.

Pain exploded and she heard Ben give a vicious swear. She was on the ground and didn't see but she assumed he had thrown a punch because an instant later, Jimmy toppled to the ground.

Somebody screamed at that point and she could only hope it wasn't her.

"HE CAN TRY to press charges, but they won't stick," Wynona said twenty minutes later. They were in McKenzie's office at city hall, the closest spot where they could find a quiet place to give their statements to her.

"Are you sure?" McKenzie pressed. She could just

see Ben being charged with assault. Wouldn't that just put the seal of doom on any hopes she had of him coming around and recommending Haven Point for the new facility?

"Positive. Two hundred people saw Jimmy knock you down. I'm willing to bet a hundred-ninety-five of those people would have taken down Jimmy if Kilpatrick here hadn't done the honors—including Eppie and Hazel, who were halfway out of their chairs."

"So you're saying I performed a civic duty by knocking out the bastard."

Wynona grinned, apparently no more immune to Ben's all-around gorgeousness than McKenzie. "That's one way of looking at it. You should have let law enforcement handle the situation. Barring that, you did what you had to do. Who knows how many other people he might have plowed down on his way out of the barbecue. There were senior citizens and children there. You should get a freaking medal, as far as I'm concerned."

"I'll pass on the medal, thanks."

"Well, Jimmy's in jail on a drunk and disorderly. He'll be there overnight to sleep it off, which gives you until tomorrow morning to decide if you want to press charges, Kenz."

She didn't. She wanted the whole thing to go away. "I'll sleep on it and call Chief Emmett in the morning."

"Sounds good. You sure you don't want to let the paramedics take a look at you? Say the word and Julio

Robles will come knocking down your door to check you out. You know he's got a thing for you."

Her face heated. Julio was barely twenty-one. She used to babysit him, for heaven's sake.

"I've got a stupid goose egg. That's it. It's not like it's a traumatic brain injury or something. I don't need paramedics."

If she had moved a little faster, she wouldn't even have had the stupid goose egg.

"Anyway, Devin took a look at it at the scene and assured me I'm fine."

Wynona's radio crackled suddenly and McKenzie recognized the dispatcher telling her of a report about underage marijuana use at Starlight Beach.

Wyn sighed. "I'm in for a fun night, if the kids are lighting up their own fireworks already. It's not even dark yet. What the hell, right? You sure you're good here?"

"Absolutely," McKenzie answered. "Thanks, Wyn."

She hugged her friend, who gave Ben a cheerful smile and headed out.

"Well. That was fun," Ben answered.

She made a face. "I'm so sorry. Jimmy is an idiot drunk but he's usually relatively harmless. His wife left him a few weeks ago. Smartest thing she ever did, but he's obviously taking it hard, especially since she took their two kids with her."

"So you're saying I should have let him get away with bad-mouthing you, shoving you? I disagree. I should have taken him out when he first started up."

It *had* been rather impressive. For a Silicon Valley

tech executive, Ben was in amazing shape to knock out a big dude like Jimmy with one punch. She imagined Welch's head would be spinning for a week.

"Well, no. I was just trying to explain that he can be a bit of a hot-tempered jerk but he's not all bad."

He gave a short laugh. "Do you see the good in everybody?"

"Not quite," she answered. If someone had asked her a week ago whether she could see any good in Ben Kilpatrick she would have been quick to argue. These past few days had shown her that perhaps she'd been unreasonably obstinate.

"Just drunks whose wives have finally had enough." He shook his head. "Maybe you shouldn't be so quick to forgive everyone."

"I'll keep that wise advice in mind," she said.

He rolled his eyes and made a little twirling gesture with his forefinger.

"Turn around. I want to get a better look at this goose egg I should have prevented."

"It wasn't your fault. I should have moved faster. Anyway, Devin already looked at it."

"Turn around," he said again, in an uncompromising voice.

"You are so bossy."

"That's one word for it."

She sighed and finally complied. She could feel the heat of him as he moved behind her. His breath whispered against the back of her neck and she had to fight to control an involuntary shiver. He made her feel small and delicate, which was totally ridiculous, since she was neither.

His fingers gently probed the bump on the back of her head but she still flinched a little as he touched the most tender spot.

"Sorry," he murmured. The low timbre of his voice seemed to slide down her spine.

"Not your fault," she murmured back.

Too soon, he dropped his hand and stepped away. "Nice little bump you've got there."

She made a wry face. "Great. As if I didn't have enough trouble getting my hair to look right."

He gave a low laugh. "Your hair is fine every time I see it. Lovely, actually."

He thought she was lovely? Really? Okay, her hair, anyway.

Her breath seemed to catch in her throat and for a long moment, she couldn't do anything but stand there, so aware of him it was like a fire sizzling through her. Suddenly, she was certain she could feel each sluggish beat of her heart, each pulse of blood through her veins.

His gaze danced to her mouth again, as it had that night in his kitchen, and she felt that seductive heat shiver between them again.

No. She wasn't going to make a fool of herself over Ben. That *wouldn't* help her cause.

She eased away and forced a smile. "Thanks again for your help."

He looked disconcerted for a moment but finally nodded. "You're welcome. You should be fine. Maybe grab a little ice from one of the vendors while you watch the fireworks show—though, really, who needs fireworks when Haven Point has you?"

"I'll have you know, I almost never got in fights with bullies before you came to town."

He laughed, a sound so rich and sweet, she wanted to stand there in her office and just let it soak through her. "I guess I'm a bad influence on you."

Oh, if he only knew. McKenzie pushed away the attraction. She had responsibilities, she reminded herself, and they didn't include standing here and mooning over Ben Kilpatrick.

"Speaking of fireworks, I need to go. I can't believe it took Wyn so long to take our statements. It's going to be dark soon and I need to go back to Lakeside Park before they light the first fuse."

It was an excuse to help her put a little distance between them and she was very much afraid he knew it.

CHAPTER ELEVEN

He wasn't sure what happened, but one moment McKenzie had been soft and warm, her lips slightly parted, her eyes dilated—all signs she wanted him to kiss her.

The next, she turned prickly and cool, easing away and returning to Mayor Shaw, brisk and businesslike.

He couldn't remember the last time a woman left him both confounded and intrigued. He didn't know what to do with her, which was an odd state of affairs.

On the one hand, he was fiercely attracted to her and wanted nothing more than to take her home and spend the night making fireworks of their own.

On the other, he knew he must tread carefully. This was a potentially explosive situation. He couldn't risk hurting her or raising false expectations. No matter how much he might like McKenzie, he still didn't think Haven Point was the right fit for Caine Tech and he didn't see changing his mind anytime soon.

Why did the situation have to be so complicated? Why couldn't she simply be a beautiful woman who was obviously attracted to him as well?

They walked down the street to Lakeside Park through gathering shadows. The sun had set some time ago, as it tended to do early in narrow valleys like this one. The charming streetlights along the downtown area had come on and he could see lights sparkling from more than a few masts and bowlines out on the water.

"I should have taken the Delphine onto the water tonight with everybody else."

"It's crazy out there," she said. "One time Wyn, Devin and I took my dad's fishing boat out. We just about capsized after some idiot tourist broadsided us."

"Scary."

"At the time, we thought it was hilarious, but then we were stupid teenage girls. When I look back, I shudder to imagine how things could have gone south quickly. The water, at night, a bunch of inexperienced boat operators, including us. Dad was furious we took the boat without asking him and Adele didn't speak to me for a month. She blamed me for the whole thing, of course, especially as my sister was in the middle of chemotherapy. It was still worth it to see Devin laugh and have a good time, for a change."

He hadn't known her sister had cancer. That must have been hard on the family, but she seemed healthy and vibrant now.

"Was it tough for you, after you came here?"

McKenzie cast a sidelong look. "You're the one who is supposed to be sharing your innermost feelings with me. Don't think I've forgotten you were going to tell me why you're pissed at your mom."

"You first," he said. He was fascinated by how a

woman from her situation could grow and thrive here, even becoming mayor.

Okay, he was fascinated with her, period.

She shrugged. "It was okay. My dad was great."

"But not Adele?"

"She tried," McKenzie said. "She really did. But what woman would be happy about having her husband's bastard daughter thrust into her family life?"

He could think of a few who wouldn't necessarily have made the daughter feel ostracized.

"Before I came to Haven Point, my name was Xochitl Vargas."

She pronounced the first name "Soshi" but he had a business associate from Mexico who spelled her name with an *X* and pronounced it the same way McKenzie just had.

"Wow. How does someone go from Xochitl Vargas to McKenzie Shaw?"

"My dad wanted me to take his last name, since I would be living with his family. I guess he didn't want me to stand out more than I already did. I was cool with that but Adele thought Xochitl Shaw was too much of a mouthful. She said nobody would be able to pronounce it, so she insisted I needed a new first name while we were going through the court proceedings to change my last name. At least she let Devin and me pick it. I have no idea why we chose McKenzie, to tell the truth. I think it was the name of a character in a book Dev was reading at the time."

He couldn't imagine how difficult it must have

been to give up everything familiar, even her name. "Wow. That's messed up."

"It wasn't so bad. I do sometimes wish I'd chosen something elegant and simple like Jane or Elizabeth or Anne with an *E*."

"I like McKenzie. Or Xochitl, for that matter."

She smiled a little. "Devin still calls me Xochitl sometimes. She was great to me, from the very beginning. She's the sweetest big sister ever."

He was glad for that, at least, that she had a loving sister. It was obvious they were still close.

"How did it happen that you came to live with your father, anyway?"

"My mom died when I was ten from complications of Type 1 diabetes. When she realized she was dying, that she wasn't going to be able to bounce back this time, she contacted my father out of desperation, I think. She didn't have any other family and she didn't want me to go into foster care, since she had come out of the system and knew how rough it could be on a kid."

"You hadn't met him before?"

"She never told him I even existed. It's not like they had a long-term thing going, just a brief relationship while he was in California on an extended business trip for a client. My mom was a paralegal for the firm he was working with. I got the impression from my mom that it was just one of those spontaneous things neither of them planned. He broke things off when the case was settled and he came back to Haven Point and his family. She didn't find out she was pregnant until a few months later and for various reasons, she decided not to tell him about his bouncing baby girl—though his name *is* on my birth certificate."

Her father had been his mother's divorce attorney after Lily died. Small world, he guessed.

"You must have been a shock to them."

McKenzie laughed without humor. "You could say that. What would you do if a kid you didn't know about was suddenly dropped into your world? Some grieving, lost, confused girl?"

"I hope I would have tried to love her."

She sent him a sideways look but her expression was indistinguishable in the dim light. After a moment, her teeth gleamed with her smile. "My dad did love me, from the very beginning. He was great. He drove to California to pick me up and made it just in time for my mom's memorial service. I already told you Devin was great, too. She had always wanted a sister, apparently, just not a half-grown one only a few years younger than she was. We all muddled through. I'm very lucky. I spent a decade with a loving mother before coming to the home of a loving father. Was it perfect? No. But what childhood is?"

He had been around that same age when his father suddenly stopped loving him. One moment, he had an attentive father who enjoyed being with him, the next…not so much.

He must have made a sour expression, which she misinterpreted.

"Don't feel sorry for me, Ben. When I came here, I instantly gained a great father and a wonderful sister, two things I had no experience with before I came to Haven Point. And truly, I loved it here. I was a part of a family for the first time ever and I was given opportunities I never would have had otherwise. My mother, Sarita, was terrific, a truly remarkable woman, generous and kind. I never spent a single second wondering whether she loved me and I still miss her. At the same time, I'm so glad I had the chance to know my dad, too."

McKenzie was remarkable. She had faced tough things and emerged stronger for them, reinventing herself along the way.

He was coming to admire her entirely too much.

They were still about a half block away from the park. From here, he could see hundreds of people on blankets or lawn chairs, ready for the excitement to begin while a bluegrass band entertained them from a stage overlooking the lake.

"Sorry I yakked your leg off, but you did ask."

"I did," he murmured.

She pointed toward the park. "You're staying, aren't you?"

"You know," he said, coming to a snap decision, "I think I've had enough excitement for the evening. I could use a little quiet. I'll have a clear view of the fireworks from the dock on Redemption Bay, won't I?"

"It's close to perfect."

"And I can have a beer there. Even better." He glanced down at her. "How's the head?"

She gingerly touched the spot. "Still tender but I should be fine."

"That was a crazy thing you did, pushing your way between me and Welch. I was handling the situation."

"I know. I was just so furious with Jimmy and didn't think things through. I've spent the last week killing myself, trying to leave you with a good impression of Haven Point, and in five minutes, that belligerent jerk ruins all my hard work."

A soft, seductive warmth seeped through him. Tenderness and amusement and that ever-present attraction.

"Not all of it," he murmured.

Though they were by no means private here, he pushed her into a doorway, where they would be relatively hidden from view, and finally, at long last, he couldn't fight it anymore.

He kissed her.

SHE WASTED ABOUT three seconds in complete shock to find herself here, in his arms. Ben Kilpatrick was kissing her as if he couldn't get enough. It couldn't be real. Perhaps she bumped her head a little harder than she thought. What else could explain something so totally unexpected?

No. It was definitely real. She had a vivid imagination, sure, but she couldn't possibly be making up the heat of his mouth on hers or the taste of him, delicious and intoxicating.

This was real. Ben was kissing her and she was squandering this once-in-a-lifetime chance by wondering what on earth was happening. Stupid girl. Better to just grab hold of the chance and savor every second, especially when this heat had been growing between them all day. No, longer. Since that night in his kitchen when she had been a coward.

She kissed him back, a little tentatively at first and then with growing enthusiasm.

The man definitely knew how to kiss a woman. It was better than Carmela's gelato, rich and heady, seductively sinful.

It might not be the most romantic of spots, pressed into the entrance of Linda Fremont's boutique, with mannequins wearing disapproving frowns and dowdy church lady dresses all around them in the window display, but McKenzie ignored all of it, lost in the moment.

She wasn't sure how long the kiss went on, there in the shadows. When she finally emerged to take a breath, she was dizzy and off balance.

She hadn't kissed a man in entirely too long. Kissing Ben Kilpatrick was a little like coming off a long fast to a thirty-course meal—too much, too fast and entirely not healthy for her.

She eased away slightly, desperate suddenly for a little space to regroup.

"We have to stop, Ben. I've got to go."

"Why?"

How was she supposed to concentrate when his tongue was doing such marvelous things? She sighed and gave in for just a moment. She only managed to find the strength to draw away again by forcing herself to focus on her responsibilities.

"I… The, um, the fireworks will be starting any minute."

He rested his forehead on hers and she was more than a little gratified to see his blue eyes looked dazed, his pupils dilated and aroused. Nice to know she wasn't the only one feeling the aftereffects here.

When he spoke, his voice was low, throaty, and she felt as if she'd swallowed one of the sparklers the kids were waving around at the park.

"I suppose I could say something totally lame—like, I don't know, maybe, I thought they already started."

She laughed a little and was rather astonished that she could, especially when that sparkler was still merrily trailing flickers of heat. "Thank you for sparing us both that."

Her dry tone amused him, at least judging by the sudden smile that left her giddy. "Anytime."

From the park, she heard a deep, distorted voice on the loudspeakers: Chief Gallegos, announcing the fun would be starting in a few moments and asking everyone to take their seats.

She really did have to go, as much as she might want to stay hidden here in this alcove with him, lost in his kiss.

"Thank you for coming to my defense and for… everything today."

"I enjoyed myself," he answered, and seemed a little surprised by the admission.

"Even punching out Jimmy Welch?"

"Maybe *especially* that part. I only wish I'd decked

him ten seconds earlier so he wouldn't have had a chance to shove you."

She would have to tread very carefully here. She'd had a terrible crush on him when she was a girl and she suspected it wouldn't take much more than another kiss or two for her to be right where she was all those years ago, only this time with a woman's wants and needs.

Distance would help, at least to give her some semblance of composure. "I really do have to go. I'm sure I'll see you later."

"Definitely," he answered.

The note of promise in his voice made her shiver, though she couldn't tell whether it was from nervousness or anticipation.

McKenzie had a tough time making it through the crowd as she headed toward the shore where Devin texted her they were saving a spot to watch the fireworks.

Everybody seemed to have something to say to her—people wanted to talk about the altercation near the dessert table or about the parade or how much they enjoyed the wooden boat festival that year.

She was stopped by at least a half-dozen people and had to remind herself each time this was what she loved about living in Haven Point, that people knew her, liked her, wanted to talk to her.

At least the conversations provided a good distraction to keep her from obsessing about Ben and that amazing kiss.

Finally, she made her way to her sister and some of their friends, who had spread out blankets in a primo viewing spot.

"How's the head?" Devin asked.

"Still fine."

"Is it true you got knocked out by Jimmy Welch and Ben Kilpatrick punched him?" Samantha Fremont asked.

"Knocked *down*," she stressed. "Big difference. But yes, the rest of it is true."

"You're so lucky," Sam exclaimed. "I would have *loved* to see that. He's rich and gorgeous and a fighter, too."

Devin rolled her eyes behind Sam's back, though she followed it up with a probing look at McKenzie. Devin was always entirely too perceptive. What could her sister see on her features? Her lips felt swollen, deliciously well-used. Surely it was too dark for Devin to notice.

No way could her sister guess that McKenzie had just spent several long, life-altering moments kissing Ben outside Sam's mother's awful boutique. Right?

To her great relief, the fireworks started before her sister could start any interrogation.

"Ooh. Here they go," Sam exclaimed. Had McKenzie sounded that young when she was twenty-one? It seemed another lifetime.

Devin patted the empty spot on the blanket next to her and McKenzie settled down, lying back so she could watch the show overhead.

While colors began to light up the sky, she couldn't help rehashing that kiss.

It hardly seemed fair to women in general that the man had everything—money, gorgeous looks, a really great dog—and he could also kiss as if his life depended on it.

She licked her lips, still tasting him there. He had been right, lame or not. The fireworks bursting across the sky were nothing compared to what the two of them had generated in those few amazing moments.

McKenzie sighed. She would have to do something about this ridiculous crush that had suddenly reawakened inside her. If she wasn't careful, he would walk away when his time here was over and leave her heartbroken.

A week ago, she had loathed the very mention of the man's name. Now, after the time she had spent with him since he came back to Haven Point, she was discovering the truth wasn't always as black-and-white as she might like to believe. He had certainly made mistakes, trusting the wrong people, and demonstrating an obvious lack of interest in his holdings here.

She could even understand it a little. If his childhood had been as unhappy as she was beginning to increasingly suspect it had, given the tension between him and his mother, he would naturally want to distance himself from his hometown.

These past few days had shown her that perhaps her perspective about him wasn't completely accurate. She still wished he hadn't closed the boatworks, especially now that Kilpatrick boats were reemerging in popularity. But she was beginning to see that perhaps the decision hadn't been as spontaneous or vindictive as she'd always thought.

She let out a soft breath. What did it matter? Even if he wasn't necessarily the villain she had always painted him, he wasn't the kind of man she needed. She wanted someone who loved Haven Point as much as she did, who could find peace in small moments like this, being surrounded by friends in this beautiful spot on a perfect July night.

Maybe she was finding a little too much peace. After a few more moments, the colors of the fireworks seemed to stir and blend together like paint on a palette and her body seemed to sink a little more deeply into the blanket on the soft grass.

This was the first time she had stopped moving since well before sunrise. She hadn't realized how very exhausted she was by the events of the day.

Something about the cessation of sound snapped her out of the Zen-like state she had slipped into. She had completely missed the entire grand finale and realized people were getting up, gathering their blankets and chairs and beginning to stream out of the park.

Devin glanced over. "Were you asleep?"

"Not quite," she said. "Close, though. It's been a long day."

"A few of us are heading over to the Mad Dog for the Lake Haven Monster Ball," Megan Hamilton said. "Want to come?"

On the last night of Lake Haven Days, the local

watering hole threw a wild party to celebrate the mythological Lake Haven Monster—which, as far as anyone could tell, no one had actually seen except a few drunk fishermen and boys trying to scare their little sisters. It sounded like fun, hanging out with her sister and girlfriends, drinking a little too much, maybe flirting with a couple of the cute guys from out of town who showed up for the marathon or the baseball tournament.

Sometimes having grown-up obligations really sucked.

"I'd better not," she said, with real regret. "I'm opening the store in the morning and then Lindy-Grace's boys are coming to stay overnight."

"Oh, man," Megan commiserated. "You definitely need to save your strength, then."

Lindy's boys were a handful but she loved having them over. "You girls have a good time. Dance with a hot tourist for me."

"We'll do that. If you change your mind, you know where to find us."

"Got it."

She wouldn't join them, McKenzie thought as she gathered up her own belongings. She wanted to be home with Rika, safe in her comfortable bed and away from the temptation of the gorgeous man living next door, who was far more appealing than any cute tourist.

CHAPTER TWELVE

THOUGH HER CAR was parked behind city hall in the special spot reserved for the town's mayor, she decided it would be easier to just walk home and get her car in the morning so she could avoid all the traffic driving slowly through town after the fireworks show.

She opted to walk along the lake trail, using the flashlight on her cell phone to light the way so she didn't stumble over any unforeseen obstacles like rocks or tree roots. The night was beautiful, cool and sweet with summer. She tugged her pashmina around her shoulders, grateful she'd had the foresight to grab it out of her car earlier. Even in summer, the temperature of these high mountain nights could drop dramatically.

The pines whispered with the breeze and out on the water, a few people were launching their own fireworks shows off their boats. The celebration would be going on long into the night.

She was enjoying the moonlit night so much, she was almost sorry when she reached her house, even as she felt the familiar sense of contentment and homecoming beckon her.

When she reached her property, a couple of creatures bounded toward her through the night. She gave an involuntary shriek until she realized it was two dogs, a regal German shepherd and a beautiful cinnamon standard poodle.

"Hello, you two. Paprika, you rascal. What are you doing out here?"

"My fault." A shadow separated itself from the darkness of the dock, stepping into a patch of moonlight.

Her heart accelerated and she suddenly couldn't think about anything but that wild kiss.

"I thought I'd better let her out again after I came back from town," Ben said. "The fireworks were just starting as I let her out. Since she didn't mind them—and since Hondo seemed to find a little more courage with her around—I let the two of them sit out here on the dock to watch with me. I wasn't sure when you'd be back and I was just about to let her inside. Here's your key from the red flowerpot."

He pulled it out of the pocket of his jeans and handed it over, still warm from the heat of his body.

She felt it press into the skin of her hand, concentrating on the hard metal shape of it. "Thanks for watching her."

"It was my pleasure, believe me. She's a great dog. How did everything go at the park? The fireworks looked nice from here."

"Good, I guess. We didn't have any major crisis this year—unlike a few years ago, when one of the volunteer firefighters accidentally let off the whole shebang at once and the show was over in about thirty seconds."

He laughed, a soft sound that rippled through the night. She could swear she felt it in the very tips of her toes.

Out on the water, somebody set off a particularly impressive display of pyrotechnics that arced across the sky before exploding in a shower of color.

"Apparently the show isn't quite over."

"Private aerials are technically illegal, especially so close to US Forest Service land, but everybody does them, anyway. People seem to think it's fine to set them off across the lake since they can't catch anything on fire. They buy them on one of the reservations or down in Wyoming and haul them in. I swear, there are some people in town who spend more for their private fireworks show than the city does for the official display."

"Looks like we've got front-row seats. We'd better take advantage while we can. It's only one night a year, right? Are you tired of fireworks yet?"

"I never get tired of them," she told him. By tacit agreement, they headed back to the dock, to the porch swing under the open wooden pergola that straddled her property and the vacation rental next door.

The breeze off the water was cool and she was grateful for her pashmina. She pulled it more tightly around her and settled into the swing. The chains rattled a little as Ben sat beside her.

Hondo came to stand in front of her, obviously still a little on edge because of the fireworks. She scratched between his ears. "There's a good, brave boy. They won't hurt you."

Rika made a sound that drew Hondo's attention and the dog padded over to her, and the two of them settled down on the dock, perfect companions.

"How's the head?" Ben asked.

"Fine. Still a little achy but I'm good."

"You must be exhausted after the long day."

Her answering shrug brushed against his shoulder. Sensations flooded through her but she did her best to ignore her reaction. A snide little warning voice suggested—just a thought—that this might not be the smartest idea, sharing a swing on a sweetly perfect summer night when she had just resolved to keep some safe distance from the man. She decided to ignore it.

"I fell asleep a little during the fireworks earlier," she admitted, "but caught my second wind during the invigorating walk home."

She paused, aware of every inch of him beside her on the swing, the heat and strength of him. In an effort to fight the attraction she knew couldn't go anywhere, she introduced the one topic she was certain would distract both of them.

"So. Here we are. Just the two of us. The perfect chance for you to tell me about your strained relationship with Lydia. You promised."

He groaned. "That again? Why ruin a perfectly lovely evening? Let's talk about something easier, like politics or religion or the China trade deficit."

"Ha. I knew you'd try to weasel out. And after I

told you about coming here to live with my dad, too. Weaselly McWeaselson."

He gave a rusty laugh. "Anybody ever tell you you're relentless, Mayor Shaw?"

"All the time. Just ask anybody on the city council or the city public works director. I'm *not* his favorite person, always after him to fix this roadway or that water line."

He was silent for a long while as the waves lapped softly against the dock and fireworks burst from a wooden sailboat to the north of them. Perhaps he wasn't going to tell her. It was really none of her business and very presumptuous of her to hound him to talk about things he didn't want to discuss.

"Sorry," she relented. "I'm just teasing you. You don't have to tell me anything. I'm being nosy and rude and I'll shut up now."

"We didn't have a very happy home," he said in response. "I guess you probably knew that, from the times when you would visit Snow Angel Cove to see Lily."

The household had always seemed on edge. She remembered that now. At the time, she assumed it was because of Lily's worsening condition and the grim inevitability the family had to live with each day.

Lydia had always been very kind to her daughter's friend, but McKenzie now recalled the lines of strain on her features, the sadness in her eyes. As for Ben, he had been a distant, rather angry figure. She rarely saw Joe, since he spent most of his time at the boatworks—or the Mad Dog, if rumors could be believed.

Only Lily had seemed oblivious to the emotional tumult in their home.

"I did pick up that things were…strained, but I didn't think twice about it," she admitted. "Every family has issues. I told you all about my own messy home life. But I wasn't dealing with a terminally ill sister, either."

Except those horrible months when Devin had first been diagnosed, she remembered, when the entire world had seemed to condense only to that.

"Lily's cystic fibrosis was tough to deal with, yes, but that wasn't the core issue." His fingers drummed out a rhythm on the armrest of the bench, his posture tight.

"My father was a son of a bitch. Everyone in town knew that. He was a bully at the boatworks, he pushed his weight around with the other merchants in town and he came home and tried to dominate his family completely. When I say family, I mean my mother and me. He was never physically abusive but he knew just how to strike out at a person's most vulnerable spot, with lethal precision."

She heard the tension in his voice and regretted ever bringing this up. She had to get over thinking she could solve everyone's problems. Some situations couldn't be solved. They just had to be endured.

"I worked hard in school and earned good grades but Joe was always telling me how stupid I was, how lazy, how I would never amount to anything. He was cold and cruel. With my mom, it was worse. So much worse."

Her chest ached at the echo of old pain in his voice. Despite the advice she had given herself earlier, about trying to keep a safe distance between them, she couldn't ignore that pain. She reached a hand over to where his fist was clenched on his thigh and folded her fingers over his. He looked startled at the contact and then she felt a little of the tension seep away.

"She wouldn't let me protect her. That was the toughest thing for me to deal with. Joe slept around with anything that moved in town and delighted in flaunting that to her. He told her she was an ugly cow and called her the most horrible names you can imagine. He controlled all the finances and withheld any spending money from her. I can remember her having to borrow cash from the housekeeper so she could buy feminine hygiene products. It was truly horrible, the way he beat her down without once using his fists."

He glanced down and seemed a little startled to find her there. "I've never told anybody else in the world that. See what happens when you're obstinate? You find out more than you probably wanted to know."

She was touched beyond words that he would confide his deepest pain in her. The subtle connection between them seemed to tighten a little more.

"May I ask the obvious?"

"What's that?"

"Why are you taking out your anger at Big Joe's cruelty on your mother, when it sounds as if she was just as much a victim as you were?"

"Intellectually, I know that. She *was* a victim. But from my perspective, she wasn't a helpless one. She chose him. She married him. She had two children with him. I just can't get past the fact that she stayed as long as she did, knowing what he was like. Lydia is a smart woman. She had to know where she could find help out there. Why didn't she leave him earlier, at the first sign of abuse?"

"Sometimes there are complicating factors, Ben. You can't know what was in her head."

"I'm sure my mom had reasons for staying. Lily was probably the biggest. For all his faults, my dad was surprisingly good with Lily. She was so frail and so needy and she simply adored him. I get that, but it doesn't make it any easier."

"I'm sorry."

"You know, he could walk out of her room after reading to her for an hour and then come to my room and rail at me for an hour about how stupid and worthless I was because I got an A-minus on my advanced calculus test."

She didn't know what to say. Compassion twisted inside her and she wished she could take away the pain of his memories. "That must have been very hard for you," she murmured.

"I suppose in some ways I'm grateful now. He pushed me to try harder and be better. I hated the bastard by the time I left that house but I wasn't about to let him be right about me. I refused to become what he said I was, so I worked my ass off to get into Cal Poly and haven't stopped since."

"So now when you're with your mother, you remember being back at Snow Angel Cove and all the pain and disappointment that she didn't do more to protect you," she guessed.

He seemed struck by her words. "That's about the size of it, yeah. Pretty pathetic, isn't it?"

She squeezed his fingers. "No. Not pathetic at all. Completely understandable. Mothers are supposed to protect their kids above all else. You felt betrayed and abandoned and that's a tough thing for a person to move past. I get it."

She paused as the party in the sailboat sent off their grand finale, a huge, exploding burst of color and light that clearly illuminated the Redemptions across the bay.

"Don't you think it's possible to find some sort of peace with your mother?" she asked quietly, when the last spark had drifted into the water. "To let go of the past and move on, somehow, so the two of you could build a better relationship now? It's obvious, even to me, that she wants that very much."

"I don't know," he said frankly.

"I would give anything to still have my mom *or* my dad right now. The saddest thing in the world to me is unnecessary regret. Take the chance now, while you still can."

He was silent, gazing out at the now-quiet lake. The Independence Day revelers had all started making their way back to the marina or to other private docks along the lake. Without the pyrotechnics to distract the eye, McKenzie could now see a wide spangle of stars above the lake and a half-moon rising above the highest peak.

Ben made the swing move with his longer legs and she was content to sit beside him, wondering what he was thinking about, feeling the heat of him, listening to the quiet night sounds around them—the dogs snuffling together, a splash here or there, where a fish jumped up after some unsuspecting insect, her friendly neighborhood owl in the pine tree.

Finally, his fingers tightened on hers. “Do you feel the need to solve everyone’s problems, or just mine?”

“It’s a bad habit, I know. Sorry.”

“Not a bad habit at all,” he argued. “It’s very sweet, actually. *You* are very sweet.”

Something about the low tenor of his voice made her swallow. Awareness seemed to swirl around them like the currents under the dock.

She wasn’t sure if she moved first or if he did, but a moment later, his mouth was on hers. It seemed inevitable, somehow, as if they had only paused for the past few hours to take a breath and now they were right back where they were in the hidden alcove of Linda Fremont’s boutique.

That first kiss had been fiery and wild. This was softer, like the evening, and every bit as seductive.

Desire seemed to sigh through her and she wanted to tug him down onto the cushions of the swing, to wrap her arms around him and forget all the reasons this was a terrible idea.

She hadn’t been with anyone in so very long, not since she left Chicago and the college boyfriend she thought she might one day marry—until her father asked her to come home and she realized how staid and meaningless their relationship had become.

Nothing would be staid and meaningless with Ben, she suddenly realized. On the contrary. The sweetness of his kiss was devastating enough. She couldn't imagine how shattered he would leave her if she slept with him.

The owl soared just offshore, his wings flashing white in the moonlight, enough to distract her and yank her back to reality, to her hands gripping Ben's shirtfront and the tangle of their mouths and her heartbeat, loud and demanding in her ears.

She drew in a shaky breath and settled back on her side of the swing, aware as she did that her hands were trembling.

She folded them tightly together, hoping he couldn't see, and tried for a casual voice. "Well. That was fun. You're a terrific kisser—but then, you probably know that already."

He gave a low laugh that trickled through her like slow-dripping honey. "You know, I don't believe that's listed on my curriculum vitae."

"It should be, trust me."

"I'll make sure to add it, then." He smiled, his mouth just a flash of white in the moonlight. At least she amused him. She found a funny kind of happiness in that, since she had the feeling he was far too serious most of the time.

"You know," he murmured, "I'm all about a person improving his strengths. I think I could use a little more practice in the kissing department. It's been a while and I'm feeling a little rusty."

Oh, it would be so very tempting to slip into his arms again, to let the night and the heat and the magic of being here with him seduce her away from all common sense.

She drew in the last bit of strength she had left and rose from the swing. "Sorry, Ben. As much as I would like to help you out, I have to go to bed."

"That would work, too."

Oh, he was a hard man to resist. She drew in a shaky little breath and forced a smile, even as his words and his intent sent her insides spinning.

"I'm not going to sleep with you," she said firmly.

"Is that right?" He rose as well, big and gorgeous and male. If she were smart, she would dive into the lake right now, both for safety and to cool herself down.

"Yes." To her mortification, her voice wobbled a little on the single word.

"Why not?" Ben asked. "Are you seeing someone? I should have asked earlier. I just assumed you weren't, for some reason."

She thought of Jonathon. Neither one of them had cared enough to pursue a long-distance relationship after she came home. Since then, she had dated here and there but nothing with any meaning, which she suddenly found rather depressing.

"First of all, if I were dating someone, we wouldn't be in this situation, since I would have shut you down the first time. Second of all, why do I have to be seeing someone to think that sleeping with you might be a bad idea?"

"Why, again, is it a bad idea?"

"On what planet would it be a *good* one, barring the immediate—and, okay, probably incredible—sexual gratification?"

He cleared his throat. "Again, why is it a bad idea?"

Men. She wanted to toss *him* into the lake.

"A hundred reasons. A thousand. Do you want the condensed version? Okay. Here it is. I don't do flings, especially with a man who has the potential to save or destroy the town I love."

"This has nothing to do with Haven Point. This is about two available adults who are attracted to each other taking that to the obvious conclusion."

"Maybe in your mind. I'm very attracted to you, yes, and I like you far more than I would have expected a week ago when I only thought you were an evil, soulless billionaire out to ruin my town."

"That's something, at least."

She shook her head, even as she felt an unwilling smile curve her mouth. "It's not enough, at least for me. I'm going to bed. Good night. Come, Rika."

Her dog rose to her feet with great reluctance to leave her new best friend. She came, though, which touched McKenzie's heart, and followed her into the house.

After the noise and chaos of the day—not to mention the past few glorious minutes in his arms—her snug little house on the bay seemed to echo with emptiness.

Usually she didn't mind the solitude and actually enjoyed it most of the time, but right now she found it more depressing than a comfort.

Had she done the right thing, walking away from him? It had been the sensible choice, a smart, wise woman's decision, but right now, if he had followed her into the house, she was very much afraid she would have traded wisdom for the heat of his arms.

CHAPTER THIRTEEN

MULTIPLE CHILDREN WERE outside his window—and by the sound of the shrieks and cries, somebody was being tortured with chains, cudgels or possibly kitchen implements.

Ben glanced out the window and saw two blond boys chasing each other around the yard next door, with Rika in hot pursuit. He watched for a moment but nobody seemed to be in imminent danger. He couldn't tell whether Rika or the boys were enjoying themselves more. Satisfied he didn't need to call in the paramedics, Ben finished the email to his executive assistant, hit Send and closed his laptop.

The day had been remarkably productive. He had finished a half-dozen projects on his to-do list for weeks and had even managed to fit in a conference call with Aidan and their marketing director overseeing a product launch for a new productivity app Aidan had developed over the holidays. Ben fully expected it to be another home run for Caine Tech—hence the need for a new facility as soon as possible.

Aidan had been right, as usual. Ben *had* needed a vacation, even if the unlikely destination was Haven Point. That morning, he and Hondo had gone hiking across the lake to Mt. Kisomma, the highest peak in the Redemption Mountain Range—named for the Blackfoot word for sun. They had been the only ones on the trail at daybreak and had hiked back into a beautiful glacial lake surrounded by towering granite peaks.

All in all, *not* something he would have done in San Jose, though he did enjoy the sea and surf and natural beauty of his adopted state.

He had come back to the rental brimming with possibilities to supplement the ideas the marketing director had for the product launch and had spent the past few hours fine-tuning everything.

He put in very long hours in California, usually up before the sun rose and not leaving the Caine Tech offices until ten or eleven at night, with very little leisure time.

He had designed his life that way on purpose. He loved his work, loved knowing his contribution mattered. Ben knew his dedication was an effort to silence the voice in his head that, not surprisingly, sounded just like his father—the one that insisted loudly and vociferously that he was worthless, that he was a waste of air, that he would never amount to anything.

He hadn't really believed those things in a long time—even before he and Aidan had created their first million-dollar idea together. The insistent voice was still there, though, pushing him on. That was probably why he hadn't yet learned to slow down a little, to relax and enjoy the fruits of all their hard work.

He was trying, though. After Aidan's health scare last year and then Marshall's death from a heart attack, Ben knew his single-minded focus on work wasn't healthy. He needed to take these little breaks from the office, even if he was ostensibly mixing business with recreation.

Hondo went to the door and whined with a pathetic sort of look.

"Do you really need to go out, or do you just want to go hang out with Rika and those kids, whoever they are?"

The dog gave him an impatient, figure-it-out sort of look and paced back and forth in front of the door, the canine equivalent of a kid dancing in place with his legs desperately crossed.

Ben gave a rueful chuckle and grabbed the leash off the hook by the door. He wasn't sure how the dog did around children—especially considering Marsh had been a confirmed bachelor without a family. Aidan didn't particularly want to risk finding out the German shepherd wasn't crazy about them.

The July afternoon was warm, with a lovely breeze drifting off the water. It looked as if plenty of people had chosen a lovely Sunday to be out on Lake Haven. He could see a couple of personal watercraft, a few sailboats and even some water-skiers.

He also spotted a couple of older model Killies and he had to wonder whether their owners lived in the area or had been visiting for the wooden boat festival.

Hondo barked and strained a little at the leash, something highly unusual for him. He didn't seem interested in taking care of business, despite his little con job earlier. Instead, he headed straight for Rika, who had come onto their lawn with the two young boys close behind.

The poodle greeted Hondo with delight, then turned to do the same to Ben.

"Hey there." He scratched her between the ears while he scanned the area for her grown-up human. All he found were the boys, freckled and blond and extremely adorable.

Were these two small creatures really the source of all the commotion of the past ten minutes? He had a tough time believing that—judging by the screaming, he would have expected an entire platoon of small fry.

But then, he didn't have any more experience with children than Hondo did. Less, probably. The dog seemed to be perfectly fine with the situation. He was writhing around in happiness, his tail wagging as he eagerly licked the two newcomers, who giggled and petted him with matching enthusiasm.

"Hello," Ben said with a healthy dose of wariness.

The boys gave him looks that seemed split between curiosity and a little apprehension.

"Do you live there?" the larger of the two demanded, pointing to the rental house.

"Temporarily," he answered.

"We're being quiet so we don't bother you," the younger one announced.

Oh, is that what they called it? He managed to hide his smile. "I appreciate that."

"Kenzie said we had to," the kid said. "Why do we

have to be quiet because of you? Were you taking a nap or something?"

It had been a very long time since he had last taken a nap—though right now, he had to admit that sounded quite appealing. That seemed the kind of thing one did when one was on a quasi-vacation.

"I was working," he said.

"Did we a-sturb you?" the younger boy asked.

"Not at all," he lied. He had to admit, they were cute. He held out his hand. "I'm Ben."

The older one looked at him with caution for an instant, then Hondo licked him again and he giggled, apparently forgetting all about stranger danger. "I'm Caleb Keegan. This is my brother, Luke."

"Nice to meet you both." He shook hands solemnly with each boy in turn.

"I'm six and a half years old and Caleb is nine," Luke announced. "How old are you?"

He had to smile again. "Old."

Luke snickered. "You're not *that* old. I bet you're not even as old as our grandpa Keegan."

"Probably not quite." He hoped not, anyway. It was one thing for his friends to all start having kids. He could get that but he wasn't quite ready to be compared to somebody's grandfather.

"What are you guys doing out here?"

"We were playing fetch with Paprika," Caleb said. "I can throw a stick really far. Want to see?"

"Sure."

Taking a chance—and figuring if the dog were

going to attack, he would have to stop licking the boys first—he took Hondo off the leash.

Caleb picked up the stick and tossed it about twenty feet across the lawn. The two dogs bounded after it. Rika reached it first and trotted back to them triumphantly.

Luke was about to take a turn when the back door of McKenzie's house burst open and she hurried outside with a panicked sort of look in her eyes. It eased a little when she spotted the two kids with him.

"Boys! What are you doing outside? I thought you were watching the show with the minions."

"We've seen it about a hundred times," Luke announced. "We were tired of it. And then Rika wanted to come outside because she had to pee, so we came, too."

"Next time, how about a little warning?"

"You were on the phone," Caleb said. "Mom says it's rude to interrupt grown-ups when they're on the phone."

"I don't mind. When you're at my house, interrupt me all you want, especially if you're coming outside by the water, got it? I need the info."

Caleb nodded. "Okay. Sorry, Kenzie."

"Not a problem, kiddo. Just remember it next time. Looks like you're playing fetch. Have you tried a tennis ball? If you do, she'll be your best friend."

Luke giggled. "I want to! Where is a tennis ball?"

"Up there on the deck. See that big white box? I keep cushions and toys and things in there. You should be able to find two or three balls in there."

The boys immediately took off at full speed toward the white box in question, with two dogs hot on their heels.

McKenzie turned to Ben with a rueful expression. "Sorry. I hope they didn't bother you. I should have been more diligent about keeping an eye on them, but a friend from college called. I haven't heard from her in years and I got distracted, catching up with her. I thought the boys were occupied watching a movie but apparently I'm the world's worst babysitter."

He smiled a little. "Surely not the *worst*. You didn't dangle them over a pit of hungry crocodiles."

"Okay. Second worst."

She looked beautiful in the warm July sunshine, wearing flip-flops, a pair of tan shorts and a peach T-shirt that made her look sweet and fresh and good enough to eat.

He sighed a little, aware of the low ache inside of him. He had it bad for her. The night before had been magical, out there on that swing on the edge of the water. He had kind of hoped the fierce desire had been a temporary condition, but it returned stronger than ever, here in the bright sunlight.

He had spent a restless night, filled with wild, tangled dreams, and had awoken restless and edgy—which might have explained why he had been compelled to get up before sunrise and take Hondo on a grueling hike into the mountains.

He pushed away the memory of those dreams and of the soft, sultry embrace that had preceded them. "So who are the munchkins?"

"Oh. These are the kids of an employee of mine, Lindy Keegan. Her maiden name was Blair. You might have known her, back in the day."

"I remember Lindy-Grace. I believe she asked me to the girl's-choice dance during my junior year."

"Yes. That's Lindy-Grace. She told me about the dance and she said you were a perfect gentleman—much to her disappointment. Anyway, LG and her husband went on a quick overnight trip to Boise for their anniversary. You probably don't know him, since he and his family moved here from the Hailey area after you left town."

"Got it."

"Anyway, I owe her about a million favors so I told her I would take the boys for the night. We have great plans. We're going to roast hot dogs and marshmallows later out here on the deck and have a *Harry Potter* marathon."

"Sounds great."

The kids came tumbling off the deck, each carrying about seven tennis balls.

"Look, Kenzie! We found some. We found some!"

"Whoa, guys. Let's work with one ball at a time. You don't want to drive the dogs bonkers trying to figure out which one to chase," McKenzie said.

"Me first!" Caleb said.

"No. Me. Me!" Luke insisted.

"Hold on. We can take turns."

"Two boys, two dogs, two balls," Ben said, paring the issue down to the essentials.

The boys dropped all the balls onto the grass and picked up one each.

For the next fifteen minutes, he enjoyed the pure loveliness of a summer afternoon, the laughter of children and the excitement of a couple of dogs doing their favorite thing—not to mention the subtle but omnipresent attraction simmering through his veins for McKenzie.

Rika and Hondo tired long before the boys did. They both headed to the lake for a drink, then wandered back up to flop on the grass.

"That was fun. Thanks, Ben," Caleb said with politeness probably drilled into him from Lindy-Grace. "You throw *far*."

So apparently his days as an all-state high school pitcher weren't *completely* behind him.

"You're very welcome. I had a great time."

"You're welcome to have a hot dog with us later, if you'd like," McKenzie said. "And you could even join us for the movie marathon, if you're into *Harry Potter*."

"Who's not? Tempting. Very tempting."

"I make excellent popcorn."

He glanced out at the water, where his Delphine gleamed in the sunlight. An idea struck him, one he found immediately appealing.

"Think they might be interested in a fishing trip instead, out on my Killy?"

She stared at him as if that was about the dumbest question she had ever heard. "Are you serious? They're boys. It's a beautiful summer afternoon at

Lake Haven. Of *course* they would love to go fishing. But do you seriously want to take a couple of crazy kids you don't even know out on your beautiful Delphine?"

The idea seemed increasingly captivating. He hadn't been out on the water in a couple of days after making the somewhat discomfiting realization that taking the boat out by himself wasn't as enjoyable as he had anticipated.

Cruising the lake with two enthusiastic boys, on the other hand, seemed a perfect idea.

"I can't imagine anything I want more right now." He paused and had to add, with perfect honesty, "Okay, I take that back. I could probably come up with a few things."

Instant heat flared between them. He saw immediately that she picked up on his meaning. Her eyes widened and her breath caught, just a little, before she frowned. "Cut it out."

"Sorry," he said, though he felt completely unrepentant. "I'm serious about taking the boys out, though. It sounds like fun, don't you think?"

She hesitated for a moment, that frown still furrowing her forehead. He wanted her to say yes, with an intensity that unnerved him more than a little.

Finally, she nodded. "Sure. It sounds like tons of fun. The boys love being out on the water and *I* would love having someone else around to help me keep them out of trouble."

"A perfect storm, then."

"I hope no literal storms. But I know what you

mean." She paused. "They're going to need to eat soon. I've found that regular infusions of protein go a long way to keeping the peace. Would you mind if I pack a picnic?"

"Even better. What could be more ideal on a July evening than dinner on the water with a beautiful woman by my side and a fishing rod in my hand?"

"I hope you can still say that after an hour with Lindy-Grace's rambunctious boys," she said with a smile, before she herded the boys into the house to help her pack dinner while he headed out to the dock to ready the boat.

SHE NEVER WOULD have expected Ben Kilpatrick to be a child whisperer, but he seemed to have an uncanny knack with the two high-spirited boys. For the past hour, Luke and Caleb seemed to be having a fabulous time out on the water.

Ben had become their new best friend. He was fun, kind and extraordinarily patient, leaving McKenzie little to do but sit back and relax.

It was a perfect day to be out on the water. Sometimes Lake Haven could be rough with wind blowing down through the Redemptions, but today was calm and lovely.

These were the idyllic days she dreamed about during January and February, when the snows piled high and the wind was bitter. She leaned her head back, enjoying the sunshine that warmed her face, even behind her sunglasses and floppy hat.

A seductive sort of peace lapped against her like

the water against the gleaming wooden hull of the Delphine. She closed her eyes, wanting to savor every sensation, from the sweet taste of the cherry licorice vines Ben had supplied to the funny but not unappealing mix of smells on the boat, gasoline and wood polish and sweaty little boys.

"I don't believe I've ever seen you so relaxed, Mayor Shaw."

She opened one eye. "What's not to be relaxed about, when you've been suckered into doing all the work?"

"Is that what happened here?"

"Let's see. You're the one driving the boat, showing the boys how to fish, helping them cast out, even baiting the hooks. I just have to sit here on this sexy boat of yours and soak up the rays. Seems like a win all around for me. Boo-yah. That's how it's done, people."

He laughed, the most lighthearted sound she had heard from him. The sound seemed to send a funny little quiver of emotion straight to her heart.

She peeked at him under her sunglasses. Out here, he seemed far more relaxed and young and even… happy.

McKenzie couldn't help remembering how he had looked the first evening he came back to Haven Point—tightly wound, humorless, hard. Right now, he looked like an entirely different man—a sexy, relaxed, *gorgeous* man.

"I think I'm getting the raw end of the deal here," he said with a mock growl.

She grinned. "What? I brought sandwiches, didn't I?"

He shook his head with a chuckle and she felt that strange tug in her chest again.

She was in serious danger of falling hard for him, she suddenly realized.

Ben Kilpatrick.

How was that even *possible*? She had nurtured so much anger and frustration toward him over the years as businesses closed one by one in the downtown area. Okay, it hadn't been *completely* his fault, but he definitely should have been more proactive about taking care of his holdings here.

She could understand his priorities had been elsewhere. She could also understand, now that she had a little better understanding about his home life, how he wouldn't have the fondest of feelings for his hometown.

She wasn't ready to completely forgive him. Too much harm had been done to good people who just wanted to make a living in the town they loved.

On the other hand, what was she accomplishing by holding on to lingering resentment?

She thought of the advice she gave him the night before, about learning to let go of the past to focus on today. She might have been referring to his relationship with his mother but she could see now it applied just as well to her own situation.

She needed to let go and find room for, if not forgiveness, at least acceptance that neither of them could change what had happened over the past five years.

Was she ready for that?

Since she didn't know the answer, she decided not to fret about it and thus ruin what was left of this perfect evening.

"Haven Point looks lovely from here, doesn't it?" she asked.

Ben followed her gaze to where the buildings of the town clustered on shore and up the hillside. The mountains behind the town were encircled with wispy clouds, the way they often were in summer. A brief, cleansing afternoon thundershower in the mountains was more the norm than the exception.

"It does indeed."

"Sometimes I have to pinch myself that I actually have the chance to live in such a beautiful place."

He snorted, obviously seeing right through her rather obvious ploy. "Nice try, Mayor Shaw."

"What? I was just thinking I honestly don't know why anyone would want to live anywhere else."

"The theater?" he suggested. "The ocean, maybe? A few more choices in restaurants?"

"We have theater here," she protested. "Every year the high school stages a big musical and a couple other plays. They do a great job—and not only that, but we also have a community theater troupe. You probably didn't know that, did you? They put on really excellent shows several times a year. Next month they're doing *Fiddler on the Roof*, with Tony Rocca playing the part of Tevye. What he might lack in actual singing ability, he makes up for in volume. And girth. He does own the gelato store, after all. It's too bad you're going to miss it."

"That almost sounds worth a return trip."

"You won't be disappointed, trust me. Plus, everybody who comes to the show gets a coupon for a single-scoop gelato of your choice. How can you lose?"

He laughed again and the sound seemed to swirl around her, sweeter and more delicious than Tony and Carmela's best stracciatella.

"You're a very good advocate for your community, Mayor. I'm not sure the people of Haven Point deserve so much devotion."

"They do," she answered firmly.

He didn't answer for a moment, his mouth suddenly tight. She couldn't see his eyes behind his sunglasses, but he seemed troubled about something. He opened his mouth to say something but before he could, Luke shrieked.

"I just felt my pole move. I think I got something!"

"Probably a snag," his brother predicted.

"Let's take a look." Ben stepped forward to help him. After a minor but dramatic battle—at least judging by the yelling of the boys—they set the hook and eventually pulled up a decent-sized lake trout.

"Did you see it, Kenzie? I caught a fish! A big one," he exclaimed, holding it up high.

"That's a nice one. Let's get a picture so we can show your mom and dad."

She snapped several with her cell phone, making sure to catch a few with Ben in them, too, whether he wanted her to or not. His high-powered associates at Caine Tech probably wouldn't believe the picture of him out here, relaxed, wearing an Oakland A's baseball cap and a blue T-shirt that clung to more muscles than he had a right to possess.

"It's a great fish, isn't it?" Luke said with pride.

"Should we take it home and have it for dinner?" she asked.

His eyes widened, aghast. "No way. I hate fish. I thought we were having sandwiches."

"Do you want to let it go, then?" Ben asked. "If you do, we need to hurry and get him back in the water."

McKenzie felt compelled to offer a suggestion. "If you don't want it, Luke, I would love to give it to my neighbor, Mr. Twitchell. He has a deep and abiding passion for lake trout, sautéed in a little butter with lemon pepper seasoning. He can't get out fishing like he used to."

"He goes to our church. He's cranky," Caleb declared.

"He's more sad than cranky," she explained, to the boys and to Ben. "His wife died last Christmas and he's not adjusting very well to being alone. Maybe it would cheer him up if somebody takes him his favorite kind of dinner."

Luke appeared to think this over. "I guess it's okay," he finally said with a solemnity that rivaled a brain surgeon over the operating table.

She smiled. "Thanks, kiddo. You can come with me to take it over as soon as we dock."

He didn't particularly look thrilled at that prospect but she figured she could make sure he was at least polite to Mr. Twitchell.

"Are we going to eat first?" Caleb asked. "I'm *starving.*"

"Me, too," Luke exclaimed. "I'm so hungry I could eat a worm."

"We wouldn't want that," McKenzie said. "Let's see what we can find so you don't have to resort to such desperate measures."

CHAPTER FOURTEEN

WHO WOULD HAVE ever guessed he could find such enjoyment out of an evening's fishing with a couple of little boys and the mayor of Haven Point? When he stopped to think about it, the idea was more than a little surreal, but Ben couldn't remember an evening he had enjoyed more.

It was one of those sweet, pure moments in life he didn't want to end.

He had always figured he would never have kids—what kind of messed-up father would he be, given the example Joe had provided—but being with the boys made him think maybe that decision had been a hasty one.

He was actually much better with the kids than he ever would have expected and he enjoyed seeing their delight in everything, from his explanation about how the boat motor worked, to watching fish jump all around them at evening feeding time, to a story he had only just remembered about one magical night when he and some high school buddies had come out on the lake and caught a fish with almost every cast into the water.

The simple meal of club sandwiches, potato chips

and a cold pasta salad seemed like gourmet fare when they were floating gently on Lake Haven as the sun began to sink behind the mountains.

After their picnic, they fished a little longer, until the sun had almost disappeared behind the cloud-shrouded peaks.

"I wish we could sleep on your boat," Luke said, his tone wistful.

"We'd be too cold, silly," his older brother said. "Plus, there's not enough room for all of us."

"Why don't we go back to the house and build a blanket fort in my living room?" McKenzie suggested. "You can sleep in your sleeping bags there and it will be like camping."

"Oh, that sounds fun," Luke said. "After we take my big fish to Mr. Twitchell, right?"

"Of course. We can't forget that." She smiled softly at the boy and tugged his ball cap down a little more firmly on his head. Something twisted inside Ben's chest. She was remarkable with them, unfailingly patient and kind. Every time he turned around, he seemed to find more things appealing about McKenzie Shaw.

He frowned a little as he drove the boat back toward the dock. Everything had seemed far easier when he thought this restless ache inside him was simply a physical attraction to a lovely woman with big dark eyes and a lush, kissable mouth.

He was beginning to suspect it wouldn't take much for that attraction to deepen into something else, something far more dangerous to his peace of mind.

"Why the frown?" she asked, when they were nearly to the dock. "Is everything okay?"

"Fine," he lied, forcing away his sudden unease. He was imagining things. He liked her and he lusted after her. That was as deep as he was willing to go. "I was just wondering how the dogs did without us. I hope it wasn't a huge mistake, leaving them inside my place together. Who knows what kind of mischief they might get up to? I hope I don't lose my deposit because they ripped down the curtains or pulled the stuffing out of the sofa pillows."

"Rika is very well-behaved," McKenzie said pertly. "She'll keep that troublemaker of yours out of trouble."

"Not mine," he said automatically. "Only on a temporary basis, until I can find him a new home."

She rolled her eyes. "Oh, give it up, Ben. You know you love Hondo now. It's time you face the truth. Somehow you're just going to have to figure out how to make a German shepherd fit into your busy life."

He didn't want to think about that, either, especially because he was very much afraid she was right.

"At least Rika and Hondo are both fixed," he said, "so we don't have to worry about any cute little Shepherdoodles showing up in a few months."

"Isn't that a relief," she said as he slowed down to approach the dock. He pulled alongside, thinking again how perfect this house had been for his needs while he was in Haven Point.

Before he could even ask, McKenzie scrambled over the side of the boat and onto the dock so she could help him tie up the Delphine, like an old pro.

Soon, she was helping the two boys over the side. He handed over the jackets they had brought along and hadn't used and the few leftovers from their picnic and then slipped the lake trout Luke had caught into a plastic bag.

"Here you go. To the victor, the spoils."

"What does that mean?" Luke asked with a confused look.

"It means you win at fishing tonight," McKenzie said with a laugh. "What do you guys have to say to Mr. Kilpatrick for taking us out on his boat today?"

"Thank you," they chimed in unison.

"It was super fun," Caleb added.

"My pleasure," he replied, with all sincerity. "I completely agree."

He wanted to add they could do it again sometime. As soon as the thought appeared in his brain, he realized that would never happen. He was leaving in less than a week and probably wouldn't see the boys again.

"Seriously," McKenzie said with a soft smile. "The fishing idea was brilliant."

Yeah, he liked Caleb and Luke but right now he had a fervent wish that he and McKenzie were alone so he could give in to the fierce urge to kiss her soundly.

"You're welcome."

She smiled again, gave him a wave, and then she and the boys took off for the neighbor's house, with Luke holding his fish offering at arm's length.

McKenzie had immediately thought of giving Luke's catch to a cranky old grieving neighbor. He wasn't sure why that touched him so much. What a great example to the boys, about how to care for other people.

He headed inside to let the dogs out, where he found them both sleeping curled together on the rug in the family room. As far as he could tell, all looked in order, with no pillow stuffing or spilled garbage in sight.

They both followed him outside eagerly and sniffed around the yard while he finished wiping out the boat. He wasn't obsessive or anything, but he figured a Killy as beautiful as this one deserved to be well cared for so she could last for decades longer.

The dogs were the first to alert him to company. Hondo barked once, going into protective stance for only a second before he relaxed and went to greet the newcomer.

He thought it might be McKenzie, returning in an odd direction from the neighbor's house, but since the woman who walked around the corner of the house didn't have two little shadows following her, he quickly discarded that idea.

As she neared, he saw it definitely wasn't McKenzie. It was his mother.

As usual, she looked trim and neat, wearing a short-sleeved lilac sweater set and tan slacks…and a nervous smile.

He climbed out of the boat and headed toward her, remembering the conversation he'd had with McKenzie the night before. She was right, though he didn't like to admit it. He needed to find some measure of peace with his mother, no matter how difficult. He wasn't sure he was ready for that but he could at least be polite to her.

"Hello, Mom," he said, leaning forward and kissing her cheek.

She looked surprised and a little flustered by the gesture, though he wasn't sure why. It wasn't exactly unusual for him to greet her that way.

"Hello, my dear. I rang the doorbell but I guess you were out here. I'm glad I took the chance to check, as I did the other night. Lovely evening, isn't it? Have you been out on the lake?"

"Yes. I took McKenzie out, along with a couple of boys she's watching for a friend. We had a picnic dinner and fished a little."

"Any luck?"

He could tell by the edgy emotions in her eyes that she had some ulterior motive there that had nothing to do with talking about fishing. "I didn't have any, but one of the boys caught a nice-sized lake trout. They're taking it to a neighbor."

"Oh, how nice. What a generous, kind woman she seems to be."

"Yes." He could feel her searching look, but to his relief, she didn't press him about his relationship with McKenzie. He wasn't sure how he would answer her if she did.

"That boat is so beautiful. I can't get over it. The Delphine model was always one of my favorites. It was one of your grandfather's, too. My father, I mean. He was so proud to have worked on them at the boatworks."

She didn't talk about her father often, who died when he was five or six. He had a few vague memories of the guy, mostly as a stern man who didn't seem to laugh much.

Her family had been poor, bordering on destitute—especially with seven children. His grandfather had been a part-time pastor paid a pittance by his small congregation and had supplemented the family's income by taking a job at the boatworks, as his father had done before him.

He should offer to take her out on the boat while he was still in town. The thought came to him out of the blue, shocking the hell out of him. Before he could act on it, McKenzie's lights came on. A few moments later, she walked out onto the terrace, most likely looking for her dog.

He could see when she spotted his mother. Her mouth made a little O and she gave him a meaningful look as she waved.

"Hello," she called. "Sorry to bother you. I'm just looking for my dog. Looks like she's here. Rika, come on, girl."

The cinnamon poodle nudged Hondo one last time before she turned and bounded up the steps to her person.

"Sorry. I'll get out of your way. Good night."

She wasn't exactly subtle, his McKenzie. She wanted him to find peace with his mother and she obviously didn't think he could achieve that with her there. He watched her go back inside, trying hard not to notice those tan shorts and her long, lusciously tawny legs.

"So," Lydia said slowly, drawing his attention back abruptly. "Mayor Shaw. Every time I see you, it seems you're with her or you've just *been* with her. Is something going on there?"

He felt that little tug in his chest again, the one he didn't want to think about yet. "She's a friend."

"I like her very much," Lydia offered, "and not only because she was a good friend to Lily. She seems like a lovely person."

Yes. She was. "I like her, too," he answered. Because he wasn't quite ready to accept how *much* he liked her—or, for that matter, to talk about her with his *mother*, of all people—he quickly changed the subject.

"Somehow I don't believe you came here to talk about boats or about my temporary neighbor. Perhaps you could tell me your real reason."

Lydia gave a nervous laugh. "Maybe I just wanted to stop and chat with my son."

"Oh?"

She seemed to grow increasingly flustered. "This is stupid. I'm sorry I bothered you."

Guilt pinched at him for not making this easier. She obviously had an agenda, something she wanted to discuss, and he was making the conversation unnecessarily confrontational. He remembered what McKenzie had said and resolved to try harder.

"If you want to chat, we can chat. I'd like to wash up first. I smell like trout."

She blinked a little, obviously caught off guard. "I… No. Of course not. I'll just stay out here on the swing. These summer evenings by the lake are too rare and beautiful to waste and you have such a spectacular view here."

"Can I bring you something?"

"No. I'm fine."

"Hondo will keep you company."

He headed inside and scrubbed his face and hands, even changing into a clean shirt that didn't smell like lake water. On impulse, he grabbed a longneck beer for him and poured a glass of wine for her.

When he walked outside, twilight had descended in all its summer magic. He found his mother on the swing, gazing up at the dark silhouette of the Redemption Mountains across the bay.

He handed her the glass. "I know you said you didn't need anything but I remembered white wine is your favorite. A friend of mine has a winery in Sonoma and she keeps me well-supplied."

"Thank you." She took the glass and took a rather large gulp of it.

Why was she so nervous? He could tell she was uneasy about being here. Her face seemed unnaturally pale and her gaze seemed to bounce from the lake to the mountains to him and then back, as if she couldn't quite figure out where to settle.

"Is something wrong?" he finally asked.

"This is hard. So much harder than I thought it would be."

He didn't press her, only sat beside her in silence. She would eventually get around to it, he figured.

"I suppose first I should ask if you would mind if I started…seeing someone."

This startled a laugh out of him. "Seriously? You've been divorced for fifteen years. Joe's been gone for five. I guess it's time, if you're sure you're ready. Is this a general question or are we talking about someone in particular?"

"Someone in particular," she said.

He couldn't see her features clearly in the pale light but he somehow had the impression she was blushing. "Anyone I know?"

She was quiet for a long time. "Russell," she finally said. "Dr. Warrick."

Ben supposed he wasn't really surprised, especially when he recalled the doctor's probing questions the day Ben returned to Haven Point.

Doc Warrick had been a constant presence in their lives when Ben lived at home. As Lily's primary care physician, he had been there every step of his sister's difficult journey.

"He's a good man," Ben said. "I've always respected him very much."

Lydia made a small sound and then to his great horror and astonishment, she burst into tears.

Tears. His mother. Two things he didn't know how to deal with separately. Throw them together, and it was like a hot, steaming pile of stress suddenly tossed into his lap.

"I don't understand. I only said he's a good man. Why would that possibly make you cry?"

Lydia sniffled. "Did you…ever make a decision you thought was exactly the right choice in the moment, the *only* choice, but later you realized what a mess you had made of things?"

He could think of plenty of decisions that had gone south but nothing that would have made him burst into tears.

Her question was apparently rhetorical.

"I did that," she said, without waiting for him to respond. "To you. To myself. Even to your…to Joe."

He raised his eyebrows, aware he hadn't heard her use his father's name in a long, long time.

She sniffled a little more but seemed to gain control over her emotions after strenuous effort. "I need to tell you the truth. Russell isn't sure he wants me to. I think he's afraid of what you'll think of both of us—of what you'll think of me, in particular. I have kept this secret for all these years. That should be enough, isn't it?"

He had no idea what she was talking about—and suddenly he wasn't so sure he wanted to know. He had the strangest feeling that something significant was about to happen, as if he was teetering on the edge of something and only needed a push to go tumbling over.

Lydia pulled her sweater more tightly around herself and released a ragged little breath.

"Okay. I just have to say it. There's no other way." She paused and finally turned to meet his gaze. "Son,

I don't know how to tell you this but Joe Kilpatrick is not your father."

The words seemed to come from far away, as if he were hearing them on a loudspeaker that wasn't quite turned up high enough. He stared at her, unable to process what he had just heard.

Joe Kilpatrick is not your father.

Even the echo of the words in his head didn't make sense.

"I know what you must be thinking," Lydia went on in a rush, "and you're absolutely right. I should have told you a long time ago. I know. Believe me, I know. I've wanted to but… How does a mother find those words, especially to her grown son, whom she loves more than anything?"

He still felt as if he were out on the Delphine, only this time a typhoon had blown through Lake Haven and the boat was rocking wildly, tossing him from stern to aft and back again.

A million thoughts raced through his head, foremost among them one central concept.

Of *course* Joe Kilpatrick was not his father.

He thought of how Joe seemed to despise him, how before Ben had left Snow Angel Cove, the man could barely look at him except to spew ugly cruelty—the same man who had once patiently baited his hook the same way he had done for Caleb and Luke that evening.

"Did he know? He must have known."

"Not at first. Oh, Ben. It's such a long and ugly story."

He barely heard her, still trying to absorb the ripples of shock that radiated around and through him.

While most of him was still reeling, a tiny corner of his brain must have been working feverishly to make the connection. He combed back over what she had said, that Dr. Warrick hadn't wanted her to tell him.

The pieces suddenly all clicked into place. He knew it was true, even as his mind couldn't absorb one more stunning revelation.

"Dr. Warrick," he said as a statement, not a question. What would be the point of asking?

She gave a gasping sort of sob, but nodded. "Yes," she whispered. "The boy I loved since I was just a girl."

"You loved someone else but you married Joe Kilpatrick, anyway?"

"That's the difficult choice I was talking about."

She was shaking, he realized. The chains of the swing trembled a little, like the effects of aftershocks.

"Let's go inside, where it's a little warmer," he said.

She shook her head. "No. I'm all right. To tell you the truth, it's…easier out here, where I can pretend you can't see me in the dark."

He couldn't see much of her, just vague shadows and hollows. Perhaps it was better this way.

Joe Kilpatrick was not his father.

He felt as if some arduous weight had been lifted from him—though, oddly, he couldn't exactly say the emotion coursing through him was relief.

"What happened?"

"Russell and I fell in love the summer before my senior year of high school, though I secretly had loved him far longer than that. Forever, it seems like. He had just started his first year of medical school. The army was paying for it and he was so busy, but he still wrote to me throughout that whole last year I was in school and would call me sometimes from a pay phone on campus. He was the one bright spot in my life. My mother was dying of an aggressive cancer and my family was struggling. We didn't have much money and little health insurance. My dad hardly slept, he was so worried about how he was going to take care of a dying wife and all her medical bills, work his job at the boatworks and take care of all of us."

She rarely talked about her mother's death. He only remembered her crying and going to the cemetery a few times a year, on her mother's birthday and on Mother's Day.

"After my mom finally died in April of that year, I knew I had to go to work to help out. I left school early, against my father's wishes, and was lucky enough to be hired as personal secretary to Mr. Kilpatrick, Joseph Senior, even though my only experience was high school typing class."

In her lap, her fingers twisted together as if she were ghost knitting.

"He was a good man who had sympathy for my family's situation. I'm sure that's the only reason he hired me." Her teeth flashed a little in the darkness as she gave a slight smile. "Oh, and he liked pretty girls, too. That probably didn't hurt—not that he ever was the sort to do anything more than tease. He was a good man, Joe Senior."

She swallowed.

"I met your…Joe Junior, after I'd been there a week. He was five years older than me and had been away at college and I guess he took an instant liking to me. Like Joe Sr., he also liked pretty girls."

Her mouth tightened a little and he felt an echo of an old fury. Joe had cheated on the marriage and made no secret of it.

"Joe asked me out a few times and I went, even though I told him I had a boyfriend."

"So why go at all?"

"My father encouraged me to go out with him. Joe Jr. was his boss's son and would one day run the company. What father *wouldn't* want his daughter to go out with him? Beyond that, Joe Sr. made no secret that he wanted his son to date me. And Joe was… very sweet to me, in those first difficult weeks after my mother died. He had lost his own mother when he was a teenager and he understood what I was going through. He was here, Russell wasn't. Though my heart belonged to someone else, I really liked Joe. He was different then."

She was quiet, then let out a soft, regretful sigh. "At the beginning of that summer, Russell came home for ten days before he had to go back and spend the summer at some army training in Georgia. We… spent every moment we could together during that time when I wasn't working or helping out at home. I think we both faced the fact that this tiny window of time was all we would ever have. The night before he left, he told me emphatically that…he didn't want me to wait for him. He was just at the beginning of his medical training, with many years to go and then his military obligation after that, which would possibly take him overseas. He knew I wasn't in a position at the time to leave Haven Point and my family to follow him, not while things were such a mess."

A breeze twirled through, rattling the leaves of the big cottonwood nearby.

"I was completely heartbroken, as only an eighteen-year-old girl can be, especially after he wrote me a letter a few weeks later carefully outlining all the sound reasons he wanted me to move on and date someone else. He specifically mentioned Joe as a good prospect for me."

"Joe."

"Yes. Ironic, isn't it?" She gave a ragged-sounding laugh. "In retrospect, I wonder what would have happened if I had thrown good sense to the wind and gone with him, anyway. My family would have survived without me. My sisters were there to help with the younger siblings, after all. But I suppose some narcissistic part of me was certain they couldn't get along unless I was there."

He remembered her spending a great deal of time with his uncles and aunts. The youngest, Aunt Mary, was only three years older than he was. That made a great deal more sense now.

"I did as he said," his mother went on. "I started dating Joe again right after Russell left town. I was hurt and, I'll admit, a little angry that he was pushing me toward someone else. After only a short time, Joe started pressuring me to marry him. Joe Sr. had already had one massive heart attack and doctors said he could have another one anytime. I think he wanted to see Joe settled before he died."

She released a heavy breath and, as if by force of will, stilled the nervous movements of her fingers, clasping them together tightly now on her lap. "A short time after Russ left, I…started to suspect I might be pregnant. I…knew the baby had to be his, since I hadn't given in yet to Joe's pressure to…well, you can imagine. It was a terrible time. I cried for days, desperate and afraid. I was eighteen, remember, and a good girl. At least I'd always tried to be. A naive preacher's daughter. I knew I couldn't raise a baby by myself, nor could I put my father through what he would have seen as a shameful situation, not when my mother had barely been gone four months.

"I… When Joe asked me to marry him the next time, it seemed the logical decision. He told me he loved me and I liked him very much and was certain I could fall in love with him. When I finally said yes, Joe was so happy and Joe Sr. was absolutely over the moon. He agreed to set up a trust to pay for all my siblings' college educations. Joe even promised I could continue to help my father out in the evenings and the little ones could even come to Snow Angel Cove, this huge house, to stay if they wanted. It seemed perfect, except for one thing. Joe wasn't Russell."

She gave another shuddery sort of sob. Was she

crying? It was too dark to tell. He couldn't see the reflection of tears in the moonlight.

"Because of Joe Sr.'s health issues, Joe didn't want to wait so we were married only a month after he asked me. We…had been together a few times in that month and when I told him a few weeks later I thought I was pregnant, he was ecstatic that we would be starting a family right away. He adored you from the very beginning. I never wanted to tell him the truth."

His only good memories of his father had been those early years. Playing catch in the backyard, horsey rides through the big house, then real horseback rides when he was a little older. Boat rides and fishing trips and long drives in the car.

Somehow, those good memories made everything that came after so much harder.

"He must have found out, didn't he? That's when everything changed."

"Yes," she whispered. "He found out. After you were born, we tried right away to have more children. Both of us wanted several because we loved you so much, but month after month I didn't become pregnant, despite how easy things seemed with you. Finally, after four long years, I became pregnant with Lily. When she was nearly six, doctors began to suspect something was wrong. She wasn't breathing normally and always had a terrible cough and after testing, they diagnosed the cystic fibrosis. It was a relatively late diagnosis for CF. Now, thank heavens, they screen infants, but not when she was born. We had no idea."

He remembered his adorable little sister, so sweet, with big eyes and big curls and a laugh that could light up the room.

Losing her had been the worst thing he had ever gone through, worse even than having a father who stopped loving him when he was ten.

"You probably don't remember, but during that difficult time after she was first diagnosed, they wanted to test you as well since both Joe and I were carriers of the particular gene mutation that caused her CF."

"Let me guess. They did blood work." He had a vague memory of going to a doctor's office at the children's hospital in Boise but it might or might not have been at that time. Lily had spent a great deal of time in the hospital and he had spent hours in waiting rooms there, which was why his personal charitable foundation gave millions to provide entertainment technology to children's hospitals around the country to help siblings and patients pass the time.

"Not only did we find out you were *not* a carrier of the mutated CF gene but the testing also revealed there was no possible way you could be Joe's son."

Everything changed when Lily got sick. He could see that with stark clarity. All this time, he never knew why Joe turned away from him. Ben had felt guilty, somehow, that *he* was the healthy child while his beloved little sister had to endure so much. At the time, he remembered thinking his father must have blamed him, somehow.

"That's why he hated me."

"Oh, darling, no," his mother whispered. "He hated

me. You were only a very unfortunate by-product of that."

He couldn't seem to think through all the shocks that had been thrown at him the past half hour and he didn't know how the hell he was supposed to respond to all of this.

"You were still his son, DNA or not. I wish he could have seen that. You were still the sweet, loving boy who was always so thrilled when his father walked through the door. He just couldn't accept it. All he saw when he looked at you was my betrayal."

He had tried so hard to earn his father's approval, never guessing it was completely impossible.

"Did he know that Warrick was my…real father?"

Again, the shock of it poured over him in waves, as if he stood under an icy waterfall somewhere up in the mountains being pounded by snowmelt.

"I never told him, but I've always believed he had to know. He knew I…loved Russell, that he had broken my heart when he ended things between us before he left. It was the logical conclusion."

Ben frowned, thinking of how often the doctor was in and out of their home. "And yet he let the man treat Lily?"

"He was the best physician in town. Your… Joe knew that. And maybe he knew how difficult it was for me, having to be calm and casual with Russell. It was yet another punishment."

The moon had come up, Ben realized. It glimmered on the lake, rippling across the waves with almost unbearable beauty. They sat in silence for a few moments before he finally asked the question he had wondered since she first threw this hand grenade into his lap.

"Did Warrick know from the beginning?"

He thought of the man's searching looks over the years, how he had paid perhaps inordinate attention to what was going on in Ben's life.

"Apparently. He never told me but…yes. He knew. He had access to the medical records. I should have realized but it never once occurred to me that he knew. He stayed quiet out of respect for his marriage and mine but…I know it was hurtful to him, not being able to say anything to you or acknowledge you or, I don't know, make things better for you."

There it was. The part of this that hurt the most. He was angry, suddenly, bitterly angry as he thought of the years and years of coldness and cruelty. He was also, he had to admit, angry that she was making him see things through a different perspective. Joe was a cruel man…but he was also a man who had once loved a woman who had cuckolded him, in the literal sense of the word.

"Why didn't you say something before now? All those years when Joe was so cold and you let me think it was something *I* did."

"I live with regret, every day of my life, that I stayed with him and let him put you through what he did."

"Why? It wasn't just me. He was worse to you, Mom. All those years, why did you put up with it? You're not a weak or stupid woman!"

She was silent for a long time, her ragged breathing the only sound between them. When she spoke, her voice was small and filled with pain.

"He would have taken Lily away from me. He threatened it often and I knew he had the money, the influence *and* the resolve to back up those threats with action. It was a terrible situation and I didn't know what to do. You were miserable, neglected, starving for his affection. Meanwhile she was happy and had everything she needed to prolong her life as long as possible. I told myself you were all right, that you were healthy and tough. I tried to convince myself my love could be enough to make up for Joe withholding his."

He couldn't soak it all in—nor did he understand why Joe had left him everything when he died. He had no other heirs, but wouldn't he have rather let some foundation somewhere inherit his property and holdings in Haven Point rather than leave them to another man's child?

Was it guilt, perhaps, at how he had treated Ben for all those years? He didn't want to think about that, not when he was still reeling. "What now? Am I supposed to just pretend we're now one big happy family? You, me, Russell."

"No. Of course not. This changes nothing. He would like a relationship with you now, an honest one, but if you don't want that or aren't ready, he understands. He's a good man, Ben. He always has been."

He had always liked Doc Warrick but he still wasn't sure he was ready to take on a new father at this point in his life.

"He would like to have dinner with both of us before you leave town. Will you…think about it?"

He would be doing nothing *but* thinking about all of this. His history, who he was, *what* he was, had just shifted into an entirely new reality.

"I'll think about it."

"I understand. I'm sorry to just drop this on you. I didn't know any other way."

"Right."

She rose from the swing with a soft rattle of chains. "I love you, my darling. You and Lily are the best things that ever happened to me, no matter what pain and loss happened later. Please remember that. I hope you can someday forgive me."

She kissed his cheek, then started to head to her car. Out of the good manners she had drilled into him, he walked her to her car and opened the door for her. She stood for a moment, her hand on the door frame, then stepped toward him and wrapped her arms around him in a quick, fierce hug.

"I made so many mistakes. I cannot tell you enough how sorry I am for them. I wish I could have had a little of the strength both of my children showed me over the years. Good night, Ben. Call me if you want to talk about any of this again."

He didn't. He didn't even want to *think* about it, but he had a feeling he would be able to focus on little else. His entire worldview had just been thrown into the air, the pieces rearranging themselves as they fell.

"Please don't forget I love you. More than anything."

She hugged him again, then slipped into her car and closed the door before he could answer.

Feeling numb inside, he watched her drive away for a long moment, until her taillights disappeared around a curve in the road. Hondo finally nudged him, probably trying to figure out why he was just standing there. After a long exhalation, he walked around the house again, drawn inexorably to the lake.

He walked all the way out to the end of the dock and sat down on the wood surface, Hondo on his haunches next to him. Together they watched the moonlight dance across the gentle waves and the stars peek out, one by one.

He wasn't sure how long he sat there, lost in thought as he tried to come to terms with the stunning news and all its implications. It was too big—impossible, even—for him to comprehend.

How had he never guessed, all these years, that Joe's change in behavior might have been caused by something like this? He should have made the connection. Some part of him had always wondered why he didn't look at all like Joe, other than similar-colored hair. They shared no other features in common and he had always been grateful for that, glad he didn't have to look at the man's face in the mirror. Now he understood.

He had a father. One who didn't think he was a waste of the very air he breathed.

He still had no idea what he was going to do with that. The idea of trying to establish a relationship with Doc Warrick left him feeling twitchy and overwhelmed.

Beside him, the Delphine bounced a little on the waves, reminding him of the other inescapable fact. The boatworks. Apparently he wasn't a Kilpatrick. He had no connection, at least paternally, to the Kilpatrick family or the boats they produced. His mother's family had worked at the boatworks for generations, so he supposed he was still linked to the history of the watercraft but not the way he had always supposed.

It seemed inevitable, somehow, when he heard a door opening in McKenzie's house. A moment later, she and Rika joined them.

She stood for a moment on the edge of the dock before she walked out to join him.

She must have sensed his upheaval, though she couldn't know the reason for it. She placed a hand on his shoulder for just a moment, enough to bring a swell of emotion to his throat.

"Is everything okay?"

He wanted to laugh at the sheer magnitude of the understatement. "Not really."

"I wondered," she murmured. "Your mom was here for a long time—not that I was spying or anything, I just happened to hear her car pull away as I was settling the boys for bed in their tent."

He was a private person by choice and by necessity. As a top-level executive at Caine Tech, he had learned early that discretion was a vital skill. He nevertheless had a powerful urge to confide in her.

Why? Why McKenzie? He realized the answer to

that almost before the question formed in his mind. She was a friend. He cared about her, more than he realized until right that moment.

Besides, after their conversation the night before, she knew more about him than anyone else he could think of. Even Aidan, his closest friend, didn't know why Ben had been so very eager to sell Snow Angel Cove at the first chance.

"She had some earthshaking news for me," he finally said. "I haven't decided yet how I'm supposed to feel about it."

She sat down beside him on the edge of the dock and wrapped her arms around her knees. "You feel how you feel. There's no 'supposed to' about it."

He trusted her discretion and her wisdom and he suddenly wanted to tell her. In a few short sentences, he relayed the information his mother had shared.

When he finished, she was silent for a long moment while the breeze off the lake curled strands of her dark, silky hair around her face. In the light of the three-quarter moon, he could see her features, soft with compassion. Something tight and hard in his chest seemed to loosen a little.

"Oh, your poor mother. It must have been so difficult keeping such a huge secret all these years."

"I'm just still not sure why she did. I would have thought after she left my…Joe, she could have come clean."

"It wasn't only her secret," she pointed out. "Maybe she was worried about the impact on Doc Warrick and his wife if she told the truth. Take it from the voice of experience. Not everybody is thrilled to find out their spouse produced a child with someone else."

If anyone could understand that, McKenzie could. This seemed yet another link between them, their tangled paternity.

"I suppose."

"Would you rather she never had told you?" McKenzie asked.

"I don't know. Right now it all just seems so… daunting."

"You'll figure it out," she murmured.

She rubbed her hand up and down his arm, a gesture solely meant for solace. Her concern seemed to seep through him, warm and comforting.

"Thanks."

She rose to her feet and he did the same, though his bones felt old and creaky suddenly.

"I wish I could stay out here with you but I left the boys asleep inside their tent in the living room. They were completely exhausted—thanks for that, by the way—but I should still probably get back to keep an eye on them. If you want to talk or something, you're welcome to come over. We can talk in the kitchen or out on the terrace without disturbing them."

"Thank you, but I'd better not. I need more time to absorb everything."

"I understand."

"Thank you, though. For…everything."

Her soft smile gleamed in the dark. "You're welcome."

Before he realized what she intended, she wrapped

her arms around his waist and hugged him hard. He stood frozen for just a moment as that sweetness and softness encircled them. Did she sense the threads that were beginning to tug between them, to tangle and bind? It was exactly what he needed, the comfort and peace of her embrace.

Something fundamental was beginning to shift inside him and it had nothing to do with the shock of learning he wasn't the person he had always believed.

"Seriously. If you need to talk, you know where to find me. My bedroom is the window right there facing the water. You can throw a pebble or something to wake me up."

If he came looking for her bedroom anytime soon, he had a feeling talking would be the last thing on his mind.

"Thanks," he murmured, then waited until she went inside before turning to his own solitary—and temporary—home.

CHAPTER FIFTEEN

"THIS IS NICE. Why don't we do this more often?"

"I saw you two days ago at Lake Haven Days," McKenzie protested to her sister. "If I recall, there were fireworks."

"Which you slept through."

She made a face. "I saw most of them. But you're right. We don't see enough of each other—maybe because you work sixteen-hour days, between the hospital and your practice with Doc Warrick, and when you're not working, I'm busy here or at city hall."

"That's really pathetic, when you think about it. We're both single, not unattractive women—thank you very much—but it's been months since either of us had a date."

She decided not to mention the few steamy kisses she had shared with Ben. None of her interactions with him qualified as a date, exactly.

He hadn't been far from her thoughts since the night before, when he had shared his mother's stunning news with her. When she woke early with the boys—who were spending the day with their grandmother until Mac and Lindy-Grace returned that evening—the Delphine was gone and she couldn't see it anywhere in sight. He must have gone for a long cruise on the lake.

How was he dealing? It was definitely a shock. She only hoped a night's rest had helped him gain a little perspective and realize he was still the man he had always been.

She forced herself to turn back to Devin and the unexpected gift of an hour with her sister. "Thanks for lunch. Sorry I couldn't go out with you. These aren't the most grand accommodations but I just can't leave the store right now."

"You know I don't mind."

They sat in the back workroom, eating Chinese takeout on the huge table she had bought at Goodwill.

This was where she taught classes on flower arranging or wire-wrapping techniques and where the Haven Point Helping Hands met regularly for their little projects and smorgasbord lunch dates.

"I don't mind," Devin assured her. "It's just my bad luck that the one day I had time to meet for lunch, you're too busy at the store to break away."

"Between Lake Haven Days last week and the general mayoral craziness all the time, I feel like I've been gone lately more often than I'm here. Lindy-Grace and Kaylee have had to hold down the ship without me but today they couldn't be here. I suppose I need to occasionally come in and at least pretend to be a business owner. Not to mention, the Foster wedding is Saturday and I've got ten corsages and four bouquets to throw together."

She didn't add to Devin that after all the excitement

of the past week—and, okay, she wasn't just thinking about having Ben Kilpatrick next door, though that was certainly enough excitement for any girl—she had actually found it a relief to slide back into her routine.

She had enjoyed changing the window display that morning, going through invoices, catching up on correspondence, finding comfort in the ordinary.

"You'll do great," Devin said with humbling confidence. "You've really found your calling here. I'll admit, I worried you were making a big mistake when you walked away from your job in Chicago after Dad got sick but you are thriving here. I love seeing it."

She smiled. "It's a good life," she said, even as she felt a little pang in the vicinity of her heart. Ben would be leaving soon. Would she still find her life here so rewarding and fulfilling once he returned to California and Caine Tech?

Yes, she told herself, especially since she fully intended to be busy helping her town get ready for a new Caine Tech facility.

"What's new with you?" she asked her sister.

"Well, Mom is coming to town in a few weeks. We Skyped last night during my break at the hospital and she broke the news."

McKenzie felt another pang. Though she had tried to keep up a cordial relationship with Adele—she was beyond grateful the woman had opened her home all those years ago—they both seemed to have given up the pretense that they could ever be close as the years passed, especially after her father died.

"How is she doing?" she asked with a forced smile.

"Good. Arizona seems to agree with her. She seems pretty happy there. She said she'd like all of us to get together while she's here."

Something to look forward to. McKenzie smiled. "That would be great. Let me know when and I'll try to clear my calendar."

"You need to slow down," Devin said.

"You first," she said.

Her sister tucked a strand of auburn hair behind her ear. "I know, right? You'll never believe what I'm doing now. I just started a yoga class at the senior center."

McKenzie stared. "You are kidding. When are you going to fit that into your schedule? At 3:00 a.m.?"

"I agree. It's crazy. I'd just like to get some of my patients moving a little bit more, you know? Maybe keep them from eating breakfast every morning at Serrano's and out taking a walk instead."

"Good luck with that."

Devin sighed around her Buddha's Delight. "They're great, though. So funny. Wait until you see what Eppie and Hazel are offering at the service auction this week."

"Oh, man. Thanks for the reminder. I've still got to figure out what I'm auctioning off. I'm thinking maybe fresh flowers every week for a month."

"Ooh. I might have to bid on that one for the office."

She and Devin talked about the auction for a few more moments. Finally, her sister asked the question McKenzie had been dreading—and the question she suspected had been the impetus behind this impromptu lunch.

"So…are you bringing your sexy new neighbor?"

McKenzie picked up her water bottle and drank quickly to hide her sudden discomfort from her sister's perceptive gaze.

"I don't know," she said after she calmed herself with a little cool water. "I hadn't given it much thought."

She had given *him* plenty of thought. Just not in the context of Ben, together with the service auction.

"You should. It's a great way to show off what a great little town Haven Point is, don't you think?"

"Yes," she admitted.

"Will he still be in town Thursday?"

Only three days away. Her tiny spicy chicken suddenly lost its flavor. "I'm not sure," she admitted.

"Well, ask him. For the good of Haven Point, of course."

"Of course," she murmured, feeling her face heat.

Devin gave her a searching look. "Is something going on between the two of you, Xochitl?"

She remembered those stunning kisses they shared on the Fourth of July, the heat and the magic of it, and then that peaceful day out on his beautiful Delphine.

"What would possibly be going on?" she obfuscated. "This is Ben Kilpatrick, remember? I can't stand the man."

It wasn't true at all anymore and she suspected Devin knew it but to her relief, the chimes rang over the door before her sister could protest.

"Customer," McKenzie said, jumping up. "Sorry."

"Don't be. This is your business. Customers always come first."

She hurried out the door—and immediately wished she had hung the Closed sign out after Devin came over with lunch when she spied Constance Martin, the wife of the Shelter Springs mayor.

She was a trim woman in her late fifties who wore too much makeup, too much jewelry and *way* too much perfume. McKenzie could smell her coming from ten feet away.

"Constance. Hello."

The other woman's fake eyelashes widened and she gave McKenzie a smile that was entirely too big to be real. "Why, hello, Mayor Shaw. I don't know why I seem to always forget this is your little store."

Right. Like McKenzie believed that for a second. "Can I help you with something?" she asked, with the same fake smile.

"Yes. I suppose. I'm in a bind and wonder if you can help me. Wallace and I are throwing a dinner party tonight for a very important guest—a genuine VIP, if you know what I mean—and I wasn't at all satisfied with what they had to offer at the floral shop in Shelter Springs. I'm hoping you can do better. I'm looking for just the right arrangement."

Constance obviously wanted her to press for details but McKenzie wouldn't give her that satisfaction. She didn't really care, anyway. A job was a job. And what a silly question. Of *course* she could do better than the florist in Shelter Springs, who used cut-rate flowers from inferior suppliers.

"Is it indoors or out? Formal or not?"

"Oh, indoors. I can't stand the bugs this time of year."

McKenzie had a sudden sharp memory of that magical dinner of sandwiches on Ben's Delphine, boys and bugs and all, with the fish jumping beside the boat and the air sweet with summer.

The weather around Lake Haven was beautiful this time of year for outdoor entertaining, warm afternoons and cool evenings, and she knew the Martins had a lovely home at the north end of the lake, perfect for hosting a party. Too bad for their guests that Constance was so fussy.

"It's really important we make a good impression," the other woman said.

"Oh?"

She peered around the small shop as if she expected spies to be lurking in the houseplant section or Rika, stretched out on her favorite rug, to be wearing a listening device. "This is all hush-hush, of course, but I can trust your discretion, I'm sure. Who knows, Haven Point might see indirect benefits, as well."

She forced away her personal irritation with the woman. As mayor of Haven Point, she had a responsibility to put aside her own feelings and focus on the good of her town.

"Indirect benefits from what?" she asked.

Again, Constance looked around. "You've heard of Caine Tech, right?"

McKenzie refrained from rolling her eyes. This was the same as asking the average person if they'd heard of McDonald's or Walmart.

"Yes. I believe I have," she said, with a dryness that sailed over Constance Martin's head like a red-tailed hawk soaring the ridges and peaks of the Redemption Mountains.

"Haven Point is pleased to have Aidan Caine as one of our own," she added, a thinly veiled gibe. Technically, Snow Angel Cove was about a mile and a half outside the city limits but she wasn't about to stress that point with Constance.

Constance's face soured a little at the reminder but then her expression changed to that same sly, secretive glee McKenzie found seriously annoying.

"I'm sure that must be nice for you. He seems like a nice man," she said with a smile. "But while you might have one man, Shelter Springs is going to get an entire Caine Tech facility."

It took a second for her words to fully register. When they did, McKenzie's stomach suddenly seemed coated in ice. Shelter Springs. Caine Tech facility.

"Wh-what did you say?"

"It's all but official." She was practically rubbing her hands together. "Think of it. Three hundred employees—highly paid employees, too, bringing those juicy salaries with them. One of Aidan's executives is coming to dinner tonight with Wallace and a few members of the city council to work out the final details. I'm sure you can see why I need something spectacular for a centerpiece, to commemorate such a grand occasion."

McKenzie couldn't seem to make her brain click

into gear. "I… Yes. Flowers. Centerpiece." She drew in a sharp breath. *Focus. You can throw a tantrum later.* She cleared her throat. "I understand why you want it to be perfect. Let's see what we can find for you."

"I don't have time to wait. I've got to run over to Serrano's and talk to Barbara about a few last-minute menu changes."

McKenzie decided not to mention the irony that the wife of the Shelter Springs mayor relied on *Haven Point* merchants to take care of her dinner-party needs in order to show her town in the best light. Constance wouldn't get it, even if McKenzie did bother to point it out.

While she might be seething inside, she was also a professional. "What sort of a budget do you have?"

"The best you can do, dear. I'm thinking roses, lilies and birds of paradise. Spare no expense. Can you have it ready in an hour?"

"I'll do my best."

Constance's gaze suddenly turned cagey. "I'll expect a discount, naturally. This is great news for all of us. What helps Shelter Springs helps Haven Point, right?"

Which town would it help most if she "accidentally" snipped off some of Constance's helmet hair bob with her shears?

Professional, she reminded herself, a little desperately.

"I'll see you in an hour. If you'll excuse me, I've got to get busy."

Constance nodded and bustled out of the store in a cloud of perfume.

Devin looked up in concern when McKenzie burst through the door to the back.

“Was that Constance Martin? What’s wrong? What did she need?”

“I don’t think you want me to answer that right now. Give me a minute to calm down.”

“Need me to do some of the yoga moves I’m teaching the senior citizens?”

“No. I just need to do a little deep breathing.”

She gave herself sixty seconds to calm down, fighting down anger and hurt and a deep sense of betrayal.

It didn’t really work but she didn’t have time to dwell. She opened her eyes and hurried around the workroom, grabbing supplies.

Devin was quiet at first, then—because her beloved sister knew her so well and must have sensed she wasn’t ready to talk yet—started filling the space with chatter about everything and nothing. The heavy rains that were supposed to be hitting the area the next day. A hike she wanted to take up to Evergreen Springs. A seventy-year-old guy who came into the emergency room with a hernia and ended up asking her out on a date.

Why was she so surprised? McKenzie asked herself, only half listening while she tossed in some lovely Colombian orchids.

All along, Ben made no secret that he didn’t want to put the new facility in Haven Point. He had even told her he was looking at Shelter Springs. Really, from a practical standpoint, the other town made so much more sense, with more available real estate, several big-box stores, more updated infrastructure. Why would he even have considered Haven Point in the first place, other than Aidan pushing the matter?

"Okay. I've officially run out of inane conversation."

She glanced up at her sister. She had almost forgotten Dev was still there.

"You're doing fine from here," McKenzie assured her, then realized what she said and winced. "Sorry."

Devin only smiled briefly before she took on that worried look again. "You're right. That's enough for both of us. You might as well tell me what's going on. What did Connie want?"

Oh, prissy Constance would *hate* being called Connie. It made her smile a little and filled her with deep love and gratitude for her sister.

"She came to gloat. That's the only reason she was here. To rub our pathetic little noses in it."

McKenzie wanted to cry suddenly. To cry and then find Ben and slug him hard, right in the gut.

She sank down into the chair where the remains of her Chinese takeout still littered the table. "How *could* he?" she practically wailed.

Devin sat down beside her, that worried look a little more pronounced. "Who are we talking about? What's going on? Who's got you so upset? Not Connie, is it?"

McKenzie drew in a deep breath. She was annoyed

with Connie. Constance. She was *furious* with someone else entirely.

"Ben. I wasn't supposed to talk about it but I guess it doesn't matter now. We were in the running for a new Caine Tech facility."

Devin's eyes widened. "Really? That would be amazing!"

"It would, except apparently Ben has decided Shelter Springs would be a better fit."

She said the other town's name like the most vile curse word she could think of, and right now it felt that way.

Devin sat back in surprise. "Really? Why? And when did he decide this?"

Had he known this whole time? When they were out on his boat with the boys last evening, or, the night before, while they watched fireworks bursting out over the lake and he had kissed her with such sweet hunger?

They were *friends*, damn it. She had confided in him about her life after coming here. He had told her about how difficult Joe had been and then his mother's shocking revelation about Dr. Warrick the night before.

She had trusted him, kissed him, embraced him. She was falling for him…

She shied away from that, focusing instead on her deep sense of hurt. Why wouldn't he have thought to mention, in all those conversations, that he had already decided the new facility should be built in Shelter Springs?

"I doubt Haven Point was ever even a serious contender," she said, in a voice that wobbled just a little. "He doesn't care about this town at all. I don't know how many times he has to prove that to me over and over again."

Devin gave her that careful look again, the one that always made her feel as if her sister could see straight through all her pretense to her very heart.

"Before you take the word of Constance Martin, maybe you need to get Ben's side of things."

"He's given me his side of things. He told me from the very beginning he had strong reservations about Haven Point and was only here because Aidan insisted."

She should have listened to him. She stupidly thought she could change his mind, that if only he spent a little time in town, he would come to love it as much as she did, as much as Eliza and Aidan did, as much as the people who lived here did.

Devin cleared the rest of their takeout from the table, stowing the leftovers in the little mini refrigerator in the corner.

"I'm going to get out of your way, since you've got to finish the arrangement and I've got to be at the senior center in half an hour. Are you sure you'll be okay?"

"I'm fine." McKenzie forced a smile. "Thank you for lunch. I'm sorry it ended like this."

"Seriously. Talk to Ben. And call me after you do, okay?"

"I will. 'Bye, sis."

Devin hugged her, reached out and adjusted one of the orchids and then hurried out of the room, leaving McKenzie with her anger.

CHAPTER SIXTEEN

Ben was so tired, right now as he walked into his vacation rental, he wanted to open every window to the breeze coming off the water, climb into bed and crash for about a week.

He hadn't slept more than an hour the night before, still reeling from the news his mother had dropped on him. He felt like the survivor of a massive earthquake, where everything in his world had been shaken, shattered and rearranged.

Finding out Joe wasn't his father—and that Dr. Warrick *was*—still seemed like an interesting abstract concept that wasn't at all grounded in reality. Every time he closed his eyes, though, he relived the moment when his mother had blurted out the truth, after all these years.

He hadn't called her. He would have to at some point but he wasn't ready. Not yet.

Hondo whined to be let out and Ben forced himself to engage instead of standing in the doorway in a stupor.

"Come on. Outside."

He headed for the back door and opened it for the dog, who immediately raced outside in relief and gratitude.

The vacation rental had definitely been a good idea. Even if Ben hadn't had Hondo with him on this trip to complicate everything, he would have favored this over an impersonal hotel room in Shelter Springs. He liked the extra room, he liked having a kitchen even if he wasn't much of a cook and he loved the private dock. If he were going to have a house on a lake somewhere, a dock was a necessity.

He stood out on the patio looking down at the lake in the moonlight. Twenty-four hours ago, his life had changed completely. He still couldn't take it in.

Hondo raced to the nearest tree to take care of business—not the kind that needed scooping, yay—then started sniffing around the yard, looking for interesting scents. Ben took a seat in the Adirondack chair on the terrace, feeling some of the tension that had gripped his shoulders in sharp talons begin to ease.

He enjoyed watching the dog. Playing with him, walking, petting him was *restful* somehow, in a chaotic, intense world.

What was he going to do about the dog when he left here in a few days?

In light of everything else that had been going on in his world, that question had slipped a little down the priority chain but now, watching the dog, it reemerged.

If only he could figure out a way to carve a space for Hondo in his world...but it wouldn't be at all fair to the dog. He worked fourteen-hour days and didn't have any live-in household help to take care of his needs. An active German shepherd would find all kinds of mischief to get into if left alone all day in that big house.

He supposed he could hire a dog sitter, but that seemed indulgent and also not really fair to the dog.

He would just bite the bullet and talk to Aidan, see if Jim and Sue, Aidan's caretakers at Snow Angel Cove, could take on another dog.

As if knowing he occupied Ben's thoughts, Hondo wandered up to the porch, tail wagging, and came closer, looking for a little attention. He complied, scratching between his ears and petting him. He would miss the dude, though.

Hondo's big, alert shepherd ears suddenly perked up and a second later he took off next door, almost before the terrace light came on and McKenzie and Rika walked out.

He was aware of a little catch in his chest as he caught sight of her, a strange shifting and settling. She greeted the dog and immediately looked over to his house. He lifted a hand in greeting, though he wasn't sure whether she could see him, since she didn't wave back or call a greeting.

He hesitated for a moment, that exhaustion weighing on him, then he decided he should at least go over and say hello and thank her for her concern the night before. He didn't remember it all with perfect clarity but he had a feeling he hadn't been at his most gracious.

"Evening," he said, when he reached her terrace.

"Hello." Her voice was as clipped as Mr. Twitchell's hedges.

She made no move to come closer to him. Indeed, he could sense by her posture and what he could see of her expression in the dim outside lighting that she didn't seem very happy to see him. He frowned, wondering what he'd done. He was too tired to deal with this tonight. Maybe he should have stayed on his own side of the property line.

He was here. He should at least do what he came to do.

"Thank you for listening to me last night. It's a strange situation and I appreciate the listening ear."

"Have you spoken with your mother?" she asked, still in that cool voice.

"Not yet. I plan to call her tomorrow."

"That's probably a good idea. It would be cruel to leave her hanging too long."

"Right."

They lapsed into an awkward silence, something unusual for the two of them. Usually he had no problem talking to her but he couldn't quite gauge her mood right now, maybe because of the fatigue that seemed to have soaked into his bones.

He was about to tell her good-night, grab Hondo and head back to the vacation rental when she broke the silence.

"How was your dinner?" she asked.

He stared at the unexpected question. Was that why she was pissed? That he dared share a meal with the mayor of the town she considered a rival? "The company was a little stuffy but the food was good," he said calmly. "Catered, I understand, from Serrano's."

"No wonder it was good, then."

He narrowed his gaze. "How did you know I was having dinner?"

"Most people do. Every day, even. It seemed a logical assumption."

He sensed more to the story. Somehow she knew *where* he'd eaten dinner and wasn't happy about it. He hadn't been all that thrilled, either, but it was all part of what he had come here to do.

"Constance Martin stopped into the store today," McKenzie finally said, her voice cool. "She came in ostensibly to order flowers, but mostly to gloat."

He had tried to keep an open mind about the Shelter Springs mayor and his wife but ten minutes into their dinner party, he had decided Wallace seemed the decent sort but Constance grated on him. She was one of those women who pretended to hang on to his every word. After ten minutes, he found her extremely annoying. He had never been the sort who needed the constant ego gratification of relentless simpering.

"To gloat about what?" he asked McKenzie. "That she and her husband were hosting a stuffy dinner party for me and a bunch of prosy city council members?"

"Don't bother pretending." Now her voice wasn't simply irritated, it was harsh and angry, a tone he had never heard from her before. Where was this coming from?

"Constance was delighted to tell me all about the new facility Caine Tech is building in Shelter

Springs—which, by the way, she informed me in a rather condescending way would be nothing but good for Haven Point. She told me you've made your decision, that you've all but signed the deal to set up shop in Shelter Springs."

He raised an eyebrow. "Is that right?"

This was all news to him.

"You never had any intention of putting the Caine Tech facility in Haven Point, did you? We were never a serious contender. You only came to appease Aidan. Admit it."

If he weren't so tired, he might have been able to handle this in a far more diplomatic way. His usual savvy communication skills seemed to be floating on the night breeze out to the middle of the lake.

"My position on the matter was never a secret to you or to Aidan," he finally said.

"You made me think otherwise! These last few days, you made me hope Haven Point might have a chance. The last thing I expected is that you would go with Shelter Springs!"

The betrayal in her voice stung—and, worse, made him question everything of the past few days. She had been so sweet to him. Those tender kisses out by the lake, the evening out on his boat with her friend's sons, that embrace on the dock the night before that had been both comforting and healing.

He couldn't help thinking of all the times in school when people only wanted to be his friend because his family was relatively well-off and lived in a huge, sprawling house by the lake, because his father owned the boatworks where many of *their* fathers were employed.

Little had changed after Caine Tech exploded onto the high-tech scene. As one of the founders and highest-ranking executives of a multi-billion-dollar company, he was used to people trying to curry favor with him.

Was she really no different from Constance Martin, just better at hiding her obsequiousness?

Anger growled to life, probably magnified by his exhaustion. He was used to exhibiting ironclad control—his childhood had taught him that—but right now it seemed beyond him.

"Is that what these last few days have been about? You just trying to push your cause? I have to say, Mayor, you really go above and beyond for your town."

She drew in a sharp breath. "I'm not going to justify that with a response."

"You seem very quick to make assumptions about my behavior. All I did was have dinner in Shelter Springs. What's so wrong about that?"

"It's not about the dinner! It's about the deception. You made me think we had a chance. Why did you even waste time coming here in the first place? You never would have considered Haven Point, even though Aidan wanted you to."

He didn't want to do this right now. He wanted to grab his dog and head back into his rental house. No, he wanted to pack up his Delphine and get the hell out of this town that had brought him nothing but trouble.

Except those sultry kisses.

And a fledgling friendship that had come to mean something to him, one he had apparently destroyed.

"You know the worst part?" she said, a wobble of pain in her voice. "I was starting to think maybe you weren't the evil creature I painted you all this time, when you didn't bother to pay more attention while your incompetent property manager was shoving this town into an early grave. I can't believe I was so wrong. You're worse. You had an unhappy childhood here. I'm sorry for that but I can't forgive you for punishing the people of this town because of it."

"I'm not punishing anyone," he exclaimed. "That's ridiculous."

"What does Shelter Springs have that Haven Point doesn't? Answer that!"

"Besides bridges that aren't falling apart, roads that have been better maintained and a wider tax base, you mean?"

"We would have all those things if not for you!"

Any last clinging tendril of restraint seemed to have gone to sleep without him. "Okay. You want truth, Mayor Shaw, I'll give you truth. Constance Martin is crazy. I don't know where she got the idea I'd settled on Shelter Springs but the reality is, I have no intention of recommending Shelter Springs *or* Haven Point to Aidan for the new facility. I think moving anywhere near Lake Haven would be a financial and strategic mistake. I am sticking with my original recommendation, that we expand our existing satellite office outside Portland, where we already have a base."

"Portland."

She sank into a chair looking defeated and small suddenly.

He ran a hand through his hair. He shouldn't have sprung it on her like this. He didn't know how he would have told her—maybe in an email or a memo, or just let Aidan do the honors. But that would have been cowardly. He supposed it was better this way, even though it hurt.

"On a purely financial basis, it would be a huge mistake to move here, sixty miles from a major airport in a mountain valley with harsh weather and no institute of higher education to cull graduates. Neither town is ideal. In Portland, we already have one facility in place, we own enough surrounding land to expand it and the infrastructure is already set up for our needs. It's the only logical decision and I'm sure Aidan will see that."

She nodded curtly once, twice. "I…see. Well. Yes. That does make sense. Logic is everything, isn't it? Thank you for being frank."

"Kenzie—" He felt terrible, suddenly, as if he'd just kicked several cute, cuddly kittens into the lake.

"No need to apologize. It's a business decision. I get it. I suppose it's some comfort to know you were stringing Shelter Springs along, too."

She placed her hands on her thighs as if she couldn't quite get up without bracing herself, then rose to her feet. "I do wonder how far you were going to let things go between us before you told me the truth. Would you have told me if I'd slept with you?"

"I didn't intend for any of this between us when I came here. It just…happened."

He had come to care for her, more than any other woman he'd ever met. Yet another thing he was too tired to deal with right now.

"Many mistakes *do* just happen," she retorted. "The only thing you can do is move on and try to make sure they don't happen again."

She grabbed Rika and headed back to her house without another word, leaving him cold, suddenly, though the evening was pleasant.

Hondo gave a pathetic sort of whine and Ben refused to think how perfectly it echoed the emotions chasing through him.

What a mess, he thought as he made his way back across the lawn to his house. The hell of it was, he didn't know what he could have done differently. He had *told* her, straight up, that he was against moving the facility to Haven Point. If she chose to believe he might be changing his mind, that wasn't on him, was it?

Right now he was heartily sick of this town. Could he leave in the morning? No, he realized. Not with everything still out there with his mother. He needed to at least meet with Doc Warrick, to figure out if they could forge some sort of new relationship, after all these years.

After that, he would load up the Delphine, drive away and leave all this pain behind.

McKenzie let herself into her house, holding tight to Rika's collar to keep the dog from lunging back outside until she could safely close the door behind them.

She couldn't believe she had been such a fool. It was one thing to pin her hopes for the town's future on the man. It was another thing entirely for her to start secretly wondering if the two of *them* might actually have a future together.

A few kisses did *not* lead to happily-ever-after. She was certainly old enough and experienced enough to realize that.

She pressed a hand to the ache in her chest. Rika must have sensed her distress with that sometimes spooky intuition she had. The dog nudged against her side and licked McKenzie's hand until she placed her fingers on the poodle's curls.

She was freezing, suddenly, though the temperature outside hadn't dipped far from the heat of the afternoon. Just now, she wanted nothing but to change into some warm pajamas, wrap a blanket around her and maybe curl up with some Häagen-Dazs she had been saving for a special occasion.

She hurried into her bedroom with that objective in mind. This wasn't the end of the world, she reminded herself, for Haven Point or for her. Aidan and Eliza still had big plans for the downtown area. They were working on bringing in new retail outlets and restaurants, and the reconstruction of the beautiful inn that had burned down before Christmas would be finished by next summer, better than ever.

As for her, she would make it through this. She had survived heartache before. She had lost the mother she loved and then the father she had grown to love. She had walked away from a job and a boyfriend in Chicago and rebuilt herself here. She had a business she loved and good friends, and the people of this town trusted her as their mayor.

Her life was happy and fulfilled and she refused to let Ben ruin that, as he had ruined so many other things.

CHAPTER SEVENTEEN

"That is really adorable," Barbara Serrano exclaimed as she looked at the quilt in browns, pinks and lavenders stretched out on a rack in the back room of McKenzie's store.

"You're so good at putting colors together. I wish I shared your skill. It must be the florist in you."

"I'd like to take credit but Louise Pennybaker at the fabric store over in Shelter Springs helped me figure out what would go well together."

"The poor kids being treated at the emergency room will love it," Samantha said. "A little bright bit of sunshine in the midst of a scary experience."

The Helping Hands were gathered for an unusual midweek potluck project, tying small child-sized quilts to be handed out at Lake Haven Hospital. It had been Devin's idea, an urgent request as activity at the emergency room always increased in the summertime.

"We need all the sunshine we can get. Holy Toledo, this rain! Where did it come from?" Linda Fremont exclaimed.

"Do I have to explain the whole condensation-evaporation-precipitation cycle to you again, Mom?"

Samantha asked with an eye roll that usually would have made McKenzie laugh.

She wasn't finding very many things amusing. A little sunshine, both literal and figurative, would be very welcome right now. The heavy rains forecasters had been predicting for the area had hit with a vengeance shortly after midnight the night of her confrontation with Ben and showed no sign of letting up. Already, Haven Point had surpassed July rainfall records and at least another day or two of rain was expected before the storm passed over.

The world seemed bleak and gray to her right now, and only partly because of the unusual summer storm.

When she awakened to find rain steadily falling outside her window the past two days, she had half expected to find that Ben had returned immediately to California, but she had seen lights on next door and his big SUV was still parked in the driveway. Before she and Rika drove into work—an unusual event for them in summer but a necessity so the dog didn't track mud from the trail all over the store—she had seen Hondo out in the yard.

The same scenario repeated itself this morning. She woke up, expecting him to be gone, only to see that light and, later, his dog.

Other than that, she hadn't seen any trace of Ben.

He was still in Haven Point, then. For how long?

She didn't care, she told herself. Her stupid infatuation with him was completely done.

"These are so beautiful. I would like one for my new grandbaby." Anita Robles, her assistant at city hall, admired one with little ducks and bunnies marching across it.

"Why don't we save a few of our favorites to auction at the dinner tonight?" Megan Hamilton suggested. "It looks like we've got plenty to cover immediate needs at the ER and this will give us an excuse to meet again in a few weeks so we can make more."

"That's a terrific idea," McKenzie said. She should have thought of that herself, if Ben Kilpatrick hadn't messed with her brain.

In theory, the service auction was supposed to be exactly that—volunteer work offered for other people to bid on. But many people didn't feel they had a skill like that so they brought goods instead. Beaded jewelry, hand-dipped chocolates, even gorgeous tooled leather saddles.

"Are you taking a certain Caine Tech executive?" Lindy-Grace asked with a teasing smile. Apparently her boys had been full of information about the trip the four of them took out on Ben's Delphine. They were completely enamored with him, Lindy-Grace informed her, and wouldn't stop talking about him. Ben this, Ben that, Ben-and-Kenzie, as if they were one unit.

Lindy-Grace had been teasing her about it since she and her husband came back to town after their quick getaway.

McKenzie could feel her face heat. "Why would I do that?" she asked, keeping her gaze determinedly down at the needle and yarn in her hand.

"Are you kidding?" Linda Fremont exclaimed. "I thought we were all supposed to be trying to show him Haven Point in the best light, weren't we? That's what you told us to do."

"Right," Megan piped up. "How many towns do you know that have a service auction where people donate their time and talents to help other people?"

"He has to come!" Samantha echoed. "What better way to convince him he won't find a better place for whatever he and Aidan Caine are doing together?"

How could she tell these dear ladies it would be a complete waste of time, even if Ben came to the auction? He had made up his mind long before he ever came to town. Nothing any of them did would make the slightest difference.

That hurt washed over again, sharp and stinging, like the relentless rain.

Maybe she never should have told them anything, even as vague as she had been about the whole thing. Now everyone would be as disappointed as she was when it never materialized.

"Yes. You have to take him with you tonight," Barbara Serrano said. "Great food, wonderful conversation and people volunteering of their time and talents. It's the perfect opportunity."

McKenzie swallowed. "I'm sure Ben has seen all he needs to of Haven Point and the good people who live here."

"It can't hurt to give him another push," Anita insisted.

"If you don't invite him to go with you tonight, I

will," Hazel said with a lascivious grin. "That man is *hot*."

This sent the other women chortling. Even McKenzie managed a tiny smile that quickly slid away. He might be gorgeous but his heart was as cold as the deep waters in the middle of Lake Haven.

She had had plenty of time to think about what he'd said the other night. In some ways, he had valid points. A major airport nearby would be more convenient but Caine Tech had several jets at company disposal and it was only a ninety-minute drive to Boise and the major airport there. She didn't see it as a deal breaker.

She happened to think the quality of life here made up for some of the area's shortcomings.

She also couldn't avoid thinking about the irony. After he closed the boatworks five years earlier and turned his holdings over to an idiot who mismanaged everything, Haven Point had struggled just to survive.

Of course they didn't have all the cool stuff a more prosperous town like Shelter Springs might offer: the big-box stores, the trail systems, the gleaming new parks. They were lucky to have any stores left, because of Ben. With a major new employer, that would change very quickly.

She sighed and told herself to get over it. Ben had made up his mind. As far as he was concerned, the only logical decision had been reached before he ever came back to town. Now they all had to live with it, unless Aidan and the Caine Tech board of directors overruled him. She would just keep praying for a miracle.

"Isn't it convenient that Ben is staying next door to you?" Lindy-Grace said with that teasing grin. "All you have to do is walk over and invite him."

She knew her friends well enough to be certain none of them would rest until she made some sort of response. "If I happen to see him, I'll mention it," she said stiffly.

This earned her a surprised look from both Megan and Lindy-Grace, who had heard her say much more positive things about Ben in the past.

Ben might have come a long way to overcoming his reputation as the town villain over the past week in the minds of many people. Once word trickled out that he had once more betrayed his hometown, the tide of public opinion would turn faster than Eppie Brewer's horrible potato salad.

SHE MANAGED TO put the conversation with the Helping Hands out of her head the rest of the afternoon. It helped that she was far too busy at the store to think much about him. She and Lindy-Grace had volunteered to do the table decorations for the dinner that night so they had twenty-five centerpieces to finish and deliver.

Whose crazy idea had it been to throw an impromptu quilt-tying party in the middle of it all? Devin's, actually. Her sister had claimed it was urgent and the Helping Hands had hurried into gear.

Aware of the time crunch—it was already five-thirty and the spaghetti dinner and auction started at seven—she made a quick trip to the small grocery store on the edge of town for dog food, which she meant to buy a week ago. Poor Rika was down to the very last dregs in her container.

As she moved into the dog food aisle, she spotted a familiar figure perusing the dog treat options with a rather dazed expression on his gorgeous features.

Why couldn't he look like a troll, darn it? If she had her way, people's appearances ought to match their personalities.

Despite her frustration and hurt with him, she had to pity him a little as she watched him look dumbfounded at the many choices on the shelves.

From the top shelf, she pulled down the gourmet treats the grocery store owner stocked just for her dog and a few other spoiled canines around the lake.

"Rika likes these," she offered. "Hondo probably would also."

He looked down, clearly surprised to see her there. An odd mix of emotions crossed his features. At first she thought he looked happy to see her—which she told herself absolutely should *not* send this shaft of warmth through her—but his initial reaction was quickly replaced by wariness, as if he expected her to start yelling and throwing dog treats and canned dog food off the shelves.

He cleared his throat. "Thanks. Actually, I think that's the one I've been looking for, now that I see the shape of the thingies. Marshall left a supply of food and treats for Hondo but they weren't in the original packaging. It's been a struggle to figure out which brands he likes."

"You're welcome." She ought to just grab her dog food and go but as she hadn't seen him since Monday night, curiosity took over for common sense. As usual.

"I'm surprised you're still in town," she commented. "Your work here is done, isn't it?"

Okay, that sounded a little more bitter than she intended, but it was too late to take back her words.

His mouth tightened a little, obviously picking up on it. "I'm going to dinner with my mother and Doc Warrick tomorrow night. My plan is to take off Saturday morning so I can be back in California for work on Monday."

The man was dealing with some serious life changes. She had been so angry with him, she had almost forgotten that element in all this.

She wanted to ask him how he was doing with everything but somehow she couldn't seem to find the words. Why did everything have to be so awkward between them now? She hated it.

She was about to make some excuse and continue on her way when she happened to look at the end of the aisle and saw Barbara Serrano pushing a cart loaded with the Diet Coke she loved. Barbara's mouth opened a little at the sight of her and Ben together, then she wagged her finger between the two of them and gave McKenzie a significant look.

Right. The service auction. She was supposed to ask him to go with her. McKenzie huffed out a breath.

She didn't *want* to, but Barbara was standing there waiting, blocking the whole darn aisle.

Okay, she would ask him, he would turn her down and she could get on with her night. At least she could tell all the Helping Hands she had tried. Let *them* be mad at Ben, too.

"Do you have plans tonight?" she mumbled.

"Tonight?"

"Yes."

He gave her a suspicious sort of look, obviously caught off guard by the question. "Hanging out with Hondo and watching the Portland Pioneers play the Rockies. Why do you ask?"

"Oh. Well. That sounds fun. I guess you're booked."

"Did you have something else in mind?" he asked slowly.

She sighed. Barbara was obviously eavesdropping. If McKenzie didn't follow through, she would go back and report to all their mutual friends.

"I can't see any point to it, for obvious reasons, but my friends thought you might be interested in coming to the annual spaghetti dinner and community service auction we're having tonight. I've been ordered to invite you. I tried to tell them all it was a waste of time, given the circumstances." She lowered her voice so Barbara couldn't hear. "Without violating the confidentiality you demanded, I obviously couldn't say much."

"Service auction?" He looked both surprised and intrigued.

"I told you about it the other day. This is where

everybody donates their skill or talent and we all bid on what we want someone else to do. It's kind of a big deal around here and all proceeds go to the library foundation."

"Right. Sure. I'll go. Sounds fun."

She stared, totally taken off guard. "Really? You actually want to go?"

"Why not? The truth is, I haven't enjoyed the Pioneers as much since Smoke Gregory left."

That distracted her a little from the shock, since she was a huge Smoke fan. "I mourned along with everybody else when he had all that trouble a few years ago. Did you know he's married to Aidan Caine's sister? Oh. Of course you would."

He was Aidan's best friend. He probably knew all the Caine family members quite well.

"He came into the store at Christmastime," she told him. "I just about had a heart attack when I saw him walk in. I expect he'll come back for Eliza and Aidan's wedding next month." She paused. "It's supposed to be a huge bash. I'm doing the flowers and I'm scared to death I'll mess it up."

"You won't."

He said that with such confidence, she was almost willing to feel a little charitable toward him, especially considering they were apparently going to be spending the evening together. Drat her luck.

"What time should we go?" Ben asked.

She hadn't really thought ahead to the two of them arriving at the event together. As much time as they spent together over Lake Haven Days, she was afraid people would already think they had a thing going.

Not that they did.

She was about to suggest they travel separately to the community center so things would be less uncomfortable but that seemed rude after she had issued the invitation.

"Um. It starts at seven. How about twenty to?"

"Perfect. I'll see you then."

Barbara grinned at the end of the aisle, gave her a thumbs-up and continued on her way with her Diet Coke.

"Can I help you get your dog food?"

"No," she managed to answer. "I'm good."

It was a bald-faced lie. The idea of an evening spent trying to be nice to Ben when she really wanted to strangle him was the exact *opposite* of good.

She didn't want to admit that a small part of her was relieved she would have the chance to see him one more time before he left town.

HE HADN'T BEEN this anxious about spending time with a woman since he was sixteen years old, taking the busty and beautiful Alice May Parsons to the junior prom.

This wasn't a date, he reminded himself. They were going together to a community event, where they would be surrounded by plenty of people who, like McKenzie, blamed him for the way the town had fallen on hard times.

Why had she invited him to attend? More important, why had he agreed? As one of the public faces of Caine Tech, he attended charity events all the time, black-tie and otherwise. In general, they weren't among his favorite activities—too many stuffy people, making boring conversation about inconsequential things, all while trying to make themselves seem benevolent and altruistic.

At least he would have another chance to spend a little time with McKenzie and try repairing the rift between them—as much as she would allow, anyway.

She was furious with him. Some part of him acknowledged she had just cause. Perhaps he should have tried harder to sell the boatworks to another company that would have been able to pour the necessary time and energy into it.

He definitely should have paid more attention to the reports he received monthly from the property management company. Perhaps he would have been more diligent if the sight of those reports hadn't filled him with memories he preferred to avoid.

He glanced at his watch and realized they would be late if he didn't hurry. He didn't need to give McKenzie another reason to be annoyed with him.

He grabbed his jacket and an umbrella. Hondo immediately raced over, hoping they were going for a walk.

"Sorry, buddy. Not now. You wouldn't want to go out in that rain, anyway. Five minutes and you'd be whining to come back inside."

This steady rain the past few days reminded him

forcefully of Portland weather from the three months he spent working on a Caine Tech project there.

Hondo sighed a little but padded back to the living room, where he plopped down on the rug.

"I'll be back in a few hours. Be good."

The dog was already closing his eyes as Ben headed outside. Rain thudded against the umbrella as he walked across the space between their houses. He rang the doorbell, anticipation curling through him.

She didn't answer right away, until he waited a moment then rang the bell again. When she came to the door, he felt his heart rate kick up several notches. Why did he always forget how lovely she was? With her silky hair down, loose and wavy, she looked fresh and lovely, bright as a summer afternoon.

It didn't matter, suddenly, whether she was angry with him or whether he deserved it. He couldn't resist leaning in and brushing his lips against hers. She smelled of laundry soap and some kind of watermelon shampoo and the almond-vanilla scent that always seemed to cling to her.

She would probably find him more than a little weird if he told her he wouldn't mind spending the whole evening with his face buried in the crook of her neck.

Too bad for him, she stepped away, a little breathlessly.

"Sorry. I'm running late. I had a phone call from the public works director just as I was finishing my hair. Do you mind waiting a moment while I finish getting ready?"

"Not at all."

Rika came over and sniffed at him, though she seemed quite disappointed that he didn't have Hondo with him. As he waited for McKenzie, he looked around her house, struck by how warm and comfortable it was, filled with pretty folk art, pillows, flowers and books.

He had given a designer free rein at his house in San Jose. The result was modern to the point of stark. He had always been fine there, but now it struck him as cold. Maybe he needed to figure out a way to add a little softness to his environment. Or maybe he just needed someone in his life to help him do that…

He shied away from that thought just as McKenzie came back in. To his disappointment, she had tamed all those luxurious waves into a French-twist thingy that only made him want to pull away all the fastenings and run his hands through it.

"I just need to grab my purse and umbrella."

"I've got one. We can share."

He held it over her as they made their way to his SUV. As he backed out, the wipers beat against the window in a steady rhythm. Even on the highest speed, they weren't clearing the water away fast enough.

"This rain," she said, shaking her head. "It's crazy this time of year in Haven Point."

"I remember rainy springs and some stormy autumns. In my memories, at least, summer days were always sunny and beautiful."

He had loved summers. The boatworks had always

been busier than the rest of the year and he hadn't had to interact much with his…Joe.

"We get rainstorms in the summer, just not this heavy and for so long. It's causing all kinds of trouble for the public works department, dealing with road rot and trying to keep the gutters cleared of leaves and debris so we don't have any flooding."

"At least it's this week and not last, in the middle of all your Lake Haven Days activities."

"I've thought of that. Believe me. It would have been a nightmare. We were lucky to have perfect weather. I'm hoping this weekend will be the same so the city workers can have a bit of a break from dealing with weather stuff. Which day did you say you were having dinner with your mother and Dr. Warrick?"

His fingers curled around the steering wheel. "Tomorrow night."

"Have you had a chance to talk to him since your mother told you?"

"No," he admitted. "I have no idea what I'm going to say to him when I do. *Hi, Dad* doesn't quite seem appropriate."

"I'm sure you'll both figure it out as you go along," she said, her voice sympathetic. It was the most warmth he had received from her since she got angry with him for having dinner in Shelter Springs and he basked in it.

"I can't help thinking how difficult things must have been for Dr. Warrick all these years, knowing you were his son but having to keep his distance from you. It's bound to be a challenge on both sides."

He had been so consumed with his own muddle of feelings, he hadn't given much thought to Dr. Warrick's. Would the man be here tonight? He also hadn't thought about that. Now, as he pulled into the parking lot, he was grateful he would have McKenzie along, just in case he needed the moral support.

The place was packed. Apparently plenty of people were looking for something to do on a rainy July night.

"Looks like a good turnout," he said as he barely managed to find a space at the edge of the lot.

"This is always one of our more popular civic events. People love feeling like they've found a good deal on work they already needed—and they love it even more when they know they're helping the whole town with their donations."

The moment she walked in, McKenzie was hit from all sides by people who needed something from her. The event organizers couldn't find the microphones to plug into the sound system at the community center, the crew organizing the low-key spaghetti dinner was afraid of running out of paper products, a new photographer in town was offering to auction a boudoir photography session and wanted to display some very racy examples that were freaking out some of the church tabbies.

She dealt with each crisis with patience and concern. Within minutes, McKenzie quickly located the microphones in their usual place, which had been concealed from view behind a few other boxes, then sent someone to the grocery store for more plastic silverware. Finally, she quietly and diplomatically spoke with the photographer and helped her select one or two photographs more appropriate for a general audience.

If Ben had worried he would feel like an outsider, that lasted for only about thirty seconds, until a friend from high school he hadn't seen since his return stopped to chat and slap him on the back, then McKenzie's sister, Devin, joined the conversation, along with two older ladies he remembered McKenzie introducing him to during the barbecue.

His cynical heart wasn't quite sure how to deal with all this warmth and welcome. After a few moments, he decided the wisest course would be to simply relax and enjoy it.

He and McKenzie ended up at a table with her sister, his high school friend and several people he didn't know. The conversation flowed over him, warm and comfortable.

They were just finishing up dessert—gelato from Carmela's, along with fresh berry and peach pies from the bakery in town—when he heard a commotion by the nearest door and a moment later heard his name.

"Ben! Ben! Hey, Ben!"

He turned and found Maddie Hayward, adorable curly-haired six-year-old daughter of Aidan's fiancée, Eliza. She waved vigorously and raced over to him, followed more slowly by Aidan and Eliza.

Maddie threw her arms around him in that big-hearted, sweet way of hers and he smiled and hugged her back.

"Hey, Mads. What are you doing here?"

"We came for spaghetti. Are we too late?"

"We can still probably find some for you in the kitchen," McKenzie assured her as Ben rose to kiss Eliza and greet Aidan.

"What a welcome surprise!" Eliza said, with a surprised look. "I knew you were in town but in a hundred years, I never would have expected to find you here, at the Haven Point service auction I've been hearing so much about."

"McKenzie invited me. She thought it would be a good chance for me to see the kindness and generosity of the good people of Haven Point."

"Is that right?" Eliza's interested gaze swiveled between him and McKenzie. Hoping she didn't pick up on any stray currents zipping between them, Ben quickly changed the subject.

"I could say the same for the three of you. Last I heard, you were spending a few more weeks in California before you came back here to get ready for the wedding."

"Maddie missed her horses and Sue and Jim too much, so we decided to fly home for a long weekend," Aidan answered.

Eliza made a face. "All that is true enough, but really we came back because we have a last-minute appointment with Maddie's cardiology team tomorrow."

"Everything okay?" He flashed a worried look at the little girl, currently chattering away to Devin Shaw.

She nodded. "Fine. Everything's just fine. We had

a regular checkup scheduled next month but turned out to be the week before the wedding, right in the midst of the craziness. When her doctors called with a last-minute cancellation, we decided to snap this one up."

"Ah. I'm glad it's only routine."

She smiled at him and Ben thought again how perfect for Aidan she was, with her generous spirit and caretaking nature. He seemed a different person now, more relaxed and comfortable in his skin.

Until that moment, Ben hadn't realized how much he envied him for finding the one person who fit him perfectly. He glanced over at McKenzie, who was hurrying from the kitchen with news that there was still plenty of spaghetti left and they even had bread sticks, Maddie's favorite.

While Aidan and the new women in his life went to fill plates, McKenzie found chairs for them and made room at their table for the newcomers.

"Did they have the auction yet?" Maddie asked when they returned.

"Not yet," McKenzie told her with a smile.

"Whew," she said in a dramatic voice.

Aidan grinned at her. "Maddie has something to donate, don't you, kiddo?"

The girl nodded but didn't speak until she'd slurped her spaghetti. "Yep. Sue is going to help me make a dozen cookies. Chocolate chip. That's my very favorite in the whole world."

The auction started only moments later and Ben

sat back in his chair, watching small-town generosity at its best.

The variety of services offered was mind-boggling. He saw teenage boys who donated their lawn-mowing services. Other residents offered handyman work or gardening advice or babysitting.

After an hour, the amount raised was staggering.

Finally, it was time for Maddie's cookies. The auctioneer held up the card where Maddie had written her donation and Aidan immediately bid ten dollars.

"A hundred," Ben said, which earned him a few gasps from the crowd and a glare from Aidan, who returned a higher bid of two hundred dollars.

And the bidding war was on.

Both of them were fierce competitors and refused to back down but finally, when the amount was ridiculously high for chocolate chip cookies, Aidan at last dropped out with a raised eyebrow.

The auctioneer slammed his gavel down. "Sold to Mr. Kilpatrick for one-thousand-one-hundred dollars."

Maddie clapped her hands with glee and jumped from her chair to hug Ben again, which made it all worth it.

"Wow. You must really like chocolate chip cookies," McKenzie said.

He shrugged. "It was for a good cause, and Sue's cookies are truly divine. Besides, it's not a bad thing for Aidan to lose at something once in a while. Sue and Maddie could make him cookies any day of the week. He's a lucky man. I'm a poor bachelor who needs all the cookies I can find."

tioned—he even helped put away tables and chairs while she was busy talking to Dale Pierson about the minor flooding a few homes had seen from the wet weather.

Finally, she managed to break away from the conversation and found Ben talking to Cade Emmett, the chief of police.

He broke away from the conversation. "Are you ready to go?" Ben asked.

"Yes. Finally. Sorry about that."

"Not a problem. Cade and I were friends in school. We just were catching up."

"I remember. The two of you were on the baseball team. My girlfriends and I used to come to the games just to watch you all in your tight baseball pants."

"Is that right? You never told me that, Kenz," Cade said with a grin. He was a notorious flirt who couldn't see what was right in front of him. Not her, of course. The two of them had dated a few times and just never had the sizzle.

"I didn't mean to break up your bro-trip down memory lane."

"I've got to take off, anyway," the police chief said. "Early shift in the morning. It was good to see you, Ben. I'm sorry we didn't have more chances to get together while you were in town. Maybe next time."

"Sounds good," Ben said. "I'll buy you a beer at the Mad Dog."

McKenzie's chest ached a little at the reminder that he would be leaving in only a few days. She doubted there would be too many "next times" in Ben's future. Once he left, would he be in any big hurry to come back?

Maybe once in a while if his mother ended up with Doc Warrick, which sounded as if it might be a possibility.

Neither of them had come to the dinner and auction. She had wondered if she and Ben would bump into them but Devin told her Dr. Warrick was working at the ER that night.

Ben would certainly be back for the wedding of Aidan and Eliza. He was obviously fond of both of them—and of that adorable Maddie. That little ache in her chest seemed to intensify when she remembered how sweet the two of them had looked together and thought of him bidding fiercely against Aidan for a dozen cookies.

After saying goodbye to Cade, she and Ben headed out. In the foyer, a figure rose from one of the chairs and stalked over to them.

"Are you finally done yakking?" Darwin Twitchell demanded with that fierce frown of his that made him look like an angry troll, bushy eyebrows and all.

"For now," she answered with the customary patient smile she tried to use with Darwin. So much for her fruitless hope that giving the man a lake trout might thaw his icy demeanor a little.

"That's the problem with a woman mayor. You don't stop flapping your lips enough to listen to your constituents."

Her smile cracked a little but held by some miraculous effort. "Probably true. What can I help you with?"

"Have you seen the pothole that's grown in front of my house today? It's the size of Crater Lake now. I tried to call that worthless Dale Pierson at the public works department about it but he won't take my calls anymore. You need to get a crew out there tomorrow to get it fixed."

"With all the rains we've had, Dale and his department are working overtime to take care of all the urgent situations around town but I'll certainly mention this to him and have him add it to his list."

"Have him put it at the *top* of his list," Mr. Twitchell demanded.

"I'll mention it to him," she repeated. She could be nice to the man but that didn't mean she could allow him to push her around, or she would be as worthless at her job as the old man believed.

"Somebody's going to lose an oil pan on that thing, see if they don't, and then they'll sue the pants off the city. If they do, I'll tell everyone I tried to warn our worthless mayor but she was too busy cuddling up to a damned Kilpatrick to listen to me," he growled, then stalked outside into the rain.

"Well. That was fun." McKenzie tried to smile at Ben, even as she felt her face heat. He wasn't a damned Kilpatrick, after all, but she had still probably spent more time than she should have "cuddling up" to him.

"Why do you put up with that kind of disrespect?" Ben asked.

She made a face. "He's an unhappy old man who has nothing else to do but complain about everything he thinks is wrong in the world."

"That doesn't give him license to be rude."

"Every time I'm tempted to snarl back at him, I remember that he has no one at home. His wife is dead, his only son and grandchildren live far away. All he has left is his dog. It can't be easy on him."

She *didn't* equate herself to Darwin Twitchell, for heaven's sake. She might live alone with her dog, but she had her sister, her friends, her business. She was busy and *happy*. Or she had been anyway, until Ben came back to town and rattled everything up in her world.

"I still say somebody should have a firm word with him. It's one thing to disagree with your job performance as mayor. It's something else to attack you personally, when you're only trying your best."

His quick defense warmed a cold, empty little corner of her heart and she hardly noticed the rain as they headed out to his SUV. He helped her inside, then went around to the driver's seat. As he started up the vehicle, she finally answered him.

"I should tell you that for all his kvetching, Mr. Twitchell is a very generous benefactor to just about every organization in town that needs a little boost, from the Girl Scouts to the Historical Society. Most of his gifts are done anonymously, too. I only found out myself after I took office in January. He cares about this town and the people in it and I have to respect that, even if he does get a little bit cranky sometimes."

She decided she was done talking about Darwin Twitchell.

"Enough about him. What did you think about the service auction?" Since she couldn't read his reaction, she might as well ask him directly. "Thanks for your donation, by the way. I could see my friends Julia and Emmie, the town librarians, were just a few dollar signs short of having heart attacks while you and Aidan were battling it out over Maddie's cookies."

He grinned at this. "I won them fair and square and I intend to enjoy every bite."

She was charmed all over, as she had been during that bidding war.

"Seriously," she pressed. "What did you think?"

"I was impressed," he admitted after a moment. "Some of those donations were extremely generous, especially in light of the struggling economy around here."

She nodded, so very proud of her neighbors and friends. "It's humbling, isn't it? Some people there tonight barely have enough money to pay their power bill but they're still willing to reach out and donate to help their neighbors—and if they can't donate financially, they donate their time and talents, which can be even more of a sacrifice."

"True."

"Take Dorothy Shields, for instance. She's the one who donated the custom-designed quilt that Eliza bid on and won. Her husband is dying of Parkinson's and requires nearly round-the-clock care. She herself has glaucoma and can barely see. She quilts at his bedside with her face just inches from the material and creates these amazing works of art."

Across the dim vehicle, she saw him blink a few times as he digested that.

"And did you see Amy Daniels? She was the woman who offered six months' worth of mani-pedis. Her husband walked out four months ago and she's barely making do while she raises their three kids by herself. Still, she is willing to donate all that labor because she loves books and reading and wants her children to love it, too."

He was silent for a long time as his headlights gleamed on the rain-drenched streets. "Okay. I get your point," he finally said. "The people of Haven Point care about each other."

"Plenty of people cared about you, too, when you lived here. Men who coached you in baseball, teachers who sparked your interest in technology and business. Friends like Cade."

"I know that," he answered, his voice stiff.

She wanted to remind him that sometimes when things were hard, it was entirely too easy to focus inward, only on the negative and the hurt, instead of on all the people who might be there lending a hand, but she was afraid she already sounded preachy enough.

Anyway, they had reached her house and he pulled into his driveway and turned off the engine.

"Thanks for coming with me," she said. "I'm really glad you got to see the town at its best, for once."

She started to open her door but he stopped her. "Hold on. I'll grab the umbrella."

"I don't mind a little rain," she answered. "You know the old cliché. Without a little rain, we can't appreciate the sunshine, right?"

Now she really *did* sound preachy. He rolled his eyes. "I don't mind a little rain, either. But why get soaked when I have a perfectly good umbrella?"

He climbed out of the car, umbrella in hand, and opened the door for her, then walked her to her door. She shivered a little in the cool breeze coming off the lake. It felt more like an evening in April than July.

She unlocked her front door, suddenly feeling awkward. This wasn't a date, she reminded herself. She didn't have to worry about the inevitable, will-he-kiss-me-or-won't-he? question. The answer was a definite *won't*. She had made sure of that.

"Thanks for coming with me, Ben," she said again. "I know you didn't have to and I appreciate that you were willing to make the effort."

"I enjoyed it," he assured her.

"I'm glad. Well, good night."

She turned to go inside but before she could, he leaned down and brushed his mouth against hers once, then twice. Okay, what did she know? Maybe she needed to stop second-guessing everything. Apparently he *was* going to kiss her good-night.

Their gazes met, only inches apart. She saw something flare there, the heat and hunger she had been fighting down for days, and a second later, he was kissing her with a ferocity that left her breathless.

At the taste of him, berries and mint and Ben, the need she had been fighting down all evening seemed to implode and she kissed him back, matching him taste for taste, lick for lick.

"You're making me crazy," he growled in her ear, then nipped at her earlobe, sending an answering heat surging through her.

"You started it," she replied, her voice ragged. She gave a soft little moan, kissing whatever skin she could reach. The strong column of his neck, his firm chin. His luscious, delicious mouth whenever it came within range.

He gave a throaty laugh. "So I did. I can't seem to help myself when you're around."

He kissed her deeply then, his mouth firm and insistent on hers. The hard, cool wall of her foyer pressed into her back and she realized he must have pushed her against it. She had no recollection of moving but somehow they were inside her house, the door closed behind him, his hands everywhere—tangling in her hair, teasing the bare skin above her waist, clutching her back.

She wanted him, right now, right here. Everything inside her ached with it, with the urge to drag him to her bedroom right now and spend the rest of the night in his arms, exploring this fire that seemed to blaze between them whenever they touched.

She wrapped her arms around him and held on, relishing the heat and strength he offered. He made her feel cherished and wanted and *safe*, as if he would take on any possible danger, any threat.

Something seemed to be unfurling inside her as the

kisses went on and on, something sweet and feathery and…dangerous.

A warning bell seemed to clang in her head but she ignored it, lost in the delicious warmth that seemed to fill all the cold hollows inside her. Her heartbeat pulsed in her ear, drowning out the warning, anyway.

Finally, after long drugging moments, she managed to wrench her mouth away just long enough to take a ragged breath. While she tried to make her brain cooperate again to grab hold of a thought, he didn't make it any easier by trailing his lips along her jawline, down her throat, to the V of her shirt.

She wanted to press his head there, to work all the buttons of her blouse free and let him explore and taste and drive her even more wild…

Wind blew off the lake, spitting raindrops against the glass, clicking and popping like pebbles. The sound jarred her from the moment and that warning bell clanged louder.

She was in love with him.

The cold, harsh realization soaked through her, every bit as brutal and relentless as that hard rain out there.

She was in love with Ben Kilpatrick—and had been for some time, maybe as far back as those years when she would watch him treat his sickly younger sister with such gentleness and caring. Watching the sweetness of his interactions with Maddie earlier in the evening had reminded her of it, one more tie binding them together.

What had she done?

She wanted to sink to the floor of her foyer, throw her arms around Rika and weep. Her heart already ached in anticipation of the pain that seemed to be waiting outside her little lake house, ready to swoop in the moment he drove away from Haven Point.

Oh, it would be so tempting to throw all her caution to the wind, to grab his hand and lead him to her bedroom, where they could spend every hour remaining to them wrapped around each other while the rain whispered against the roof.

She obviously didn't have the best track record in the common-sense department, at least when it came to Ben, but somehow she knew making love with him would only make the inevitable pain so much worse.

Sensing the shift in mood, he pulled away, his gaze searching hers. That beautiful mouth that could work such magic tightened now and he eased away. "This is the part where you tell me you want me to leave, isn't it?"

Oh, she didn't. She wanted him to stay here forever, wrapped in her arms and her love. "It's not a matter of what I want," she began.

"The hell it's not," he burst out, his eyes hot, aroused and suddenly angry. "It's been about what you want since the moment I walked into town. You want a shiny new Caine Tech facility for this damned town you love so much and you can't see anything beyond that. Because you can't have it, you won't consider anything else between us."

She inhaled sharply at his words. Because they stung—and because, okay, she sensed some element of truth to them she wasn't quite ready to face—she parried the thrust and lashed out in return.

"At least I care about *something*! I'm not some cold, insulated billionaire so afraid of being hurt that I wall myself off from anybody who might get close!"

Something flared in his eyes, something she almost thought might be hurt. "Cold? You think I'm cold?"

No. He was hot, sizzling temptation.

"I think you're like some kind of…*Vulcan*. The only difference is, you have emotions, you just refuse to show them to the world."

A muscle flexed in his jaw and she wanted to weep. She was a fine one to talk to him about hiding emotions when she was lashing out so he wouldn't realize she loved him.

She folded her hands together to keep from reaching for him again, from pushing away that strand of dark hair falling in his eyes, from kissing away his sudden frown.

If Joe Kilpatrick were still alive, she would like to take him out on that Delphine to the deepest part of the lake, hog-tie him and toss him overboard for what he had done to a little boy who had only ever wanted the love of the man he thought was his father.

"You're wrong. I feel things, deeply," he said, his gaze suddenly intense.

What did he feel? She felt breathless, suddenly, like that moment just before that first dive into the lake in spring, when she knew the waters would be painfully cold.

She opened her mouth, suddenly frightened and

exhilarated all at once, but before she could ask him, her cell phone rang, vibrating the little table in the foyer where she had set it when she first unlocked the door.

She stared at it as if it were a rattlesnake and then looked back at Ben. His expression was once more shielded, the mask firmly in place, and she suddenly wanted to cry.

"I have to take it. It's Dale. It could be an emergency."

Coward, that little voice in her head taunted. She knew she was using the phone call as an excuse, seizing on the first one that came along.

"Someone else can take care of it, can't they?"

"I'm the mayor."

"And that's the only thing that matters to you, isn't it?"

She didn't answer, she only gazed at him wordlessly.

After a moment, when the phone continued to ring, he made a rough, frustrated sound.

"You'd better answer it," he said. "I wouldn't want to keep you from something *important.*"

He turned and stalked from her house, closing the door hard behind him.

ANGER AND FRUSTRATION seemed to coil through him like barbed wire as he stomped back to his place.

He had left the damn umbrella in her entryway and the rain poured down like crazy, cold and unforgiving. By the time he made it the short distance to his rental house, he was soaked to the skin and freezing.

He didn't care. A little outward misery was the perfect match for the storm raging inside.

When he unlocked the door, Hondo barked his hey-where-have-you-been? greeting and planted his haunches next to Ben for a little love. Ben gave him a perfunctory scratch, then headed immediately into his bedroom to rip off his rain-soaked shirt.

He didn't know what to do with this turmoil raging inside him, this jumbled mess of raw feeling he wasn't sure he even wanted to look at.

At least I care about something! I'm not some cold, insulated billionaire so afraid of being hurt that I wall myself off from anybody who might get close!

How did she see him so clearly? He had spent so many years not revealing his emotions, exhibiting a cool, contained facade to the world. He had found it invaluable in business, that ability to use logic and reason.

He suddenly remembered being eleven years old, a desperate boy who used to pretend he had a Teflon super suit that deflected every barb, every criticism.

Now he realized how ridiculous that was.

The suit had deflected *nothing*. Every hurt had shoved its way under his skin and sometimes he still felt as if it quivered around him with every step.

He picked up his shoe and hurled it at the wall. Not surprisingly, he didn't feel any better.

Through the anger and frustration, he was aware of something deeper. An aching, completely unexpected sense of loss.

It was only thwarted sexual arousal, he tried to

tell himself. Somehow the words weren't any more believable than the ridiculous idea that Joe's steady criticisms had bounced harmlessly off his Teflon skin.

He had feelings for McKenzie, unlike anything he had known for another woman. Yes, she was exuberant with her emotions. Very different than he was—which was no small part of her appeal to him, he realized. She was sweet and funny, with so much love to give the entire world. She was patient with cranky old men, she pulled in friends wherever she went, she cared passionately about her community and her neighbors.

He had seen her compassion firsthand, when she used to be one of the few friends to visit Lily during those last days, this big-eyed, dark-haired girl with the ready smile and the infectious laugh. She had brightened Lily's world immeasurably, just with her visits.

Tenderness seemed to unfurl inside him like new aspen leaves in springtime.

Yes, she loved Haven Point. Of course she did. She wanted so desperately to belong. Xochitl Vargas, who had changed her name to fit in with her father's family when she had been left with nothing.

His chest ached suddenly and he sat down hard on the bed. Hondo immediately moved in, resting his head on Ben's knee. He petted the dog, yet another thing he had to let go of so he could return to his real life.

When the hell had his world become so complicated? Before he came to Haven Point, everything had seemed so straightforward. He loved his job working with Aidan Caine and he was good at it. He thought he was happy in California, working long hours and running the company he and Aidan had founded.

Suddenly, he had to deal with a father he hadn't known about, a dog he didn't know what to do with and a woman who had somehow crawled into his heart when he wasn't looking.

She thought he didn't let himself feel things deeply. Ha. He was a jumbled mess of emotions. Now the only problem was figuring out what the hell to do with them all.

HER PHONE RANG shortly before dawn—just an hour after she finally fell asleep.

She reached for it in a blind panic and knocked it off the bedside table where it had been charging. By the time she could turn on the lamp to find it on the floor, the blasted thing had rung four times and the call was about to go to voice mail. She managed to answer just in time.

"Yeah. Hello?"

"Mayor. Sorry to wake you. It's Dale again. We've got a problem."

"Is it Lake Road again?"

His reason for calling last night—she could only think of it as a fortuitous interruption before she said or did something she would deeply regret—had been to inform her about a section of asphalt on the road circling the lake that had begun to erode away from all the water. A section of shoulder about ten feet long by two feet wide had crumbled and would need major repairs.

"I only wish. This is big. Really big."

She sat up in bed, alarmed by the gravity in his voice. At the movement, she stifled a groan. Her whole body seemed like one big ache, a combination of too little sleep and too much stress.

"What's going on?" she asked after clearing the sleep from her voice so she didn't sound like a trucker with a six-pack-a-day habit.

"I just got word from the Corps of Engineers. The Elkwood Dam is critically unstable and they're worried it's going to breach. They're doing the best they can to fix the situation but they wanted to warn all the downriver communities that the Hell's Fury might be rising to dangerous levels within a matter of hours."

She sat up, now fully awake as cold dread seized her. There were thirty homes and businesses along the river within her city limits that would be impacted if water levels rose—and more upriver from them.

"How could this happen?" she demanded.

"Beats the hell out of me. I know it passed the last inspection last month. I read the report myself. Could be there was a structural anomaly they didn't know about, could be all the rain we've had that's weakened something. Doesn't matter, when you get down to it. The river is rising, either way."

All those houses, all those people. Eppie and Ronald lived along the river, with Hazel in her little house next door. The Smiths. The Pipers. Wynona. Her mind went through each house, cataloging the potential disaster for people who already had troubles, thinking of the ramifications.

"What do you want to do?" Dale asked. He was looking for guidance from *her*. The owner of a floral shop.

She pushed away the quilt, ignoring the chill. As much as she might want to stay here in her warm bed curled up under the covers with Rika asleep on the floor beside her, she didn't have time to indulge her heartache right now.

She could do all that later, after Ben left Haven Point for good. Right now, people depended on her. She drew in a breath. She could do this. This was one of the reasons she had agreed to accept the nomination last fall, so she could help when the people of Haven Point needed her.

"Call Chief Gallegos and Chief Emmett and everybody else on our emergency management team. Have the police and volunteer fire departments start going door to door to the houses on the river, letting people know what's going on and helping them evacuate. At this point, it's people and pets first, then belongings. Let's mobilize everybody we can to start filling sandbags. Scout groups, church congregations, the Haven Point High School football team. I'd like to see everybody who's physically able helping out."

"Got it."

"Meanwhile, I'll call Anita and have her set up a command center at city hall. We can use the city council meeting room and the conference room next door. I'll be in as soon as I can. A half hour, tops.

Keep me apprised if you hear anything new from the people up in Elkwood."

"Got it. Thanks, Mayor."

To her surprise, she actually heard a note of respect in his voice, for the first time ever, but she didn't have time to dwell on it. Not when her town was threatened by outside forces.

TWENTY MINUTES LATER, she walked into chaos. Her office was filled with people, each of whom seemed to be on a cell phone having different conversations.

It wasn't yet 7:00 a.m. but the city employees and the emergency management team were on the job, taking care of business.

Anita was at her desk, with her office phone at one ear and her cell at her other and writing something on a pad in front of her at the same time.

"Right. Yes. That's great. Thanks." She hung up the cell phone and held the other phone away long enough to jump up and hug her when McKenzie neared.

"Don't interrupt your call," she demanded.

"I'm on hold," Anita said. "Hell of a thing to wake up to, right? I got here as soon as I could. I barely had time for mascara."

Anita always looked perfectly made up to McKenzie, who had managed only a shower and a quick braid.

Anita handed her a stack of notes. "We're getting calls from the media already. Word is out about the potential breach and they want the human-interest angle from the downriver towns. I've already fielded two calls and I'm sure there will be more. Somebody will have to take point on that."

"Why didn't you talk to them? Everybody knows you're the one who *really* runs this town. I'm just the figurehead."

Anita gave a modest shrug. "They want to talk to the mayor, not the mayor's secretary. Makes better copy that way."

"Returning media requests will have to come second—or third or fourth. Where are we on the sandbag operation?"

"I've been contacting all the quarries in a twenty-mile radius and they're sending dump trucks full of sand to the elementary school parking lot. That's where we're going to fill them up, since it's the closest public building to the river. Do you really think it will do any good?"

Again, that yawning sense of inadequacy threatened to swallow her whole. "I have no idea. We have to do something, though."

Anita squeezed her shoulder. "We'll get through this. You'll see. Haven Point is tough."

She wished she had a little of her friend's optimism. Right now she felt helpless and overwhelmed by the pressure suddenly bearing down on her shoulders.

She wouldn't let it be destroyed, no matter what she had to do.

CHAPTER NINETEEN

HE NEEDED TO BE back at work.

Feeling muddle-headed and numb after only a few hours of sleep, Ben stood at the wide windows overlooking the deck, sipping at his coffee and watching the rain drizzle down. Everything was gray—the lake, the mountains, even the lovely landscaping around the rented lake house.

His restlessness was like an itch just between his shoulder blades that he couldn't seem to reach no matter what he used to go after it.

He needed to be back at Caine Tech, where he felt in control of his world, in his element. That was the problem here. Something about the rugged vastness of the mountains, the sheer, wild beauty of the lake, left a man feeling exposed and vulnerable.

Since he had come to town, he had been buffeted by memories he didn't want and emotional entanglements he didn't need. His mother, Joe, Warrick. McKenzie. Hondo. They all circled around inside his brain, leaving him a little dizzy.

The day stretched ahead of him, too rainy to go hiking, too dismal for the boat. If he didn't have this damned dinner to get through with Lydia and Warrick, he would be out of here and back home in California by evening.

He would just have to do his best to focus on catching up with work so he would be up to speed Monday back at Caine Tech. If the clouds cleared, he would call the marina and arrange to have someone drive the boat back there so he could hitch it to his SUV.

Maybe when he returned to San Jose, he would sell the Delphine. A few acquaintances had already offered far more than she was worth. He wasn't a Kilpatrick. Why hold on to something that was just one more emotional entanglement, one more connection to his past?

He sighed and stepped away from the window just as Hondo gave his low-throated bark and hurried to the front door seconds before it rang.

Why did he even need a doorbell, when he had an alert German shepherd?

He headed for it, aware of the ridiculous part of him that half hoped and half dreaded it might be McKenzie. He wasn't sure he was up for another confrontation with her but he hated leaving town with bitter words between them.

Instead, when he opened the door, he was shocked to see Russ Warrick standing there.

His father.

Some threads from that tangled mess of emotions he kept trying to shove down seemed to tug free—sadness, anger, betrayal, all coated in that damned awkwardness. He didn't have the first idea how to deal with this man he had always admired and respected.

He could at least be polite and let the man in out of the rain. “Dr. Warrick. This is a surprise. Come in.”

“I can’t stay. I’m headed to the community center to fill sandbags. I just wanted to apologize in person that we’re going to have to cancel our dinner plans. I was hoping we would have the chance to talk about… everything. But in light of this town crisis, I think we had better take a rain check. No pun intended, believe me. I wanted to let you know, earlier, rather than later, in case you wanted to change your plans and take off for California today and I thought it would be better to do it in person instead of over the phone.”

Apparently the coffee hadn’t taken the edge off his mental torpor. He tried to process the overload of information but couldn’t seem to make the pieces fit.

He tried to filter through the salient points. “I’m afraid I don’t know what you’re talking about. What sandbags? What crisis?”

Warrick—he couldn’t think of him as his father yet—looked shocked. “You must not have had the radio or the TV on.”

“No. I was on a conference call until a few moments ago.”

“We’re facing heavy flooding along the river within the next few hours. An upriver dam is failing, though they’re trying their best to fix the situation. It’s all hands on deck right now, between helping with evacuations for those who will most likely be hit by floodwaters and sandbagging as much as we can to protect property. I fear it’s a losing battle, but Mayor Shaw is determined.”

McKenzie. His heart twisted a little and he could almost picture her, right in the middle of the action, trying to save the town she loved.

"I'm sure you understand that we have to cancel our dinner plans. For one thing, all the restaurants in town will be closed except to provide food to the relief workers and I wouldn't feel good about leaving town for Shelter Springs in the midst of a crisis. I'm sorry. I was…looking forward to it, son."

Son. Ben couldn't deal with the word, especially when he thought back over the years to how many times Warrick had called him that.

"I understand," he said.

Warrick studied him, then spoke carefully. "I also wanted to warn you there's a real chance the bridge on the way out of town might be under water by this evening, if the river crests like they're afraid it might. If you leave now, you could make it out before the bridge is impassable. Otherwise, you might be stuck an extra day or two or have to drive hours out of your way in the other direction."

Again, he couldn't think what to say. "Thanks for the information."

"All right. Well. I should go." Doc Warrick rubbed at the back of his neck, a mannerism Ben suddenly realized was one he did frequently himself.

"How are you doing with all this?"

He didn't need the doctor to explain what he meant. From that ball of emotions, the tenuous threads of their father-son relationship seemed to coil between and around them.

"It's been a shock," he admitted. "I'm still having a tough time taking it in."

"Understandable."

Warrick's kind eyes seemed to look right through Ben's carefully calm facade. "This isn't the time or place for it," he said quietly, "but I wanted you to know, I loved your mother with all my heart, from the first time I met her. I made some mistakes along the way, I'll be the first to admit, but I never stopped loving her. Even after she got married and I met and married—and loved—someone else, too, one part of my heart always belonged to Lydia. She's an amazing woman who had some hard choices to make and did the best she could under the circumstances. I hope you fully appreciate that."

Ben wanted to bristle at what suddenly sounded like a fatherly lecture. He was a little too old for paternal discourse.

On the other hand, he found it oddly refreshing, after so many years spent with a father who either belittled or ignored him.

"I do. Thanks."

"If you do end up taking off today, God bless. Maybe your mother and I could drive to California in a few weeks for that dinner."

Driving to California just for dinner would be ridiculous, especially when he had a private jet. He was about to say so, when he remembered something. "I'll be back in town in a month for Aidan and Eliza's wedding. Perhaps we can reschedule during that time."

"Perfect. In that case, we'll definitely see you then."

Before Ben realized what he intended, Doc Warrick reached out and embraced him, just briefly but enough to leave a peculiar warmth behind.

"I know things are…awkward between us now. It's only to be expected, but in time, I hope you can come to accept me. I've wanted to tell you the truth for a long, long time. I'm so happy that it's finally out there, even though I know it can't be easy for you."

An understatement.

"I'll see you soon," Warrick promised. "Now I'd better go. Safe travels, son."

This time the word didn't strike him nearly as odd.

After the doctor left, Ben returned to the window, gazing at the lake and the Redemption Mountains. The Delphine bounced on the high water.

He had no reason to stay now. McKenzie obviously didn't want him here. He didn't have to wait to meet his mother and Warrick for dinner. The town was in crisis and he ought to get out of the way and leave the people of Haven Point to deal with it.

He looked out toward the little jewellike town that provided the only spots of color in the dreary rain. He couldn't see the river from here but he could imagine it, frothing and wild. It wasn't called the Hell's Fury for nothing. Under certain conditions, it could rage through town to the lake, swollen with runoff and rain—and now, apparently, floodwaters from a dam breach.

He pictured McKenzie in the middle of the action,

trying desperately to save her town. He thought of all the people he had seen in action the night before—the little old lady quilting at her husband's bedside, Eppie and Hazel, the teenage boys who had offered lawn-mowing services.

His little fishing buddies, Caleb and Luke. Even the jackass he had decked at the Lake Haven Days barbecue, Jimmy Welch. He was somehow absolutely certain everybody was out in force, working together to help each other.

How could he duck and run, even though he was no longer part of the town?

Yeah. He wasn't leaving.

He glanced down at Hondo. "I have to take off for a while, dude. You can handle things here, right?"

The dog barked in agreement and Ben hurried to grab his boots and his jacket before he headed off to see where he might be needed most.

IF ONLY THIS blasted rain would stop, they might have a chance to beat back the impending disaster.

McKenzie gazed up at the sky as she drove from city hall to the parking lot of the elementary school to check on the sandbag operation. If anything, the clouds looked more ominous and ugly. Weather forecasters had been saying the clouds were supposed to lift, but before they did they were supposed to receive one more big thundershower—the *last* thing they needed.

The weight of responsibility on her shoulders felt heavier than the Redemptions and for a moment, she could barely breathe. According to the latest update, the engineers working to restore the upriver dam's integrity were down to their last option. If that failed, a vast amount of water would be pouring through her town, sweeping through everything in its path with its dangerous power.

They were doing all they could to minimize the destruction. All residents of the houses along the river had been evacuated and dozens of volunteers had helped people remove their most valuable possessions. Emergency shelters had been set up for them at various churches, though most of the evacuated residents had friends or neighbors out of the danger zone who had gladly taken them in to wait out the potential disaster.

While city hall was command central, the true epicenter of the action was the elementary school, where the sandbag effort was underway. As McKenzie pulled up, the scene in the parking lot almost made her burst into tears.

It looked as if everyone in town was here working together, hundreds of people. In an effort to keep as dry as possible, people had brought little canvas pop-up shelters and set them up around the huge piles of sand. Others didn't even bother, working with water streaming down their faces.

From what she could see, children, teenagers, adults—even a few senior citizens in wheelchairs—were all working together to help each other.

Some were filling sandbags with shovels while still others were hauling those sandbags to a waiting flatbed trailer to be hauled to the river. She knew there were even more volunteers at the homes along the river, trying to build up the bank on both sides as high as possible.

Oh, how she loved this town.

She walked through, greeting friends and neighbors, taking a moment to offer her heartfelt thanks. She was looking for Dale to give him the latest update from the Corps when she spotted an astonishing sight.

Under one of the canvas shelters, Ben was shoveling sand into a bag held open by little Caleb and Luke Keegan. His hair was plastered to his head; his T-shirt, straining over his bunched muscles, was drenched with either sweat or rain, she didn't know.

He had never looked more gorgeous to her.

What was he doing there? He wasn't part of the town. He didn't even *like* it here. She wouldn't have expected it in a thousand years, but here he was, working every bit as hard as those whose neighbors were threatened by the potential disaster.

Oh, he was a hard man to resist.

She watched the scene for only a few seconds—more than she could spare. Just as she was about to head off to look for Dale again, Ben turned as if he felt her watching him.

He met her gaze for one supercharged moment while everything else seemed to slough away—the crisis and the town and all the people who needed her. She stood with rain pelting the hood of her raincoat, wishing she had time to speak with him, to thank him for his effort, but she had no time to even breathe.

With a half smile she hoped conveyed at least a little of her gratitude, she turned away, just as an annoyingly perky young woman in a parka bearing the logo of one of the Boise television stations hurried toward her carrying a huge red umbrella that made her impossible to miss. She was followed by a man carrying an even larger camera.

"Mayor Shaw. Mayor Shaw. What do you have to say about accusations from some citizens that your administration was caught unprepared for this situation?"

What citizens? Probably Jimmy Welch, who lived in one of the houses along the river and was already talking about suing over being ordered out of his home.

She didn't have time for ridiculous made-up controversies or diplomacy right now, when her town was in trouble.

"We had an emergency plan in place for high water levels and, as you can see, that is being implemented right now."

"Is it true that you had advance warning of the impending disaster and did nothing until this morning?"

"We were notified at 6:30 a.m. By seven, the town's emergency management protocol was operational, and before seven-thirty, we were filling the first sandbags. All people and animals have been safely evacuated and we are doing everything we can to minimize the possibility of property damage. Look around and you can see the tremendous outpouring of support. Only thirty homes are threatened along the river. The rest are safely removed from the flood zone. As you can see, nearly everyone in town is out here in the pouring rain because they want to help their neighbors. I would say that's a pretty amazing response, wouldn't you?"

The young reporter didn't seem to know what to say when the tables were turned. Her mouth opened a little and her gaze shifted away—and landed on something she apparently found far more interesting than any small-town mayor.

"Oh, my word. Isn't that Aidan Caine?"

McKenzie followed her gaze and spotted Aidan working with his caretaker and a few other men. "Yes. Aidan has a home outside the boundaries of Haven Point."

"And Ben Kilpatrick is here, too?" she exclaimed with a reverent sort of look at him. "Any other Caine Tech executives out here shoveling sandbags?"

"Not that I'm aware of, no," McKenzie said as drily as she could manage, considering she was drenched, despite her raincoat.

"You should get sound bites from them," her cameraman said. "That would make great footage. It might even go national. Billionaire tech executives aren't too busy to help out flood-threatened small town."

"Yes!" An almost giddy look crossed the reporter's perfectly made-up features and she immediately headed toward Aidan without even saying a polite goodbye to McKenzie.

She didn't care. Let Aidan and Ben handle *all* the media, if they wanted. They were both probably far more experienced at it than she was.

She quickly dismissed the reporter from her mind and went in search of Dale.

After relaying the information from the Corps of Engineers and discussing the latest threat assessment, she decided to spend the few minutes she had until she needed to return to city hall taking bottled water donated by the grocery store to as many volunteers as she could.

Inevitably, it seemed, her path led to Ben and the boys.

"Hi, Kenzie," Caleb said. "We're helping Ben."

"I can see that. Good work, guys. Need some water?"

"I'm so thirsty I'm gonna *die*," Luke declared.

"We can't have that. Here you go."

He took the bottle and took a few swallows, which were apparently all he needed to stave off perishing of dehydration.

"Thanks," Ben said, taking a bottle from her. "Not the way you expected to be spending the day, I imagine."

She shook her head. "Nor you. I'm surprised to see you."

He glanced down at the boys, who weren't paying any attention to them.

"I can see why you would be, me being a self-absorbed, walled-off billionaire and all."

Had she really said that to him? She winced, mortified at herself. She should probably apologize but this didn't seem quite the time. Before she could figure out what to say, he gestured toward the reporter, still standing with her bright red umbrella, trying to get a comment out of Aidan.

"Are you the one who sicced the media on him?"

"No. She spotted him about thirty seconds before I did. It's apparently big news when the Geek God deigns to walk among us mortal people."

"Don't let him hear you call him that. He hates it."

She could imagine. Aidan was not only brilliant but gorgeous, in a nerdy way that made women swoon.

Not her. Apparently she preferred the brooding Paul Newman sort to sexy intellectuals. Aidan had never done a thing for her, while Ben only had to crack that rare smile for her to turn into mush.

Go figure.

He gave her a careful look. "How are you holding up?"

She gave her best publicly upbeat smile, the one that made her feel as if her teeth were going to fall out from the pressure of gritting them together. "Fine. Just fine."

"Really?"

He had every reason to be furious with her after their ridiculous fight the night before but somehow here he was, exhibiting a soft compassion that seemed to work its way past all her defenses like water seeping through a wall of sandbags.

"No. Not really. Right about now, I'm asking myself why I was ever crazy enough to agree to run for mayor. Everybody needs me for something, a hundred decisions about things I know nothing about. And whatever decision I end up making, somebody isn't going to like it and will be ready to throw me into the Hell's Fury."

He gave her a solemn look. "Being the one in charge is never comfortable, is it? You can't keep everybody happy all the time, no matter what you do, so at some point you have to focus on making not the *easy* choice but the right one. Every leader has to face that truth at some point."

The words resounded in her mind and in her heart as the cold rain battered her.

Hard decisions—like whether to evacuate now or wait until the threat seemed more imminent or whether to build a multi-million-dollar facility in Haven Point—*weren't* easy.

At some point, the hardest decisions had to be motivated by logic, not emotion, or the world would devolve into chaos. She had seen that amply demonstrated that difficult day.

"You're right," she began, but before she could continue, her phone rang. She pulled it out and saw by the caller ID it was from Cade Emmett.

"I need to take this. It's Chief Emmett. I'm sorry."

He waved a hand. "I need to get back to supervising my team."

By *team* she assumed he meant Caleb and Luke Keegan, which she found rather adorable.

“Thank you for helping, especially when you don’t have to.”

“In this case, logic had nothing to do with it,” he said quietly, giving her that rare smile before turning back to the job.

CHAPTER TWENTY

SHE WAS SO TIRED, she wanted to sink into her bed and not crawl out again for days.

As McKenzie drove up to her house, the dashboard clock on her SUV read 12:56 a.m.

The worst of the crisis had passed. They were calling it the July Miracle in the media. Twelve houses and four businesses sustained minor flooding but a combination of the sandbags, geography and a healthy dose of luck had kept it from being much, much worse.

The Elkwood Dam had indeed failed—not completely but enough that other towns upriver from Haven Point were flooded before the Corps of Engineers was able to contain the situation and divert most of the flow through another channel.

The Hell's Fury was still running high and fast and probably would be for several days. Since the rain had finally stopped several hours ago, there was hope that most of the flow would run into the lake and then back through the Hell's Fury outlet on the other side without causing significant damage along the way.

She hadn't wanted to leave the emergency command center at city hall but the overnight crew monitoring the situation had promised to contact her if the situation changed. Nobody expected it to but she intended to sleep with her cell phone on her pillow next to her, anyway.

Sleep. The very idea of it was seductive. A few hours and perhaps she might feel human again instead of gritty and achy and exhausted.

As she pulled into her driveway, light spilled from a few windows at Ben's house next door and she wondered for a fleeting moment if he had been waiting for her, to make sure she made it home safely. Even if the idea was completely crazy, it still warmed her.

He had to be exhausted, too. All that day, he seemed to be everywhere she turned around—filling sandbags, loading them, handing out sandwiches and bags of chips to volunteers.

He had worked as hard as anyone that day—all for a town he claimed meant nothing to him.

Actions speak louder than words, Kilpatrick, she thought as she turned off her motor and headed for the house.

She let herself in, bracing for the frenzied gyrations of a dog who had been on her own entirely too long. In the midst of all the chaos, she had sent Kaylee, her high school employee at the flower shop, to let Rika out and give her food and water around dinnertime—but that had nearly been eight hours earlier. She should have asked Ben to check on the dog. He knew where the key was, after all.

She was a terrible pet owner and apparently she was being punished for it by a pouting poodle.

"Rika? Honey? I'm sorry, sweetie. Come."

No excited dog came racing to greet her—or even gave one of those disdainful sounds the poodle could make when she was annoyed.

The house echoed with emptiness. Where was she? Worried now, McKenzie walked through the house turning on lights.

"Rika?"

Perhaps Kaylee had forgotten to let the dog back in and she was waiting impatiently outside. She headed toward the backyard, then stopped, her hand frozen on the slider. It was slightly ajar, just wide enough for a thin, gangly standard poodle to squeeze through.

Her heart started to pound and her knees suddenly felt shaky.

Could Kaylee have left it unlatched, enough that Rika could nudge it open and head outside?

She slid open the door, hoping against hope her dog would come trotting inside, wet and goofy and happy to see her. Only a few moths flew around the security light. The yard was empty.

"Rika," she called softly. "Come on, girl."

No cinnamon poodle came bounding toward her. Her insides churned.

"Rika," she tried again. "Here, girl. Come on."

Still no response. She glanced over at the light on next door, torn. Perhaps Ben had seen something. Perhaps he let the dog out with the key under the planter and hadn't latched the screen tightly. Maybe right now she was curled up with Hondo on the rug next door, waiting for McKenzie to come home.

Though she didn't want to disturb him this late, she had to know.

Before she reached his terrace, he opened the door and walked outside.

"Something wrong?" he called softly.

"Rika's gone."

She didn't bother to hide the panic from her voice. It seemed an indescribable relief to share the worry with him as it seemed suddenly too great to bear by herself after everything she had been through that day. "The patio door was ajar and I think she must have slipped out. She's not over with you and Hondo, is she?"

He walked closer and she saw his hair was damp and he wore a pair of Levi's, unbuttoned at the top. "No. I'm sorry. I didn't see her when I returned about an hour ago. I let Hondo out when I got home and he didn't bark or anything to indicate he saw her, but she's probably not far. We can help you look for her."

She wanted so much to lean on him, to let him carry the weight of this worry. How could she ask it, when he had been working so hard that day for her town?

"Thank you. I really appreciate it but it's late and I know you must be tired."

"We'll help you look for her," he said firmly. "I just need to throw on some shoes."

She looked down at his feet, pale in the moonlight. A man's bare feet seemed such a vulnerable thing, for some reason.

"Thank you," she said softly. "She never, ever runs off—but then, I never leave her alone all day."

She probably ought to just tell him they could look for Rika in the morning. She would probably be okay until daylight, when it would be much easier to find her.

Then McKenzie thought of the high waters of the Hell's Fury, of traffic on rain-slick streets and a hundred other dangers a dog on her own might face out there.

She had to look. What choice did she have?

"Maybe we should split up," she suggested when Ben came back wearing shoes and grabbing his phone and keys off the little table in the foyer.

He gave her a careful look. "Under the circumstances, I would feel better if we stuck together. You look like you're ready to fall over and I'm not sure I'm comfortable with you driving on your own."

She couldn't deny some measure of truth in that. Adrenaline and fear spread a thin layer of energy over her exhaustion but she knew it was as crackly and fragile as November ice. The day had been draining, emotionally and physically, and this new stress seemed beyond her capability right now.

She was so very tired of solving all the problems in town. Right now, she wanted to let him take charge. That very desire made her nervous. How very foolish it would be to lean on a man who would be leaving as soon as he could arrange it.

"I should be okay," she said with a conviction she didn't really feel.

"Humor me, then. I've had a long day and I have a strong suspicion we'll both be better together tonight than we are apart."

With a pang in her heart, she acknowledged the truth of that—though she couldn't help wishing that could be true for more than only tonight while they looked for her dog.

"I suppose you're right," she answered.

"I'll drive and you and Hondo can be the lookouts."

She nodded and followed him through the cool darkness to his SUV, Hondo trotting along as if they were all heading on a grand adventure.

As soon as she was strapped into her seat belt, Ben reached across the vehicle and squeezed her fingers.

"Don't worry. We'll find her. I'm sure she's fine."

She took great comfort from his confidence. He knew what the dog meant to her, her last gift from her father. Rika had been a comfort and a joy, her dearest companion, and she didn't know what she would do without her. Somehow McKenzie had a feeling she would need the dog's quiet, calm companionship in the days ahead after Ben left Haven Point, while she tried to figure out how to move forward with part of her heart missing.

They had to find the dog. She wasn't sure she could bear losing both of them at the same time.

"I can't thank you enough," she murmured.

He squeezed her fingers again and didn't move his hand as he backed out of the driveway and began the search.

FINDING A SINGLE DOG in the middle of the night when they had no idea where to start—or even how long she had been gone—wasn't as easy in practice as he might have guessed.

They had driven through every street in town, into the Eagle Crest subdivision, along the still-swollen Hell's Fury, even in the foothills outside of town filled with sprawling ranches.

He drove slowly with the windows down and the cool night air blowing in. Hondo had his head out, tongue lolling. Several times, Ben had told him to find Rika, but he wasn't sure how much the German shepherd understood. For all Hondo probably knew, they were all out having a good time together, on a pleasant moonlit drive through town.

McKenzie's dog could be anywhere. She could have run into the mountains or she could be curled up on somebody's back porch or she could be exploring the Boy Scout camp on the other side of the lake.

For all he knew, she could have run all the way to Shelter Springs.

McKenzie was growing increasingly worried. He could feel the tension radiating off her in waves. Shadows pooled beneath her eyes and her mouth was tight with fatigue and strain.

"This is crazy," she finally said. "It's after two-thirty. We can't keep this up all night. Let's go get some sleep and I'll call in Lindy-Grace to open for me at the store tomorrow so I can mount a search party with friends."

That was the smart, logical decision. They seemed

to be spinning their wheels, wandering aimlessly through the night. If he were the cold, unfeeling businessman she accused him of being, he would seize the chance to be done with this—for her sake, if nothing else. She would make herself sick with worry. She needed rest, especially after the long, difficult day.

He almost turned the vehicle around and headed back home. He even slowed down to pull into the nearest driveway but something made him keep going.

Some decisions needed to be made with the gut, not with logic.

The realization seemed to echo through his mind as he continued driving toward the downtown of Haven Point, with its peeling paint and shuttered businesses.

Every single point of logic he had researched in the past few weeks told him unequivocally that Haven Point wasn't the best location for a new Caine Tech facility. Financially, logistically, geographically, it made absolutely no sense.

After today—after working side by side with the people of his hometown, seeing their caring for each other and the lengths they went to watch out for each other—he was beginning to question that analysis.

He had seen the town in a completely different light. In a crisis, everyone had come together. Children. Senior citizens. Teenagers. All pitching in to help their neighbors.

McKenzie was right. There was something very special about this town and the people who lived in it.

Logic might insist the company would be strategically smarter to simply expand existing infrastructure of their Portland facility. But sometimes a person had to throw logic out the window and go with his gut.

As he drove through the darkened streets past the houses of people who had fought so hard to help their neighbors that long day, he had the strangest feeling that Haven Point and Caine Tech would be a perfect fit.

Haven Point *needed* the new Caine Tech facility. More important, something told him Caine Tech needed the people of Haven Point just as much, for their determination and their heart.

That was exactly what he would report to Aidan and the board.

He opened his mouth to tell McKenzie, then closed it again. Not yet. He could make the recommendation and the board could still go in another direction. He didn't want to raise false hope—beyond that, she didn't need more emotional upheaval tonight, when she was so worried about her beloved dog.

She would find out later, when he could be more sure what the final decision would be.

"Really, Ben. Let's go home. We've driven through here twice already."

He glanced over at her, worried about the lines of fatigue around her mouth. He wanted to tuck her against him and hold her while she slept.

"We'll look for twenty more minutes. If we can't find her in that time, I'll take you home so you can try to sleep for a few hours."

She nodded, swallowing hard, then turned to look out the window. Unable to help himself, he reached for her fingers again, which he had somehow lost hold of during the search. She gave a weak little smile and squeezed his hand and they drove that way, connected skin to skin.

On a hunch, he turned toward the downtown area. If he was going to go with his gut about the Caine Tech facility, he might as well trust his instincts about this.

He slowed down when he reached Point Made Flowers and Gifts. The dog came here each day with McKenzie. Maybe some instinct, some internal compass, had led her back here. He parked and turned off the engine. Hondo immediately went to the side of the vehicle closest to the storefront, his head out the SUV window, and barked once, then again.

The entryway to her store was in shadows but he thought he saw movement there in the depths. An instant later, they heard an answering bark and a shape emerged from the darkness into the glow from the little antique-looking streetlights.

"Rika!" McKenzie exclaimed. The joy in her voice touched a deep chord inside him.

She thrust open her door and rushed out just as her funny, gangly dog bolted over to her, fluffy tail wagging furiously.

"There you are! Where have you been? Oh, sweetheart!"

The dog barked in excitement and Hondo was trying to squeeze through the window to join in the fun. Ben opened the door for him and the shepherd and the poodle had an equally joyous reunion.

"I don't understand," McKenzie said. "We already drove past here twice and she wasn't anywhere to be found."

"Maybe she was looking for you while you were looking for her and we kept missing each other."

All exhaustion was gone from her features, replaced with vast relief. She looked sweet and lovely and he wanted to tuck that loose strand of hair behind her ear and kiss her until neither of them could think about anything else but how perfectly they fit together.

"Oh, Rika. You stink. What have you been into?"

"Given my limited experience with Hondo, you probably don't want to know."

"It smells like fish guts and cow manure. She probably rolled in anything nasty she could find. You don't want her in your car, trust me. We'll walk home."

"Forget it. Get in."

"Ben—"

"I'm not letting you walk a mile in the dark after the day you've had. Get in. I've got rubber mats in the back. I can just hose them off."

He opened the cargo doors and both dogs bounded inside. Ben closed the door behind them, then let McKenzie in.

By the time he made it around to the driver's side, her eyes were half-closed, her features far more relaxed than he had seen all day. Without the tension and worry for her dog, all the remaining energy seemed to have seeped out of her, leaving her limp and boneless.

As he started the vehicle, she opened her eyes and gave that pure, lovely smile that made his heart ache with emotions he still wasn't ready to face.

"I can't believe we found her. *You* found her. That was amazing. *You're* amazing. Thank you."

For her, he wanted to be.

"You're welcome."

She closed her eyes again and they drove in silence the short distance home. He thought again of the decision he had made about the Caine Tech facility.

The empty boatworks would be the perfect location. Aidan owned it already—it had been part of the deal the two of them came to last year, when Aidan had taken over Ben's holdings here—and it would provide the necessary acreage to house a large complex, if necessary.

Somehow, it seemed fitting. The world making a full turn on its axis and coming back to the beginning. He had taken jobs and livelihoods away from this town. Logically, he knew it had been the smart choice at the time. Now he had the chance to bring some back.

His mind raced over the possibilities and he started to get more excited with each passing moment. Aidan would be ecstatic. He and Eliza loved it here and wanted to build their family at Snow Angel Cove. Aidan could split his time between the Haven Point facility and their San Jose operation.

Ben would have plenty of occasion to be back as well, to see McKenzie…

He jerked his gaze away. No. She had made it plain she didn't want that. Didn't want *him*.

His chest ached at the reminder. She didn't have room for him in her life. She had made that abundantly clear.

She was half-asleep by the time they reached his driveway. "I don't have the words to thank you, Ben. Seriously."

He loved her.

The realization seemed to wash over him like the storm-tossed waves of the lake.

He loved her. How was he possibly going to live without her?

"Are you okay?" she asked, and he realized he hadn't answered her for at least sixty seconds.

"Yes. Sorry. My mind wandered for a moment there." His chest ached and he couldn't seem to take a deep breath but he forced himself to focus. She needed rest more than anything and he would do whatever it took to watch out for her. "I'm just glad we found her. Get some sleep now, if you can."

"You, too. Rika needs a bath first and I need to get cleaned up myself, then I'm going to drop like a stone."

She was amazing—sweet and warm, compassionate and stubborn and wonderful. He wanted to tell her that, too, but the words seemed to lodge in his throat.

When she unlocked her front door, he couldn't help himself. He leaned in and gave her a soft, tender kiss on the forehead. It was goodbye and thank you and a hundred other sentiments rolled into one. He was leaving in the morning and wasn't sure he would see her again before he left.

"Good night, McKenzie."

She gave him a sleepy smile as she held Rika's collar to keep the dirty, smelly dog from racing through the house. "Good night. And thank you."

As he waved one more time and headed down the steps, he knew he would take that memory of her with him—her hair tangled, exhaustion in her deep brown eyes, but her mouth lifted in that sweet smile that broke his heart.

IN THE MORNING, he was gone before she woke.

She slept in, something she never did. It was nearly eight-thirty when she finally let Rika out. She stood at the back door, trying to figure out what was different.

It took her a few moments before she realized the change. The beautiful wooden Delphine that had been moored at the dock for two weeks wasn't there. She had a clear view across the bay at the Redemption Mountains, soaring up into a blue July sky punctuated by only a few fluffy clouds.

He could have taken it out for a cruise around the lake but somehow she knew he hadn't. Not this time.

She went to the front door and looked out. No big, sleek SUV was parked in the driveway next door and the lights of the house were all out, the curtains drawn.

Pain, huge and raw and terrible, reached out and grabbed her by the throat and she sagged onto the sofa, almost doubled over with it.

Oh. How would she bear it? He was gone and she didn't know what to do. The sunny, beautiful day suddenly seemed cruel, somehow, taunting her with its perfection, even as she wanted to huddle away here in her misery.

In only a few weeks, he had completely invaded every corner of her life. All the places she usually turned for refuge were now filled with memories of Ben. Throwing a ball for the dogs in the backyard, helping her carry her kayak to the shed, swinging softly out there on the edge of the dock while the night air swirled around them.

How was she going to make it through without him?

Her throat was tight and she could feel the burn of tears behind her eyes. What was the point of holding them back? She sniffled and grabbed a tissue off the table in front of her.

She would let herself indulge in a few moments of heartache and then she would brush herself off and try to figure out how to start the process of healing.

She couldn't seem to shake the image of Ben the day before, helping during the flood crisis. Everywhere she turned around, he had been there quietly lending his support—not just to her but to everyone.

She had even heard a rumor from Anita that someone had mysteriously paid the hotel bill in Shelter Springs for any families who had been temporarily displaced because of the flooding.

It might have been Aidan but somehow she knew

otherwise. Of the two of them, Aidan was the dreamer, the genius behind the ideas.

Ben was about action and results, logic and reason.

She thought of his hands, suddenly, calloused and blistered from the shovel and the sandbags. Yet he had also held her hand with sweet, comforting tenderness as he drove her around town helping her look for her missing dog.

He was a good man and she had done nothing but push him away, so afraid to risk her heart.

She was such a hypocrite.

She thought of what she had said to him, that he was cold, that he pushed down his emotions because of what his father had done to him, that he didn't let people close to him.

They were the same in that respect. She had many, many friends and she valued each one, but very few of them were close enough to see inside her heart, to the frightened little girl trying to carve out a place for herself in a foreign world.

Most people in town knew and liked McKenzie. They had voted her mayor, after all. But very few of them—except maybe Devin—knew *Xochitl's* heart.

Ben had seen the real her—and he had cared about her anyway, despite her fears and insecurities.

She should have told him how she felt.

He had endured a terribly difficult childhood. It hadn't beaten him down. Instead, he had become stronger for it, more determined to do something good and right in the world.

He had become a strong, caring man, much more like his birth father despite Joe Kilpatrick's cruelty.

Oh, how she loved him.

She drew in a shuddering breath as Rika scratched on the door to be let back inside. McKenzie rose and opened the door for her, then sank back onto the sofa again. The dog immediately padded over and licked at her tears, obviously concerned at her distress.

She couldn't do this all day. She had to go check on the flooding situation, the evacuees, the shop. Yes, her heart was breaking but she didn't have time to indulge herself. She had a feeling that would be a good thing in the days ahead. Keeping busy was probably the only way she would get through this.

She made herself shower and change. She had just finished fixing her hair when she heard the deep rumble of a big vehicle engine out front.

Probably a delivery, she thought—though it was Saturday and she wasn't really expecting anything.

She hurried to the window and her breath caught at the sight of a big dark SUV hitched to a gleaming wooden Killy Delphine.

Rika began to bark in excitement as Ben let Hondo out of the passenger side. The dog raced to the front door and McKenzie had no choice but to let her suddenly frantic dog out to join her friend.

The two dogs brushed noses, delighted to see each other after their long six-hour absence. Ben waded through their gyrations to come to the door and McKenzie walked down to meet him on the sidewalk, her heart pounding. She hoped he couldn't see her red-rimmed eyes, her splotchy face.

She loved him so very much.

She had to tell him.

What had she said that night? That unnecessary regret is the saddest thing she could imagine. If she didn't tell him how she felt, she would regret it the rest of her life.

"When I didn't see the Delphine this morning, I was certain you had left."

"I'm about to." He stood, a little awkwardly. "After everything, I couldn't take off without a proper goodbye."

How can I say goodbye, proper or otherwise, when I don't want you to go? She thought the words but couldn't quite bring herself to say them, despite all her brave convictions earlier.

It was easier, far easier, to focus on details. "What have you decided about Hondo?"

A shadow drifted across his blue eyes as he watched the two dogs cavorting. "I talked to Aidan about taking him. He says there's plenty of room at Snow Angel Cove. It will be good for him to be around other dogs and Maddie would love one more creature for her imaginary friend to play with."

"Right. Bob the horse."

"Ah. You've met him."

She would have smiled, if her heart didn't hurt so much.

"He loves you, you know."

"Bob? What can I say? I've always been able to get along very well with imaginary horses."

"You know who I mean. Hondo. He's bonded to you now. It's going to be tough for him when you leave, losing two humans in a short time."

"He'll adapt, I'm sure." The dog came over, tail wagging, looking at Ben with hero worship in his eyes. He gave him an absent sort of scratch, those shadows darkening.

"What else can I do?" he asked. "I don't have a place in my life for a dog. I can't give him what he needs. It wouldn't be fair to him. This way is better."

"Don't be so sure. Maybe all he really needs is your love."

To her dismay, her voice wobbled a little on the last two words. Ben flashed her a searching look. Did he know her words were layered with meaning far beyond Hondo?

"McKenzie—" he started to say.

"I owe you…an apology," she said at the same time.

He waited, a confused expression on his face. "Why?"

"I owe you several, actually. I'm glad you stopped by so I could tell you in person. I…said things the other night that weren't true. I called you cold, unfeeling. It was hurtful and not the way I feel, anyway. I'm sorry."

"I appreciate that."

"You were right. I made everything between us about Haven Point, because I was scared. It was easier for me to focus on what I wanted for the town instead of…what I might have wanted personally."

"What was that?"

She had to tell him. It was one of those very difficult but completely *right* things to do. "I've never been in love before," she whispered. "It's...not as easy as I might have expected."

He stared at her, eyes wide. His features had paled a shade and he looked as if she had just poured cold lake water over him. "In love?"

Oh, she shouldn't have said anything. Once more, she had waded in and made a mess of everything.

"You don't have to say anything. In fact, it would be better if you didn't. Just forget I said a word. Goodbye. Have a safe trip. The bridge should be good for you to get out of town. We were worried about it yesterday but Dale emailed me this morning and said everything is fine. Just be careful and maybe take a route away from the Hell's Fury so you don't run into problems upstream with residual flooding."

She was babbling, as she was prone to do when she was nervous.

He took a step closer and she instinctively moved back, aware suddenly that her feet were freezing without slippers or flip-flops or anything.

Oh, she was an idiot.

"No way. You're not going to distract me by telling me where and how to drive on my way out of town. You're also not going to boss me around by telling me to forget something that suddenly seems like the only important thing in the world."

Her heart started to pound and she wanted to be

anywhere on earth right now except here, on her front walkway with Ben moving inexorably toward her.

"I'm also not going to let you order me about and instruct me on what I can and cannot say."

"You're not?"

"If I wanted to tell you, for instance, that I think you're the most amazing woman I've ever known, a woman of strength and compassion and courage, you will just have to stand there and take it."

She opened her mouth to argue that she wasn't, but he cut her off with an intense look that stole her remaining breath.

"And if, for example, I wanted to tell you that you've captured me completely, that I am a different man than I was two weeks ago—a better man—because of you, you'll have to listen to that, too."

She swallowed hard as joy and disbelief warred within her. Suddenly, she didn't want to be anywhere but right here, being softly and quietly seduced by words and by the blazing expression in his eyes that promised so much more than she had ever dared hope.

"Oh, and one more thing," he murmured. "If I wanted to tell you I'm so deeply in love with you I know I'll never be able to climb back out, I would insist you listen to that, too."

The joy took over, bursting through her like the sunlight and wildflowers and summertime on the lake, all the things she loved. She still had a hard time believing it, but how could she fight against the truth in his expression?

"Okay," she said meekly.

He looked down at her with that half smile she loved so much. "That's it? You're not going to argue with me?"

"What would be the point? That would just be stupid and would only waste time, when we could be kissing."

"Excellent point, Mayor Shaw. I like the way you think."

He took the final step forward and the tenderness in his gaze stole her breath, her reason, the very last of her defenses. When he kissed her, all the pain of the morning seemed to skim away, spiraling up into the vivid blue sky.

She wrapped her arms around him, never wanting to let go, desperately grateful for this miracle she had been given.

They kissed for a long time and when he finally eased back, both of them were breathing hard. "Have you spoken with Aidan this morning?" he asked.

It seemed a very odd question, given the magic and wonder of the moment. She shook her head, nonplussed. "No. Why would I have spoken with Aidan?"

He smiled and pressed his forehead to hers. "I thought as much. You *are* amazing. It's no wonder I'm crazy in love with you."

The words still didn't seem real but she was going to grab hold of them with both hands and never give them back.

"Why are you bringing Aidan into this?"

"Because I *have* spoken with him this morning."

"You said so. He was going to take Hondo for you."

He glanced down at the dog and she knew even before he lifted his gaze that everything had changed. He wasn't getting rid of the dog. Just as he had made room in his heart for her, he would find a place for Hondo, too.

"That's not going to happen, is it?" he said with a resigned sigh.

She smiled against his mouth. "You'll figure out how to make it work. You're very good at that."

"I suppose. I did talk to Aidan about Hondo but also about something else."

"Oh?"

How was she supposed to concentrate on anything but how wonderful she felt here in his arms, how the world seemed such a bright and lovely place, with sailboats gleaming in the sunlight and the Redemptions rising up from the blue, blue water?

"I told him I finally have a recommendation for the new Caine Tech facility."

McKenzie instinctively tensed, then pushed it away. No. She wouldn't let that come between them. Not now. Whatever happened, Haven Point would survive and thrive. The flood threat the day before and the overwhelming response to it had proven that unequivocally.

"I know. Portland. It's okay, Ben. I completely understand. You said it yourself. Sometimes leaders have to make the tough decisions simply because they're right."

"In this case, the logical decision is *not* the right one. I told Aidan we should build the new facility here. I suggested using the boatworks property, which he thought an excellent idea. We're going to fast-track it with the board and should be able to break ground before the snow flies."

She stared at him, this man she loved with all her heart. She wouldn't have believed she could be any happier than her state a few moments earlier but now the joy and shock was so huge, she started to laugh and cry at the same time.

"Seriously? You're not just saying that?"

He shook his head. "I realized last night while we were driving around looking for Rika that Caine Tech needs Haven Point, maybe even more than the town needs us. It's a good fit, Kenz."

"The perfect fit. You'll see. Oh, Ben. I can't wait to tell everyone!"

"We're still a long way from any official announcement," he warned. "It's going to take time and paperwork and red tape. You know how these things go."

"Yes. But you have one big advantage."

"What's that?"

"You've got the mayor in your back pocket." She smiled at him with all the love she had been storing up since she was a girl.

"I don't need her in my back pocket," he murmured. "Just as long as she's in my arms."

He leaned down and kissed her again while the lake gleamed in the sunlight and two dogs wrestled on the grass and the mountains watched over it all.

EPILOGUE

"BEN! HEY, BEN! Can Bob and me play with your dog?"

Ben, his arms full, looked down at Maddie Hayward. She was perched on a padded wrought-iron love seat on the terrace of Snow Angel Cove, watching crowds of people bustling around the immaculate grounds.

Her dark hair was in twisty rollers for the upcoming nuptials of her mother and Aidan Caine in a few hours and she had a doll on her lap whose hair was *also* in curlers.

Ben decided he could use a breather himself. He set the box down on the table next to her and took a seat beside her on the love seat. "Hondo's not here, honey. He's over at McKenzie's house, hanging out with her dog for the day."

"Rika's not here, either?" she asked, disappointment clear in her big eyes.

"With the big party in a few hours, things are bound to get a little crazy over here," he explained. "Hondo and Rika probably will have more fun hanging out at home, where it's a little quieter, don't you think?"

"I guess."

She sagged into the chair and flopped her doll on her lap a few times in a listless sort of way.

He didn't consider himself the most observant sort of guy when it came to females in general, particularly females of the under-three-foot-tall variety, but even *he* could see something was wrong.

"You don't look very happy right now, kiddo. This is supposed to be a great day. What's up?"

"Nobody can play with me. Sue and Jim are too busy, my mom's getting her hair done and my new cousins Carter and Faith aren't here yet. I am *sooo* bored."

He glanced across the grounds at all the preparations underway for the wedding—between the caterers, decorators, florists and lowly assistants like himself, the place was hopping. "That's tough, kiddo. Everybody's trying to make this a great day for your mom and Aidan. Maybe you can help."

She looked up. "Nobody wants my help. I told Jim I could help him feed Cinnamon and the other horses and he said I might get my hair messed up. I don't care about my stupid hair."

He had to smile. Give her a few years and she would probably be singing a different tune.

He glanced at the tray filled with flowers he was supposed to be delivering. "You can help me. I'm McKenzie's assistant today and I believe this assistant needs an assistant."

"Why?"

"Those are a lot of flowers for one person to

carry," he lied. "I definitely need a helper. You can carry these hydrangeas. Just be careful. They're very fragile."

He held out a small bundle of flowers to her and Maddie immediately set her doll down on the love seat beside her and hopped to the ground with an expression of eager delight.

"I won't even drop them or crush them, I promise!"

"Great. I trust you."

"Where are we going?"

He pointed down the sloping lawn toward the lake. "See McKenzie over there by the arbor?"

"What's an arbor?"

"That arch thingy. That's where your mom and Aidan will stand when they get married. That's where the flowers need to go."

"Got it." With a determined look on her face, she marched down the sweeping green lawn toward the flower-bedecked trellis, holding the bouquet as if it were a newborn puppy.

He followed the little girl, heady with the scent of flowers and fresh-cut grass and the pines and spruce that grew in abundance around the grounds of Snow Angel Cove.

It felt strange for him to be here at his childhood home again, but not unpleasant. Memories crowded him. A few were ugly but he pushed them away, focusing instead on the good. Playing football with friends on the lawn, diving off the long dock into icy cold water, helping his mother cut flowers from the gardens to set around the house.

Lydia was there now, actually, part of the decorating crew that consisted of Aidan's sister-in-law, Genevieve—most definitely in charge—Aidan's sister, Charlotte, and a few other women he didn't know. He had been a little surprised to see his mother there that morning, but he knew she and McKenzie had met several times over the past month for lunch and shopping and had become quite close. Apparently he wasn't the only one whose help McKenzie had enlisted.

A month ago, it might have bothered him that Lydia and McKenzie hit it off so well, given his own tangled relationship with his mother. Now it only seemed *right*, somehow, that the woman he loved and his mother could be friends. McKenzie had been starved for maternal-type affection after her own mother died, growing up with her father and a polite but distant stepmother, while Lydia had so much love to give and only him to shower it upon.

His own relationship with his mother seemed to have undergone a fundamental shift in the past month as well, more easy and relaxed all the way around. McKenzie's influence helped, he knew. She was so warm and happy, it was difficult for any tension to linger around her.

He couldn't say he was completely comfortable around Doc Warrick yet, but they were both working on it.

"I'm being careful," Maddie assured him as they neared the arbor.

"You're doing great," he assured her.

"Hi, Kenz," she called out. "I'm helping you and Ben."

McKenzie glanced down from her perch on a stepladder, where she was attaching a lush, colorful flower garland to the arbor that perfectly framed the lake and the mountains.

She smiled at the little girl. "Thank you, my dear. I need all the helpers I can find today."

Her smiling gaze met Ben's and his heart seemed to thump in his chest. All the vibrant flowers seemed brighter, suddenly, the lake a more breathtaking blue, the snowcapped Redemption Mountain Range in the background more raw and overwhelming.

It didn't matter that he'd been standing beside her ten minutes earlier, that she had spent the night in his arms, that they had seen each other every weekend of the past month.

His world just seemed *better* because of her.

"Oh, I was looking for those very flowers. Thank you both."

"You're welcome," Maddie said. "I was super careful."

"Wow. How did you know that's important with flowers?"

"Ben told me."

McKenzie smiled again as she climbed down from the stepladder. "He's pretty smart, isn't he?"

"I guess." Maddie looked over the arbor. "That looks pretty."

"Thanks! Do you want to help put it together?"

She frowned a little. "Do I have to go up on the ladder?"

"Nope. You can help me with the flowers that need to be down low."

She grabbed the hydrangeas and knelt down, then patiently showed Maddie how to attach them to the arbor. After the girl did two or three bundles, McKenzie sat back on her heels and hugged the girl.

"Now you can tell your mom and Aidan you decorated for their wedding."

"Mom!" Maddie suddenly exclaimed. "Mom, look! I'm helping!"

Ben glanced up and found Eliza walking toward them. While her hair was intricately fixed, she still wore jeans and a casual shirt with flip-flops, pink toenail polish peeking out.

She was glowing, though, eyes bright and happy. Ben was suddenly fiercely happy for Aidan, that he had found someone who fit him so perfectly.

"I can see that. Oh, Kenz. Everything looks exquisite."

"Especially the bride, I must say." McKenzie grinned and hugged the other woman, taking care not to mess up the elegant hairstyle. "You aren't supposed to be here yet, though. Aren't you supposed to be sitting with your feet up, reading a magazine or having your nails done or something?"

"I feel like I've been doing that for the last twenty-four hours. I'm not at all comfortable with all this primping and pampering. I feel like I need to be doing something."

Charlotte and Genevieve joined them, both looking militant. The women in Aidan's family were a formidable force to be reckoned with.

"Not this time," Genevieve insisted. "You aren't supposed to do a thing. That's the whole point of being a bride—not having to do everything, for once."

Charlotte snorted. "Right. Like you sat around during *your* wedding prep last summer."

"That was different," Genevieve answered pertly. "I'm a decorator and organizer by nature."

"You have all done so much. It truly looks stunning. It's like a fairy tale." Eliza looked as if she were about to cry. Ben didn't know much about women's makeup but he didn't think she would appreciate having to redo it.

"You need to get out of here," he said, hoping to head off the waterworks. "You don't want Aidan seeing you down here, do you?"

"No. You're right. Thank you all. Just…thank you." She hugged all of them—including Ben—then grabbed her daughter's hand. "Let's go see if those curlers are ready to come out."

"Okay. I need to grab my doll. Maybe *her* curlers are ready, too."

With a last brilliant smile at them all, Eliza and her daughter walked hand in hand into Snow Angel Cove, the house she had effectively transformed into a warm and welcoming home.

Genevieve and Charlotte followed behind, making noises about trying to find a few missing tablecloths, leaving him alone with McKenzie.

"Eliza's right. Everything looks beautiful."

"We're almost there. Whew. I've got one more load of flowers in the van. Can I borrow your muscles for a minute?"

"You know they're yours."

Her eyes softened and she gave him that secret smile that made him want to wrap his arms around her, right there in front of the whole decorating crew.

Knowing how busy and stressed she was, he shoved down the impulse and followed her back up the lawn to the driveway and the van with her store's logo on the side.

In the back were several trays containing vases overflowing with blooms—white roses, blue hydrangeas, yellow daisies and others he didn't recognize.

"Where are we taking them?"

"They're for the tables set up on the terrace, where the dinner and dancing will be."

"Nice."

She worried her bottom lip. "Are you sure they look okay? I've never done flowers for a gazillionaire's wedding before."

He didn't know anything about flowers, but he knew the arrangements were charming, elegantly simple.

"Everything is lovely, Kenz. You're helping to give Aidan and Eliza an unforgettable day."

"I hope so."

She looked so adorably uncertain that he decided to indulge himself, only for a moment. He wrapped his arms around her. "Relax. You heard Eliza. She's blissfully happy with everything and Aidan won't care. He only wants her and Maddie."

He could absolutely relate to that. Though he and McKenzie hadn't started talking about the future yet, Ben knew what he wanted. Her, in his life, forever.

He had already talked to Carole about purchasing the Sloane property he had rented next door to McKenzie's. Eventually, he could see combining the two lake properties into one huge, rambling, wonderful house filled with dogs and children and love.

He kissed her now, amazed all over again at the warmth and tenderness in his heart. She gave a happy little sigh that never failed to humble him and wrapped her arms around him.

"You're right," she finally said after a long moment. "I'm being silly. I know this is some of my best work. I just wish the orchids were a little more fresh. I'm so frustrated at that stupid supplier, after he promised me and everything."

"They look perfect to me."

"One more day and they would have been all wilty."

"One more day won't matter," he pointed out. "The wedding will be over. The flowers can turn brown, for all anyone will care."

She made a face but kissed him again, smelling of flowers and sunshine and McKenzie. "Why do you always have to be so darn logical?"

"It's a curse," he said, kissing the top of her head.

He had news for her, news he had been saving for later in the evening after the ceremony when she wasn't so frantic, maybe while they were dancing under the stars. He decided he couldn't wait, that now would be the perfect time.

"I know you're busy but I've got something to tell you that I think will distract you a little from the crazy."

"You're enough of a distraction," she muttered, though he caught her dimple flash before she tried to look stern again. He loved seeing her here, in this serene setting, with the lake and the mountains in the background. This was where their paths had crossed so many years ago. Maybe even then, they were planting the seeds of the love that seemed to grow stronger each day.

It seemed strange, but every moment with her here seemed to replace a few of the bad memories with lightness and joy.

"You're going to want to hear this."

"This better be good. I've got to finish the arbor and then decorate twenty tables."

"I'll hurry and then I'll help you finish up so you'll still have time to get ready for the big event." He paused, for dramatic effect, then smiled. "We received the final assessment from the utility providers today. I had a memo earlier today from my assistant."

That definitely caught her attention. "And?"

He grinned. "And they signed off on the design. Everything is a go. We can go ahead with plans to start work on the new Caine Tech facility in Haven Point next month."

She gave a sound halfway between a gasp and a squeak. "Are you serious?"

"I'm the serious, logical one, remember? I wouldn't joke about this."

She hugged him hard, excitement rippling off her. "Ben! Oh! That's fantastic news! I thought we wouldn't be able to start until next summer."

"Everything has gone smoothly so far. We were able to cut through all the red tape much more easily than anyone expected."

"This is absolutely the best day *ever*."

Until their own wedding day, sometime in the not-so-distant future, he thought, but didn't want to say. Not yet. Instead, he kissed her, his heart overflowing with love for her and all the many gifts she had given him.

She had helped him become part of a community, to begin looking for the good in people instead of holding so much of himself distant, to become excited again about his work. She had helped him find peace with his mother and their past and to begin nurturing a new relationship with Russ Warrick.

"I love you," he murmured. The words came much more easily than they had a month ago, still inadequate somehow, but also filled with power and strength and amazing potential.

Her smile was sweet and contained so much happiness, it took his breath away. "I'll never get tired of hearing you say that."

"Good. I anticipate you'll hear it plenty for the next, oh, fifty or sixty years."

Her mouth trembled just a little before she smiled with warmth and breathtaking joy, and kissed him with a tenderness that seemed to heal all the cold, empty places inside him.

* * * * *

Return to Mustang Creek, Wyoming, with
#1 *New York Times* bestselling author

LINDA LAEL MILLER

for her new *Brides of Bliss County* series!

Will their marriage pact be fulfilled?
Pick up your copies today!

www.HQNBooks.com

PHLLMTBBCSR

RAEANNE THAYNE

77907 SNOW ANGEL COVE	___$7.99 U.S.	___$8.99 CAN.
77859 WILD IRIS RIDGE	___$7.99 U.S.	___$8.99 CAN.
77769 WILLOWLEAF LANE	___$7.99 U.S.	___$9.99 CAN.
77747 CURRANT CREEK VALLEY	___$7.99 U.S.	___$9.99 CAN.
77670 SWEET LAUREL FALLS	___$7.99 U.S.	___$9.99 CAN.

(limited quantities available)

TOTAL AMOUNT $__________
POSTAGE & HANDLING $__________
($1.00 FOR 1 BOOK, 50¢ for each additional)
APPLICABLE TAXES* $__________
TOTAL PAYABLE $__________

(check or money order—please do not send cash)

To order, complete this form and send it, along with a check or money order for the total above, payable to HQN Books, to: **In the U.S.:** 3010 Walden Avenue, P.O. Box 9077, Buffalo, NY 14269-9077; **In Canada:** P.O. Box 636, Fort Erie, Ontario, L2A 5X3.

Name: ______________________________
Address: ____________________ City: ____________
State/Prov.: ____________________ Zip/Postal Code: ____________
Account Number (if applicable): ____________________

075 CSAS

*New York residents remit applicable sales taxes.
*Canadian residents remit applicable GST and provincial taxes.